THE FALLEN MAN

Also by Tony Hillerman
In Large Print:

Finding Moon
Sacred Clowns
Talking God
A Thief of Time
Skinwalkers
The Dark Wind
People of Darkness
Listening Woman
Dance Hall of the Dead
The Fly on the Wall
The Blessing Way
The Ghostway

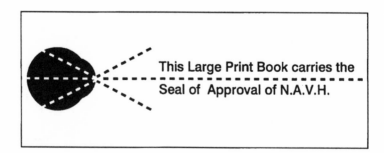

This Large Print Book carries the
Seal of Approval of N.A.V.H.

THE FALLEN MAN

TONY HILLERMAN

Thorndike Press • Thorndike, Maine

Published in 1997 by arrangement with
HarperCollins Publishers, Inc.

Thorndike Large Print ® Basic Series.

The tree indicium is a trademark of Thorndike Press.

The text of this Large Print edition is unabridged.
Other aspects of the book may vary from the original edition.

Set in 16 pt. Bookman Old Style by Al Chase.

Printed in the United States on permanent paper.

Library of Congress Cataloging in Publication Data

Hillerman, Tony.
    The fallen man / Tony Hillerman.
      p.   cm.
    ISBN 0-7862-0936-4 (lg. print : hc).
    ISBN 0-7862-0935-6 (lg. print : sc).
    1. Large type books. I. Title.
    [PS3558.I45F65 1997b]
    813'.54—dc21   96-48187

Acknowledgments

In writing fiction involving Navajo Tribal Police, I lean upon the professionals for help. In this book, it was provided by personnel of both the N.T.P. and the Navajo Rangers, and especially by old friend Captain Bill Hillgartner. My thanks also to Chief Leonard G. Butler, Lieutenants Raymond Smith and Clarence Hawthorne, and Sergeants McConnel Wood and Wilfred Tahy. If any technical details are wrong, it wasn't because they didn't try to teach me. Robert Rosebrough, author of *The San Juan Mountains*, loaned me his journal of a Ship Rock climb and gave me other help.

This book is dedicated to members of the Dick Pfaff Philosophical Group, which for the past quarter-century has gathered each Tuesday evening to test the laws of probability and sometimes, alas, the Chaos Theory.

1

From where Bill Buchanan sat with his back resting against the rough breccia, he could see the side of Whiteside's head, about three feet away. When John leaned back, Buchanan could see the snowcapped top of Mount Taylor looming over Grants, New Mexico, about eighty miles to the east. Now John was leaning forward, talking.

"This climbing down to climb back up, and climbing up so you can climb back down again," Whiteside said. "That seems like a poor way to get the job done. Maybe it's the only way to get to the summit, but I'll bet we could find a faster way down."

"Relax," Buchanan said. "Be calm. We're supposed to be resting."

They were perched on one of the few relatively flat outcrops of basalt in what climbers of Ship Rock call Rappel Gully. On the way up, it was the launching point for the final hard climb to the summit, a slightly tilted but flat surface of basalt about the size of a desktop and 1,721 feet above the prairie below. If you were going down, it was where you began a shorter but even harder almost vertical climb to reach the slope that led you downward with a fair chance of not killing yourself.

Buchanan, Whiteside, and Jim Stapp had just been to the summit. They had opened the army surplus ammo box that held the Ship Rock climbers' register and signed it, certifying their conquest of one of North America's hard ones. Buchanan was tired. He was thinking that he was getting too old for this.

Whiteside was removing his climbing harness, laying aside the nylon belt and the assortment of pitons, jumars, etriers, and carabiners that make reaching such mountaintops possible.

He did a deep knee bend, touched his toes, and stretched. Buchanan watched, uneasy.

"What are you doing?"

"Nothing," Whiteside said. "Actually, I'm following the instructions of that rock climber's guide you're always threatening to write. I am getting rid of all nonessential weight before making an unprotected traverse."

Buchanan sat up. He played in a poker game in which Whiteside was called "Two-Dollar John" because of his unshakable faith that the dealer would give him the fifth heart if he needed one. Whiteside enjoyed taking risks.

"Traversing what?" Buchanan asked.

"I'm just going to ease over there and take a look." He pointed along the face of the cliff. "Get out there maybe a hundred feet and you can see down under the overhang and into the honeycomb formations. I can't believe there's not some way to rappel right on down."

"You're looking for some way to kill yourself," Buchanan said. "If you're in such a damn hurry to get down, get yourself a parachute."

"Rappelling down is easier than up," Whiteside said. He pointed across the little basin to where Stapp was preparing to begin hauling himself up the basalt wall behind them. "I'll just be a few minutes." He began moving with gingerly care out onto the cliff face.

Buchanan was on his feet. "Come on, John! That's too damn risky."

"Not really," Whiteside said. "I'm just going out far enough to see past the overhang. Just a peek at what it looks like. Is it all this broken-up breccia or is there, maybe, a big old finger of basalt sticking up that we could scramble right on down?"

Buchanan slid along the wall, getting closer, admiring Whiteside's technique if not his judgment. The man was moving slowly along the cliff, body almost perfectly vertical, his toes holding his weight on perhaps an inch of sloping stone, his fingers finding the cracks, crevices, and rough spots that would help him keep his balance if the wind gusted. He was doing the traverse perfectly. Beautiful to watch. Even the body was perfect for the purpose. A little smaller and slimmer than Buchanan's. Just bone, sinew, and muscle, without an ounce of surplus weight, moving like an insect against the cracked basalt wall.

And a thousand feet below him — no, a quarter of a mile below him lay what Stapp liked to call "the surface of the world." Buchanan looked out at it. Almost directly below, two Navajos on horseback were riding along the base of the monolith — tiny figures that put the risk of what Whiteside was doing into terrifying perspective. If he slipped, Whiteside would die, but not for a while. It would take time for a body to drop six hundred feet, then to bounce from an outcrop, and fall again, and bounce and fall, until it finally rested among the boulders at the bottom of this strange old volcanic core.

Buchanan looked away from the riders and from the thought. It was early afternoon, but the autumn sun was far to the north and the shadow of Ship Rock already stretched southeastward for miles across the tan prairie. Winter would soon end the climbing season. The sun was already so low that it reflected only from the very tip of Mount Taylor. Eighty miles to the north early snows had already packed the higher peaks in Colorado's San Juans. Not a cloud anywhere. The sky was a deep dry-country blue; the air was cool and, a rarity at this altitude, utterly still.

The silence was so absolute that Buchanan could hear the faint sibilance of Whiteside's soft rubber shoe sole as he shifted a foot along the stone. A couple of hundred feet below him, a red-tailed hawk drifted along, riding an updraft of air along the cliff face. From behind him came the click of Stapp fastening his rappelling gear.

This is why I climb, Buchanan

thought. To get so far away from Stapp's "surface of the earth" that I can't even hear it. But Whiteside climbs for the thrill of challenging death. And now he's out about thirty yards. It's just too damn risky.

"That's far enough, John," Buchanan said. "Don't press your luck."

"Two more feet to a handhold," Whiteside said. "Then I can take a look."

He moved. And stopped. And looked down.

"There's more of that honeycomb breccia under the overhang," he said, and shifted his weight to allow a better head position. "Lot of those little erosion cavities, and it looks like some pretty good cracking where you can see the basalt." He shifted again. "And a pretty good shelf down about — "

Silence. Then Whiteside said, "I think I see a helmet."

"What?"

"My God!" Whiteside said. "There's a skull in it."

2

The white Porsche looming in the rear-view mirror of his pickup distracted Jim Chee from his gloomy thoughts. Chee had been rolling southward down Highway 666 toward Salt Creek Wash at about sixty-five miles per hour, which was somewhat more than the law he was paid to uphold allowed. But Navajo Tribal Police protocol this season was permitting speeders about that much margin of error. Besides, traffic was very light, it was past quitting time (the mid-November sunset was turning the clouds over the Carrizo Mountains a gaudy pink), and he saved both gasoline and wear on the pickup's tired old engine by letting it accelerate downhill, thereby gathering momentum for the long climb over the hump between the wash and Shiprock.

But the driver of the Porsche was making a lot more than a tolerable mistake. He was doing about ninety-five. Chee picked the portable blinker light off the passenger-side floorboard, switched it on, rolled down the window, and slapped its magnets against the pickup roof. Just as the Porsche whipped past.

He was instantly engulfed in cold air and road dust. He rolled up the window and jammed his foot down on the accelerator. The speedometer needle reached 70 as he crossed Salt Creek Wash, crept up to almost 75, and then wavered back to 72 as the upslope gravity and engine fatigue took their toll. The Porsche was almost a mile up the hill by now. Chee reached for the mike, clicked it on, and got the Shiprock dispatcher.

"Shiprock," the voice said. "Go ahead, Jim."

This would be Alice Notabah, the veteran. The other dispatcher, who was young and almost as new on the job as was Chee, always called him Lieutenant.

"Go ahead," Alice repeated, sounding slightly impatient.

"Just a speeder," Chee said. "White Porsche Targa, Utah tags, south on triple six into Shiprock. No big deal." The driver probably hadn't seen his blinker. No reason to look in your rearview when you pass a rusty pickup. Still, it added another minor frustration

14

to the day's harvest. Trying to chase the sports car would have been simply humiliating.

"Ten four," Alice said. "You coming in?"

"Going home," Chee said.

"Lieutenant Leaphorn was in looking for you," Alice said.

"What'd he want?" It was actually former lieutenant Leaphorn now. The old man had retired last summer. Finally. After about a century. Still, retired or not, hearing that Leaphorn was looking for him made Chee feel uneasy and begin examining his conscience. He'd spent too many years working for the man.

"He just said he'd catch you later," Alice said. "You sound like you had a bad day."

"Just a total blank," Chee agreed. But that wasn't accurate. It was worse than blank. First there had been the episode with the kid in the Ute Mountain Tribal Police uniform (Chee balked at thinking of him as a policeman), and then there was Mrs. Twosalt.

Cocky kid. Chee had been parked high on the slope below Popping Rock where his truck was screened from view by brush and he had a long view of the oil field roads below. He'd been watching a mud-spattered blue two-ton GMC pickup parked at a cattle guard about a mile below him. Chee had dug out his binoculars and focused them, and was trying to determine why the driver had parked there and if anyone was sitting on the passenger's side. All he was seeing was dirt on the windshield.

About then the kid had said *"Hey!"* in a loud voice, and when Chee had turned, there he was, about six feet away, staring at him through dark and shiny sunglasses.

"What's you doing?" the kid had asked, and Chee had recognized that he was wearing what looked like a brand-new Ute Mountain Tribal Police uniform.

"I'm watching birds," Chee said, and tapped the binoculars.

Which the kid hadn't found amusing.

"Let's see some identification," he'd said. That was all right with Chee. It was proper procedure when you run across something that maybe looks suspicious. He'd fished out his Navajo Tribal Police identification folder, wishing he hadn't made the smart-aleck

16

remark about bird-watching. It was just the sort of wisecrack cops heard every day and resented. He wouldn't have done it, he thought, if the kid hadn't sneaked up on him so efficiently. That was embarrassing.

The kid looked at the folder, from Chee's photograph to Chee's face. Neither seemed to please him.

"Navajo police?" he'd said. "What's you doing out here on the Ute reservation?"

And then Chee politely explained to the kid that they weren't on the Ute reservation. They were on Navajo land, the border being maybe a half mile or so east of them. And the kid had sort of smirked and said Chee was lost, the border was at least a mile the other way, and he'd pointed down the slope. The argument that might have started would have been totally pointless, so Chee had said good-bye and climbed back into his truck. He had driven away, thoroughly pissed off, remembering that the Utes were the enemy in a lot of Navajo mythology and understanding why. He was also thinking he had handled that encounter very poorly for an acting lieutenant, which he had been now for almost three weeks. And that led him to think of Janet Pete, who was why he'd worked for this promotion. Thinking of Janet always cheered him up a little. The day would surely get better.

It didn't. Next came Old Lady Twosalt.

Just like the Ute cop, she'd walked right up behind him without him hearing a thing. She caught him standing in the door of the school bus parked beside the Twosalt hogan, and there wasn't a damn thing he could do but continue standing there, stammering and stuttering, explaining that he'd honked his horn, and waited around and hollered, and did all the polite things one does to protect another's privacy when one visits a house in mostly empty country. And then he'd finally decided that nobody was home. Finally, too, he stopped talking.

Mrs. Twosalt had just stood there, looking politely away from him while he talked instead of looking into his eyes — which is the traditional Navajo way of suggesting disbelief. And when he'd finally finished, she went right to the heart of it.

"I was out looking after the goats," she

said. "But what are you looking for in my school bus? You think you lost something in there, or what?"

What Chee was looking for in the school bus was some trace of cow manure, or cow hair, or wool, or any other evidence that the vehicle had been used to haul animals other than schoolkids. It involved the same problem that had him peering through his binoculars at the big pickup over by Popping Rock. Cattle were disappearing from grazing land in the jurisdiction of the Shiprock agency, and Captain Largo had made stopping this thievery the first priority of Chee's criminal investigation division. He put it ahead of dope dealing at the junior college, a gang shooting, bootlegging, and other crimes that Chee felt were more interesting.

He'd rolled out of the cot in his trailer house in the cold dawn this morning, put on his jeans and work jacket, and fired up the old truck intending to spend the day incognito, just prowling around looking for the kind of vehicles into which those cattle might be disappearing.

The GMC pickup was a natural. It was

a fifth-wheel model designed to pull heavy trailers and known to be favored by serious rustlers who like to do their stealing in wholesale, trailer-load lots. But he'd just happened to notice the school bus while jolting down the trail from Popping Rock, and just happened to remember the Twosalt outfit not only raised cattle but had a shaky reputation, and just happened to wonder what they would want with an old school bus anyway. None of that helped him come up with the answer for which Mrs. Twosalt had stood there waiting.

"I was just curious," Chee said. "I used to ride one of these things to school when I was a kid. I was wondering if they'd changed them any." He produced a weak laugh.

Mrs. Twosalt hadn't seemed to share his amusement. She waited, looked at him, waited some more — giving him a chance to change his story and to offer a more plausible explanation for this visit.

In default of a better idea, Chee had fished out his identification folder. He'd said he'd come by to learn if the Twosalts were missing any cattle or sheep or had seen anything suspicious.

Mrs. Twosalt said she kept good track of all their animals. Nothing was missing. And that had been the end of that except for the lingering embarrassment.

It was almost dark as he topped the hill and looked down at the scattering of lights of Shiprock town. No sign of the Porsche. Chee yawned. What a day! He turned off the pavement onto the gravel road, which led to the dirt road, which led to the weedy track down to his trailer under the cottonwoods beside the San Juan River. He rubbed his eyes, yawned again. He'd warm up what was left of his breakfast coffee, open a can of chili, and hit the sack early. A bad day, but now it was over.

No, it wasn't. His headlights reflected off a windshield, off a dusty car parked just past his trailer. Chee recognized it. Former lieutenant Joe Leaphorn, as promised, had caught him later.

3

Chee's trailer had been chilly when he left it at dawn. Now it was frigid, having leaked what little warmth it had retained into the chill that settled along the San Juan River. Chee lit the propane heater and started the coffee.

Joe Leaphorn was sitting stiff and straight on the bench behind the table. He put his hat on the Formica tabletop and rubbed his hand through his old-fashioned crew cut, which had become appropriately gray. Then he replaced the hat, looked uneasy, and took it off again. To Chee the hat looked as weatherworn as its owner.

"I hate to bother you like this," Leaphorn said, and paused. "By the way, congratulations on the promotion."

"Thanks," Chee said. He glanced around from the coffeepot, where the hot water was still dripping through the grounds, and hesitated. But what the hell. It had not seemed plausible when he'd heard it, but why not find out?

"People tell me you recommended me for it."

If Leaphorn heard that, it didn't show on his face. He was watching his folded hands, the thumbs of which he had engaged in circling each other.

"It gets you lots of work and worry," Leaphorn said, "and not much pay goes with the job."

Chee extracted two mugs from the cabinet, put the one advertising the *Farmington Times* in front of Leaphorn, and looked for the sugar bowl.

"How you enjoying your retirement?" Chee asked. Which was a sort of oblique way of getting the man to the point of this visit. This wouldn't be a social call. No way. Leaphorn had always been the boss and Chee had been the gofer. One way or another this visit would involve law enforcement and something Leaphorn wanted Chee to do about it.

"Well, being retired there's a lot less aggravation," Leaphorn said. "You don't have to put up with — " He shrugged and chuckled.

Chee laughed, but it was forced. He wasn't used to this strange new version of Leaphorn. This Leaphorn, come to ask him for something, hesitant and diffident, wasn't the Lieutenant

Leaphorn he remembered with a mixture of puzzlement, irritation, and admiration. Seeing the man as a supplicant made him uneasy. He'd put a stop to that.

"I remember when you told me you were retiring, you said if I ever needed to pick your brains for anything, to feel free to ask," Chee said. "So I'm going to ask you what you know about the cattle-rustling business."

Leaphorn considered, thumbs still circling. "Well," he said, "I know there's always some of it going on. And I know your boss and his family have been in the cow business for about three generations. So he probably doesn't care much for cow thieves." He stopped watching his thumbs and looked up at Chee. "You having a run of it up here? Anything big?"

"Nothing very big. The Conroy ranch lost eight heifers last month. That was the worst. Had six or seven other complaints in the past two months. Mostly one or two missing, and some of them probably just strayed off. But Captain Largo tells me it's worse than usual."

"Enough to get Largo stirred up," Leaphorn said. "His family has grazing

24

leases scattered around over on the Checkerboard."

Chee grinned.

"I'll bet you already knew that," Leaphorn said, and chuckled.

"I did," Chee said, and poured the coffee.

Leaphorn sipped.

"I don't think I know anything about catching rustlers that Captain Largo hasn't already told you," Leaphorn said. "Now we have the Navajo Rangers, and since cattle are a tribal resource and their job is protecting tribal resources, it's really their worry. But the rangers are a real small group and they tend to be tied up with game poachers and people vandalizing the parks, or stealing timber, or draining off drip gasoline. That sort of thing. Not enough rangers to go around, so you work with whoever the New Mexico Cattle Sanitary Board has covering this district, and the Arizona Brand Inspection Office, and the Colorado people. And you keep an eye out for strange trucks and horse trailers." Leaphorn looked up and shrugged. "Not much you can do. I never had much luck catching 'em, and the few times I did, we could never get a conviction."

"I don't think I'm going to get much return on the time I've been investing in it either," Chee said.

"I bet you're already doing everything I suggested." Leaphorn added sugar to his coffee, sipped, looked at Chee over the rim. "And then, of course, you're getting into the ceremonial season, and you know how that works. Somebody's having a sing. They need to feed all those kinfolks and friends who come to help with the cure. Lots of hungry people and maybe you have them for a whole week if it's a full-fledged ceremony. You know what they say in New Mexico: nobody eats his own beef."

"Yeah," Chee said. "Looking through the reports for the past years I noticed the little one or two animal thefts go up when the thunderstorms stop and the sings begin."

"I used to just snoop around a little. Maybe I'd find some fresh hides with the wrong brands on 'em. But you know there's not much use arresting anybody for that. I'd just say a word or two to let 'em know we'd caught 'em, and then I'd tell the owner. And if he was Navajo, he'd figure that he should have known they needed a little help and butchered something for them and saved 'em the trouble of stealing it."

Leaphorn stopped, knowing he was wasting time.

"Good ideas," Chee said, knowing he wasn't fooling Leaphorn. "Anything I can do for you?"

"It's nothing important," Leaphorn said. "Just something that's been sort of sticking in my mind for years. Just curiosity really."

Chee tried his own coffee and found it absolutely delicious. He waited for Leaphorn to decide how he wanted to ask this favor.

"It was eleven years this fall," Leaphorn said. "I was assigned to the Chinle office then and we had a young man disappear from the lodge at Canyon de Chelly. Fellow named Harold Breedlove. He and his wife were there celebrating their fifth wedding anniversary. His birthday, too. The way his wife told it, he got a telephone call. He tells her he has to meet someone about a business deal. He says he'll be right back and he drives off in their car. He doesn't come back. Next morning she calls the Arizona Highway Patrol. They call us."

Leaphorn paused, understanding that such a strong reaction to what seemed like nothing more sinister than a man taking a vacation from his wife needed an explanation. "They're a big ranching family. The Breedloves. The Lazy B ranch up in Colorado, leases in New Mexico and Arizona, all sorts of mining interests, and so forth. The old man ran for Congress once. Anyway, we put out a description of the car. It was a new green Land Rover. Easy to spot out here. And about a week later an officer spots it. It had been left up an arroyo beside that road that runs from 191 over to the Sweetwater chapter house."

"I'm sort of remembering that case now," Chee said. "But very dimly. I was new then, working way over at Crownpoint." And, Chee thought, having absolutely nothing to do with the Breedlove case. So where could this conversation possibly be leading?

"No sign of violence at the car, that right?" Chee asked. "No blood. No weapon. No note. No nothing."

"Not even tracks," Leaphorn said. "A week of wind took care of that."

"And nothing stolen out of the car, if I remember it right," Chee said. "Seems like I remember somebody saying it still had an expensive audio system in it, spare tire, everything still there."

Leaphorn sipped his coffee, thinking. Then he said, "So it seemed then. Now I don't know. Maybe some mountain climbing equipment was stolen."

"Ah," Chee said. He put down the coffee cup. Now he understood where Leaphorn was heading.

"That skeleton up on Ship Rock," Leaphorn said. "All I know about it is what I read in the *Gallup Independent.* Do you have any identification yet?"

"Not that I know of," Chee said. "There's no evidence of foul play, but Captain Largo got the FBI laboratory people to take a look at everything. Last I heard, they hadn't come up with anything."

"Nothing much but bare bones to work with, I heard," Leaphorn said. "And what was left of the clothing. I guess people who climb mountains don't take along their billfolds."

"Or engraved jewelry," Chee added. "Or anything else they're not using. At least this guy didn't."

"You get an estimate on his age?"

"The pathologist said between thirty

and thirty-five. No sign of any health problems which affected bone development. I guess you don't expect health problems in people who climb mountains. And he probably grew up someplace with lots of fluoride in the drinking water."

Leaphorn chuckled. "Which means no fillings in his teeth and no help from any dental charts."

"We had lots of that kind of luck on this one," Chee said.

Leaphorn drained his cup, put it down. "How was he dressed?"

Chee frowned. It was an odd question. "Like a mountain climber," he said. "You know. Special boots with those soft rubber soles, all the gear hanging off of him."

"I was thinking about the season," Leaphorn said. "Black as that Ship Rock is, the sun gets it hot in the summer — even up there a mile and a half above sea level. And in the winter, it gets coated with ice. The snow packs in where it's shaded. Layers of ice form."

"Yeah," Chee said. "Well, this guy wasn't wearing cold-weather gear. Just pants and a long-sleeved shirt. Maybe some sort of thermal underwear, though. He was on a sort of shelf a couple of hundred feet below the peak. Way too high for the coyotes to get to him, but the buzzards and ravens had been there."

"Did the rescue team bring everything down? Was there anything that you'd expect to find that wasn't there? I mean, you'd expect to find if you knew anything about the gear climbers carry."

"As far as I know nothing was missing," Chee said. "Of course, stuff may have fallen down into cracks. The birds would have scattered things around."

"A lot of rope, I guess," Leaphorn said.

"Quite a bit," Chee said. "I don't know how much would be normal. I know climbing rope stretches a lot. Largo sent it to the FBI lab to see if they could tell if a knot slipped, or it broke, or what."

"Did they bring down the other end?"

"Other end?"

Leaphorn nodded. "If it broke, there'd be the other end. He would have had it secured someplace. A piton driven in or tied to something secure. In case he slipped."

"Oh," Chee said. "The climbers who went up for the bones didn't find it. I doubt if they looked. Largo asked them to go up and bring down the body. And I remember they thought there'd have to be two bodies. Nobody would be crazy enough to climb Ship Rock alone. But they didn't find another one. I guess our fallen man was that crazy."

"Sounds like it," Leaphorn said.

Chee poured them both some more coffee, looked at Leaphorn and said, "I guess this Harold Breedlove was a mountain climber. Am I right?"

"He was," Leaphorn said. "But if he's your fallen man, he wasn't a very smart one."

"You mean climbing up there alone."

"Yeah," Leaphorn said. "Or if he wasn't alone, climbing with someone who'd go off and leave him."

"I've thought about that," Chee said. "The rescue crew said he'd either climbed up to the ledge, which they didn't think would be possible without help, or tried to rappel down from above. But the skeleton was intact. Nothing broken." Chee shook his head.

"If someone was with him, why didn't they report it? Get help? Bring down the body? You have any thoughts about that?"

"Yeah," Chee said. "Makes no sense either way."

Leaphorn sipped coffee. Considered.

"I'd like to know more about this climbing gear you said was stolen out of Breedlove's car," Chee said.

"I said it might have been stolen, and maybe from the car," Leaphorn said.

Chee waited.

"About a month after the guy vanished, we caught a kid from Many Farms breaking into a tourist's car parked at one of the Canyon de Chelly overlooks. He had a bunch of other stolen stuff at his place, car radios, mobile phones, tape decks, so forth, including some mountain climbing gear. Rope, pitons, whatever they call those gadgets. By then we'd been looking for Breedlove long enough to know he was a climber. The boy claimed he found the stuff where runoff had uncovered it in an arroyo bottom. We had him take us out and show us. It was about five hundred yards upstream from where we'd found Breedlove's car."

Chee considered this.

"Did you say the car hadn't been broken into?"

"It wasn't locked when we found it.

The stuff kids usually take was still there."

Chee made a wry face. "You have any idea why he'd just take the climbing gear?"

"And leave the stuff he could sell? I don't know," Leaphorn said. He picked up his cup, noticed it was empty, put it down again.

"I heard you're getting married," he said. "Congratulations."

"Thanks. You want a refill?"

"A very pretty lady," Leaphorn said. "And smart. A good lawyer." He held out his cup.

Chee laughed. "I never heard you use that adjective talking about a lawyer before. Anyway, not about a defense lawyer." Janet Pete worked for Dinebeiina Nahiilna be Agaditahe, which translates more or less literally as "People who talk fast and help people" and was more likely to be called DNA, or public defenders, or with less polite language by Navajo Police.

"Has to be a first time for everything," Leaphorn said. "And Miss Pete —" Leaphorn couldn't think of a way to finish that sentence.

Chee took his cup and refilled it.

"I hope you'll let me know if anything interesting turns up on your fallen man."

That surprised Chee. Wasn't it finished now? Leaphorn had found his missing man. Largo's fallen man was identified. Case closed. What else interesting would there be?

"You mean if we check out the Breedlove identification and the skeleton turns out to be the wrong size, or wrong race, or Breedlove had false teeth? Or what?"

"Yeah," Leaphorn said. But he still sat there, holding his replenished coffee cup. This conversation wasn't finished. Chee waited, trying to deduce the way it would be going.

"Did you have a suspect? I guess the widow would be one?"

"There seemed to be a good reason for it in this case. But that didn't pan out. Then there was a cousin. A Washington lawyer named George Shaw. Who just happened to also be a mountain climber, and just happened to be out here and looked just perfect as the odd man in a love triangle if you wanted one. He said he'd come out to talk to Breedlove about some sort of mineral lease proposal on the Lazy B ranch. That seemed to be true from what I could find out. Shaw was representing the family's business interests and a mining company was dickering for a lease."

"With Harold? Did he own the place?"

Leaphorn laughed. "He'd just inherited it. Three days before he disappeared."

"Well, now," Chee said, and thought about it while Leaphorn sipped his coffee.

"Did you see the report on the shooting over at Canyon de Chelly the other day?" Leaphorn asked. "An old man named Amos Nez shot apparently by somebody up on the rim?"

"I saw it," Chee said. It was an odd piece of business. Nez had been hit in the side. He'd fallen off his horse still holding the reins. The next shot hit the horse in the head. It had fallen partly across Nez and then four more shots had been fired. One hit Nez in the forearm and then he had pulled himself into cover behind the animal. The last Chee'd seen on it, six empty 30.06 cartridges had been recovered among the boulders up on the rim. As far as Chee knew that's where the trail in this case ended. No suspects. No motive. Nez was listed in fair condition at the Chinle hospital — well enough to say he had no idea why anyone would want to shoot him.

"That's what stirred me up," Leaphorn said. "Old Hosteen Nez was one of the last people to see this Hal Breedlove before he disappeared."

"Quite a coincidence," Chee said. When he'd worked for Leaphorn at Window Rock, Leaphorn had told him never to believe in coincidences. Told him that often. It was one of the man's cardinal rules. Every effect had its cause. If it seemed to be connected and you couldn't find the link it just meant you weren't trying hard enough. But this sounded like an awfully strained coincidence.

"Nez was their guide in the canyon," Leaphorn said. "When the Breedloves were staying at the lodge he was one of the crew there. The Breedloves hired him to take them all the way up Canyon del Muerto one day, and the main canyon the next. I talked to him three times."

That seemed to Leaphorn to require some explanation.

37

"You know," he said. "Rich guy with a pretty young wife disappears for no reason. You ask questions. But Nez told me they seemed to like each other a lot. Having lots of fun. He said one time he'd been up one of the side canyons to relieve himself and when he came back it looked like she was crying and Breedlove was comforting her. So he waited a little before showing up and then everything was all right."

Chee considered. "What do you think? It could have been anything?"

"Yep," Leaphorn said, and sipped coffee. "Did I mention they were celebrating Breedlove's birthday? We found out that he'd turned thirty just the previous week, and when he turned thirty he inherited. His daddy left him the ranch but he put it into a family trust. It had a provision that the trustee controlled it until Breedlove got to be thirty years old. Then it was all his."

Chee considered again. "And the widow inherited from him?"

"That's what we found out. So she had a motive and we had the logical suspect."

"But no evidence," Chee guessed.

"None. Not only that. Just before

Breedlove drove away, our Mr. Nez arrived to take them on another junket up the canyon. He remembered Breedlove apologized for missing out, paid him in advance, and gave him a fifty-dollar tip. Then Mrs. Breedlove and Nez took off. They spent the day sight-seeing. Nez remembered she was in a hurry when it was getting dark because she was supposed to meet Breedlove and another couple for dinner. But when they got back to the lodge, no car. That's the last Nez saw of her."

Leaphorn paused, looked at Chee, and added, "Or so he says."

"Oh?" Chee said.

"Well, I didn't mean he'd seen her again. It's just that I always had a feeling that Nez knew something he wasn't telling me. That's one reason I kept going back to talk to him."

"You think he had something to do with the disappearance. Maybe the two of them weren't up the canyon when Breedlove was supposed to be driving away?"

"Well, no," Leaphorn said. "People staying at the lodge saw them coming out of the canyon in Nez's truck about seven P.M. Then a little after seven, she

39

went over to the lodge and asked if Breedlove had called in. About seven-thirty she's having dinner with the other couple. They remembered her being irritated about him being so late, mixed with a little bit of worry."

"I guess that's what they call an airtight alibi," Chee said. "So how long did it take her to get old Hal declared legally dead so she could marry her coconspirator? And would I be wrong if I guessed that would be George Shaw?"

"She's still a widow, last I heard," Leaphorn said. "She offered a ten-thousand-dollar reward and after a while upped it to twenty thousand and didn't petition to get her husband declared legally dead until five years later. She lives up near Mancos, Colorado. She and her brother run the Lazy B now."

"You know what?" Chee said. "I think I know those people. Is the brother Eldon Demott?"

"That's him."

"He's one of our customers," Chee said. "The ranch still has those public land leases you mentioned on the Checkerboard Reservation and they've been losing Angus calves. He thinks maybe some of us Navajos might be stealing them."

"Eldon is Elisa Breedlove's older brother," Leaphorn said. "Their daddy was old man Breedlove's foreman, and when their daddy died, I think Eldon just sort of inherited the job. Anyway, the Demott family lived on the ranch. I guess that's how Elisa and the Breedlove boy got together."

Chee stifled a yawn. It had been a long and tiring day and this session with Leaphorn, helpful as it had been, didn't qualify as relaxation. He had accumulated too many memories of tense times trying to live up to the man's high expectations. It would be a while before he could relax in Leaphorn's presence. Maybe another twenty years would do it.

"Well," Chee said. "I guess that takes care of the fallen man. I've got a probable identification of our skeleton. You've located your missing Hal Breedlove. I'll call you when we get it confirmed."

Leaphorn drained his cup, got up, adjusted his hat.

"I thank you for the help," he said.

"And you for yours."

Leaphorn opened the door, admitting

a rush of cold air, the rich perfume of autumn, and a reminder that winter was out there somewhere, like the coyote, just waiting.

"All we need to do now —" he said, and stopped, looking embarrassed. "All that needs to be done," he amended, "is find out if your bones really are my Breedlove, and then find out how the hell he got from that abandoned Land Rover about a hundred fifty miles west, and way up there to where he could fall off of Ship Rock."

"And why," Chee said. "And how he did it all by himself."

"If he did," Leaphorn said.

4

The strange truck parked in one of the Official Visitor slots at the Shiprock headquarters of the Navajo Tribal Police wore a New Jersey license and looked to Jim Chee anything but official. It had dual back wheels and carried a cumbersome camper, its windows covered by decals that certified visitation at tourist traps from Key West to Vancouver Island. Other stickers plastered across the rear announced that A BAD DAY FISHING IS BETTER THAN A GOOD DAY AT WORK, and declared the camper-truck to be OUR CHILDREN'S INHERITANCE. Bumper decals exhorted viewers to VISUALIZE WHIRLED PEAS and to TRY RANDOM ACTS OF KINDNESS, and endorsed the National Rifle Association. A broad band of silver duct tape circled the camper's real panel, sealing the dust out of the joint and giving the camper a ramshackle, homemade look.

Chee stuck his head into Alice Notabah's dispatcher office and indicated the truck with a nod: "Who's the Official Visitor?"

Notabah nodded toward Largo's office.

"In with the captain," she said. "And he wants to see you."

The man who drove the truck was sitting in the comfortable chair Captain Largo kept for important visitors. He held a battered black hat with a silver concha band in his lap and looked relaxed and comfortable.

"I'll catch you later," Chee said, but Largo waved him in.

"I want you to meet Dick Finch," Largo said. "He's the New Mexico brand inspector working the Four Corners, and he's been getting some complaints."

Chee and Finch shook hands. "Complaints?" Chee said. "Like what?"

" 'Bout what you'd expect for a brand inspector to get," Finch said. "People missing their cattle. Thinking maybe somebody's stealing 'em."

Finch grinned when he said it, eliminating some of the sting from the sarcasm.

"Yeah," Chee said, "we've been hearing some of that, too."

Finch shrugged. "Folks always say that nobody likes to eat his own beef. But it's got a little beyond that, I think. With bred heifers going at sixty dollars a hundred pounds, it just takes three

44

of 'em to make you a grand larceny."

Captain Largo was looking sour. "Sixty dollars a hundred, like hell," he said. "More like a thousand dollars a head for me. I've been trying to raise purebred stock." He nodded in Chee's direction. "Jim here is running our criminal investigation division. He's been working on it."

Largo waited. So did Finch.

"I'm here on something else now," Chee said finally. "I think we may have an identification on that skeleton that was found up on Ship Rock."

"Well, now," Largo said. "Where'd that come from?"

"Joe Leaphorn remembered a missing person case he had eleven years ago. The man disappeared from Canyon de Chelly but he was a mountain climber."

"Leaphorn," Largo said. "I thought old Joe was supposed to be retired."

"He is," Chee said.

"Eleven years is a hell of a long time to remember a missing person case," Largo said. "How many of those do we get in an average month?"

"Several," Chee said. "But most of 'em don't stay missing long."

Largo nodded. "So who's the man?"

"Harold Breedlove was the missing man. He used to own the Lazy B ranch south of Mancos. Or his family owned it."

"Fella named Eldon Demott owns it now," Finch said. "Runs a lot of Herefords down in San Juan County. Has some deeded land and some BLM leases and a big home place up in Colorado."

"What have you got beyond this Breedlove fella's been missing long enough to become a skeleton and him being a climber?" Largo asked.

Chee explained what Leaphorn had told him.

"Just that?" Largo asked, and thought a moment. "Well, it could be right. It sounds like it is and Joe Leaphorn never was much for being wrong. Did Joe have any notion why this guy left his wife at the canyon? Or why he'd be climbing Ship Rock all by himself?"

"He didn't say, but I think he figures maybe Breedlove wasn't alone up there. And maybe the widow knew more than she was telling him at the time."

"And what's that about Amos Nez getting shot last week down at Canyon de Chelly? You lost me on that connection."

"It was sort of thin," Chee said. "Nez happened to be one of the witnesses in the disappearance case. Leaphorn said he was the last person known to have seen Breedlove alive. Except for the widow."

Largo considered. Grinned. "And she was Joe's suspect, of course," he said. And shook his head. "Joe never could believe in coincidences."

"They still had that mountain climbing gear in the evidence room at Window Rock and I had them send it up," Chee said. "It looks to me a lot like the gear they found on our Fallen Man, so I called Mrs. Breedlove up at Mancos."

"What'd she say?"

"She'd gone into town for something. The housekeeper said she'd be back in a couple of hours. I left word that I was coming up this afternoon to show her some stuff that might bear on her missing husband."

Finch cleared his throat, glanced up at Chee. "While you're there why not just kind of keep your eyes open? Tell 'em you've heard good things about the way they run their place. Look around. You know?"

Finch looked to Chee to be about fifty.

He had a hollowed scar high on his right cheek (resulting, Chee guessed, from some sort of surgery), small, bright blue eyes, and a complexion burned and cracked by the Four Corners weather. He was waiting now for Chee's response to this suggestion.

"You think Demott's sort of augmenting his herd with some strangers?" Chee asked.

"Well, not exactly," Finch said, and shrugged. "But who knows? People losing their cattle. Maybe the coyotes are getting 'em. Maybe Demott's got fifteen or twenty head he's shipping off to the feedlot and he thinks it would be nice to round it off at twenty or twenty-five. No harm in looking. Seeing what you can see."

"I'll do that," Chee said. "But were you telling me you don't have anything specific against Demott?"

Finch was studying Chee, looking quizzical. He's trying to decide, Chee thought, how stupid I am.

"Nothing I could take in to a judge and get a search warrant with. But you hear things." With that, Finch broke into a chuckle. "Hell, you hear things about everybody." He jerked a thumb at Largo. "I've even been told that your captain here has some peculiar-looking brands on some of his stock. That right, Captain?"

"I've heard that myself," Largo said, grinning. "We have a barbecue over at the place, all the neighbors want to go out and take a look at the cowhides."

"Well, it's a lot cheaper than buying beef at the butcher shop. So maybe somebody's eating Demott's sirloin and the Demotts are eating theirs."

"Or mutton," added Largo, who was missing some ewes as well as a calf or two.

"How about me going along for the ride?" Finch said. "I mean up to the Lazy B?"

"Why not?" Chee said.

"You wouldn't have to introduce me, you know. I'll just sort of get out and stretch my legs. Look around a little bit. You never know what you might see."

5

They came into view of the headquarters of the Lazy B with the autumn sun low over Mesa Verde, producing shadow patterns on Bridge Timber Mountain. Chee had been thinking more of home sites lately and he thought now that this little valley would be a beautiful place for Janet and him. The house in the cluster of cottonwoods below them would be far, far too large for him to feel comfortable in. But Janet would love it.

Finch had been doing the talking on the drive up from Shiprock. After the first fifty miles of that, Chee began listening just enough to nod or grunt at the proper intervals. Mostly he was thinking about Janet Pete and the differences between what they liked and what they didn't. This house, for example. Women usually had most to say about living places, but if he retained veto power, theirs certainly wouldn't be anything as huge as the fieldstone, timber, and slate mansion the Breedlove family had built for itself. Even if they could afford it, which they certainly never would.

That reminded Chee of the white Porsche that had zipped past him yesterday. Why did he connect it to Janet? Because it had class, as did she. And was beautiful. And, sure, she'd like it. Who wouldn't? So why did he resent it? Was it because it was a part of the world she came from in which he would never be comfortable? Or understand? Maybe.

But now he was about to walk in and see if he could get a widow to identify a bunch of stuff that would tell her that her husband was truly dead. Tell her, that is, unless she already knew — having killed him herself. Or arranged it. He'd worry about the Porsche later. The Breedlove mansion was now just across the fence.

According to Finch, old Edgar Breedlove had built it as a second home — his first one being in Denver, from which he ran his mining operations. But he'd never lived in it. He'd bought the ranch because his prospectors had found a molybdenum deposit on the high end of the property. But the ore price fell after the war and somehow or other the place got left to a grandson, Harold. Hal had adopted his granddad's policy of overgrazing it and letting it run down.

"That ain't happening now," Finch had told him. "This place ain't going to go to hell while Demott's running it. He's sort of a tree-hugger. That's what people say. Say he never got married 'cause he's in love with this place."

Chee parked under a tree a polite distance from the front entrance, turned off the ignition, and sat, killing the time needed by hosts to get decent before welcoming guests. Finch, another empty-country man, seemed to understand that. He yawned, stretched, and examined the half dozen cows in the feedlot beside the barn with a professional eye.

"How do you know all this about the Breedlove ranch, and Demott and everything?" Chee asked. "This is Colorado. It's not your territory."

"Ranching — and stealing cows off of ranches — don't pay much attention to state lines," Finch said, not taking his eyes off the cows. "The Lazy B has leases in New Mexico. Makes 'em my business."

Finch extracted a twenty-stick pack of chewing gum from his jacket pocket, offered it to Chee, extracted two sticks for himself, and started chewing them. "Besides," he said, "you got to have something going to make the job interesting. I got one particular guy I keep looking for. Most of these cow thieves are 'hungries.' Folks run out of eating money, or got a payment due, and they go out and get themselves a cow or two to sell. Or, on the reservation, maybe they got somebody sick in the family, and they're having a sing for the patient, and they need a steer to feed all the kinfolks coming in. I never worried too much about them. If they keep doing it, they get careless and they get caught and the neighbors talk to them about it. Get it straightened out. But then there's some others who are in it for business. It's easy money and it beats working."

"Who's this one you're specially after?"

Finch laughed. "If I knew that, we wouldn't be talking about it, now would we?"

"I guess not," Chee said, impressed with how insulting Finch could be even when he was acting friendly.

"We'd just go out and get him then,

wouldn't we?" Finch concluded. "But all I know about him is the way he operates. Modus operandi, if you know your Latin. He always picks the spread-out ranches where a few head won't be missed for a while. He always takes something that he can sell quick. No little calves that you have to wean, no big, expensive, easy-to-trace breeding bulls. Never messes with horses, 'cause some people get attached to a nag and go out looking for it. Has some other tricks, too. Like he finds a good place beside a back road where there wouldn't be any traffic to bother him and he'll put out feed. Usually good alfalfa hay. Do it several times so the cattle get in the habit of coming up and looking for it when they see his truck parking."

Finch stopped, looked at Chee, waited for a comment.

"Pretty smart," Chee said.

"Yes, sir," Finch agreed. "So far, he's been smarter than me."

Chee had no comment on that. He glanced at his watch. Another three minutes and he'd go ring the doorbell and get this job over with.

"Then I've found a place or two where

he fixed up the fence so he could get 'em through it fast." He paused again, seeing if Chee understood this. Chee did, but to hell with Finch.

"You could cut the wire, of course," Finch explained, "but then the herd gets out on the road and somebody notices it right away and they do a head count and know some are missing."

Chee said, "Really?"

"Yeah," Finch said. "Anyway, I've been after this son of a bitch for years now. Every time I take off from home to come out this way, he's the one I'm thinking of."

Chee didn't comment.

"Zorro," Finch said. "That's what I call him. And this time I think I'll finally get him."

"How?"

Silence, unusual for Finch, followed. Then he said, "Well, now, that's sort of complicated."

"You think it might be Demott?"

"Why you say that?"

"Well, you wanted to come up here. And you've collected all that information about him."

"If you're a brand inspector you learn to pick up on all the gossip you can

55

hear if you want to get your job done. And there was some talk that Demott paid off a mortgage by selling a bunch of calves nobody knew he owned."

"So what's the gossip about the widow Breedlove?" Chee asked. "Who was the lover who helped her kill her husband? What do the neighbors say about that?"

Finch was wearing a broad smile. "People I know up in Mancos have her down as the broken-hearted, wronged, abandoned bride. The majority of them, that is. They figured Hal ran off with some bimbo."

"How about the minority?"

"They think she had herself a local boyfriend. Somebody to keep her happy when Hal was off in New York, or climbing his mountains or playing his games."

"They have a name for him?"

"Not that I ever heard," Finch said.

"Which bunch you think is right?"

"About her? I never thought about it," Finch said. "None of my business, that part of it wasn't. Talk like that just means that folks around here didn't like Hal."

"What'd he do?"

"Well, for starters he got born in the

56

East," Finch said. "That's two strikes on you right there. And he was raised there. Citified. Preppy type. Papa's boy. Ivy Leaguer. He didn't get any bones broke falling off horses, lose a finger in a hay baler. Didn't pay his dues, you know. You don't have to actually do anything to have folks down on you."

"How about the widow? You hear anything specific about her?"

"Don't hear nothing about her, except some fellas guessing. And she's a real pretty woman, so that was probably just them wishing," Finch said. He was grinning at Chee. "You know how it works. If you're behaving yourself it's not interesting."

The front door of the Breedlove house opened and Chee could see someone standing behind the screen looking out at them. He picked up his evidence satchel and stepped out of the vehicle.

"I'll wait here for you," Finch said, "and maybe scout around a little if I get too stiff from sitting."

Mrs. Elisa Breedlove was indeed a real pretty woman. She seemed excited and nervous, which was what Chee expected. Her handshake grip was hard, and so was the hand. She led him into a huge living room, dark and cluttered with heavy, old-fashioned furniture. She motioned him into a chair, explaining that she'd had to run into Mancos "to get some stuff."

"I got back just before you drove up and Ramona told me you'd called and were coming."

"I hope I'm not —" Chee began, but she cut him off.

"No. No," she said. "I appreciate this. Ramona said you'd found Hal. Or think so. But she didn't know anything else."

"Well," Chee said, and paused. "What we found was merely bones. We thought they might be Mr. Breedlove."

He sat on the edge of the sofa, watching her.

"Bones," she said. "Just a skeleton? Was that the skeleton they found about Halloween up on Ship Rock?"

"Yes, ma'am. We wanted to ask you to look at the clothing and equipment he was wearing and see if — tell us if it was the right size, and if you thought it was your husband's stuff."

"Equipment?" She was standing beside a table, her hand on it. The light slanting through windows on each side of the fireplace illuminated her face. It was a small, narrow face framed by light brown hair, the jaw muscles tight, the expression tense. Middle thirties, Chee guessed. Slender, perfectly built, luminous green eyes, the sort of classic beauty that survived sun, wind, and hard winters and didn't seem to require the disguise of makeup. But today she looked tired. He thought of a description Finch had applied to a woman they both knew: "Been rode hard and put up wet."

Mrs. Breedlove was waiting for an answer, her pale blue eyes fixed on his face.

"Mountain climbing equipment," Chee said. "I understand the skeleton was in a cleft down the face of a cliff. Presumably, the man had fallen."

Mrs. Breedlove closed her eyes and bent slightly forward with her hips against the table.

Chee rose. "Are you all right?"

"All right," she said, but she put a hand against the table to support herself.

"Would you like to sit down? A drink of water?"

"Why do you think it's Hal?" Her eyes were still closed.

59

"He's been missing for eleven years. And we're told he was a mountain climber. Is that correct?"

"He was. He loved the mountains."

"This man was about five feet nine inches tall," Chee said. "The coroner estimated he would have weighed about one hundred and fifty pounds. He had perfect teeth. He had rather long fingers and —"

"Hal was about five eight, I'd say. He was slender, muscular. An athlete. I think he weighed about a hundred and sixty. He was worried about gaining weight." She produced a weak smile. "Around the belt line. Before we went on that trip, I let out his suit pants to give him another inch."

"He'd had a broken nose," Chee continued. "Healed. The doctor said it probably happened when he was an adolescent. And a broken wrist. He said that was more recent."

Mrs. Breedlove sighed. "The nose was from playing fraternity football, or whatever the boys play at Dartmouth. And the wrist when a horse threw him after we were married."

Chee opened the satchel, extracted the climbing equipment, and stacked it on the coffee table. There wasn't much: a nylon belt harness, the ragged remains of a nylon jacket, even more fragmentary remains of trousers and shirt, a pair of narrow shoes with soles of soft, smooth rubber, a little rock hammer, three pitons, and a couple of steel gadgets that Chee presumed were used somehow for controlling rope slippage.

When he glanced up, Mrs. Breedlove was staring at them, her face white. She turned away, facing the window but looking at nothing except some memory.

"I thought about Hal when I saw the piece the paper had on the skeleton," she said. "Eldon and I talked about it at supper that night. He thought the same thing I did. We decided it couldn't be Hal." She attempted a smile. "He was always into derring-do stuff. But he wouldn't try to climb Ship Rock alone. Nobody would. That would be insane. Two great rock men were killed on it, and they were climbing with teams of experienced experts."

She paused. Listening. The sound of a car engine came through the window. "That was before the Navajos banned climbing," she added.

"Are you a climber?"

"When I was younger," she said. "When Hal used to come out, Eldon started teaching him to climb. Hal and his cousin George. Sometimes I would go along and they taught me."

"How about Ship Rock?" Chee asked. "Did you ever climb it?"

She studied him. "The tribe prohibited that a long time ago. Before I was big enough to climb anything."

Chee smiled. "But some people still climbed it. Quite a few, from what I hear. And there's not actually a tribal ordinance against it. It's just that the tribe stopped issuing those 'back country' permits. You know, to allow non-Navajos the right to trespass."

Mrs. Breedlove looked thoughtful. Through the window came the sound of a car door slamming.

"To make it perfectly legal, you'd go see one of the local people who had a grazing permit running up to the base and get him to give you permission to be on the land," Chee added. "But most people don't even bother to do that."

Mrs. Breedlove considered this. Nodded. "We always got permission. I climbed it once. It was terrifying. With Eldon, Hal, and George. I still have nightmares."

"About falling?"

She shuddered. "I'm up there looking all around. Looking at Ute Mountain up in Colorado, and seeing the shape of Case del Eco Mesa in Utah, and the Carrizos in Arizona, and Mount Taylor, and I have this dreadful feeling that Ship Rock is getting higher and higher and then I know I can never get down." She laughed. "Fear of falling, I guess. Or fear of flying away and being lost forever."

"I guess you've heard our name for it," Chee said. "Tse' Bit' a'i' — the Rock with Wings. According to the legend it flew here from the north bringing the first Navajos on its back. Maybe it was flying again in your dream."

A voice from somewhere back in the house shouted: "Hey, Sis! Where are you? What's that Navajo police car doing parked out there?"

"We've got company," Mrs. Breedlove said, barely raising her voice. "In here."

Chee stood. A man wearing dusty jeans, a faded jean jacket with a torn sleeve, and well-worn boots walked into the room. He held a battered gray felt hat in his right hand.

"Mr. Chee," said Mrs. Breedlove, "this is my brother Eldon. Eldon Demott."

"Oh," Demott said. "Hello." He shifted his hat to his left hand and offered Chee the right one. His grip was like his sister's and his expression was a mixture of curiosity, worry, and fatigue.

"They think they've found Hal," Elisa Breedlove said. "You remember talking about that skeleton on Ship Rock. The Navajo police think it must be him."

Demott was eyeing the little stack of climbing equipment on the table. He sighed, slapped the hat against his leg. "I was wrong then, if it really is Hal," he said. "That makes him a better climber than I gave him credit for, climbing that sucker by himself and getting that high." He snorted. "And a hell of a lot crazier, too."

"Do you recognize any of this?" Chee asked, indicating the equipment.

Demott picked up the nylon belt and examined it. He was a small man. Wiry. A man built of sun-scorched leather, bone, and gristle, with a strong jaw and a receding hairline that made him look older than he probably was.

64

"It's pretty faded out but it used to be red," he said, and tossed it back to the tabletop. He looked at his sister, his face full of concern and sympathy. "Hal's was red, wasn't it?"

"It was," she said.

"You all right?"

"I'm fine," she said. "And how about this jumar? Didn't you fix one for Hal once?"

"By God," Demott said, and picked it up. It reminded Chee of an oversized steel pretzel with a sort of ratchet device connected. Chee had wondered about it and concluded that the ratchet would allow a rope to slip in one direction and not the other. Thus, it must be used to allow a climber to pull himself up a cliff. Demott obviously knew what it was for. He was examining the place where the ratchet had been welded to the steel.

"I remember I couldn't fix it. Hal and you took it into Mancos and had Gus weld it," Demott said to Elisa. "It sure looks like the same one."

"I guess we can close this up then," Chee said. "I don't see any reason for you going down to Shiprock to look at the bones. Unless you want to."

Demott was inspecting one of the

climbing shoes. "The soles must be all the same," he said. "At least all I ever saw was just soft, smooth rubber like this. And his were white. And he had little feet, too." He glanced at Elisa. "How about the clothing? That look like Hal's?"

"The jacket, yes," she said. "I think that's Hal's jacket."

Something in her tone caused Chee to glance back at her. She held her lips pressed together, face tense, determined somehow not to cry. Her brother didn't see that. He was studying the artifacts on the table.

"It's pretty tore up," Demott said, poking the clothing with a finger. "You think coyotes? But from what the paper said, it would be too high for them."

"Way too high," Chee said.

"Birds, then," Demott said. "Ravens. Vultures and —" He cut that off, with a repentant glance at Elisa.

Chee picked up the evidence valise and stuffed the tattered clothing into it, getting it out of Elisa's sight.

"I think I should go to Shiprock," Elisa said. She looked away from Chee and out the window. "To take care of things. Hal would have wanted to be cremated,

I think. And his ashes scattered in the San Juan Mountains."

"Yeah," Demott said. "Over in the La Plata range. On Mount Hesperus. That was his very favorite."

"We call it Dibe Nitsaa," Chee said. He thought of a dead man's ashes drifting down on serene slopes that the spirit called First Man had built to protect the Navajos from evil. First Man had decorated the mountain with jet-black jewelry to fend off all bad things. But what could protect it from the invincible ignorance of this white culture? These were good, kind people, he thought, who wouldn't knowingly use corpse powder, the Navajo symbol for the ultimate evil, to desecrate a holy place. But then climbing Ship Rock to prove that man was the dominating master of the universe was also a desecration.

"It's our Sacred Mountain of the North," Chee said. "Was that what Mr. Breedlove was trying to do? Put his feet on top of all our sacred places?" Having said it, Chee instantly regretted it. This was not the time or place to show his resentment.

He glanced at Demott, who was looking at him, surprised. But Elisa Breed-love was still staring out the window.

"Hal wasn't like that," she said. "He was just trying to find some happiness," she said. "Nobody had ever taught him anything about sacred things. The only god the Breedloves ever worshiped was cast out of gold."

"I don't think Hal knew anything about your mythology," Demott agreed. "It's just that Hesperus is over thirteen thousand feet and an easy climb. I like them high and easy and I guess Hal did too."

Chee considered that. "Why Ship Rock, then? I know it's killed some people. I've heard it's one of the hardest climbs."

"Yeah," Demott said. "Why Ship Rock? And why by himself? And if he wasn't by himself, how come his friends just left him there? Didn't even report it."

Chee didn't comment on that. Elisa was still staring blindly out the window.

"How high did he get?" Demott asked.

Chee shrugged. "Close to the top, I think. I think the rescue party said the skeleton was just a couple hundred feet down from the crest."

"I knew he was good, but if he got that

high all by himself he was even better than I thought," Demott said. "He'd gotten past the hardest parts."

"He'd always wanted to climb Ship Rock," Elisa said. "Remember?"

"I guess so," Demott said thoughtfully. "I remember him talking about climbing El Diente and Lizard's Head. I thought they were next on his agenda." He turned to Chee, frowning. "Have you fellows looked into who else he might have climbed with? I have trouble believing he did that alone. I guess he could have and he was reckless enough to try it. But it damn sure wouldn't be easy. Not getting that high."

"It's not a criminal case," Chee said. "We're just trying to close up an old missing person file."

"But who the hell would go off and leave a fallen man like that? Not even report so the rescue people could go get him? You think they was afraid you Navajos would arrest 'em for trespassing?" He shook his head. "Or the way things are now, maybe they thought they'd get sued." He laughed, put on his hat. "But I got to get moving. Good to meet you, Mr. Chee," he said, and was gone.

"I've got to be going too," Chee said. He dumped the rest of the equipment in the valise.

She walked with him to the door, opened it for him. He pulled at the valise zipper, then stopped. He should really leave this stuff with her. She was the widow. It was her property.

"Mr. Chee," she said. "The skeleton. Were the bones all broken up?"

"No," Chee said. "Nothing broken. And all the joints were still articulated."

From Elisa's expression he first thought she didn't understand that anthropology jargon. "I mean, the skeleton was all together in one piece. And nothing was broken."

"Nothing was broken?" she repeated. "Nothing." And then he realized the expression reflected disbelief. And shock.

Why shock? Had Mrs. Breedlove expected her husband's body to be broken apart? Why would she? If he asked her why, she'd say it must have been a long fall.

He zipped the valise closed. He'd keep these artifacts from the Fallen Man, at least for a while.

6

He met Janet at the Carriage Inn in Farmington, halfway between his trailer at Shiprock and the San Juan County courthouse at Aztec where she had been defending a Checkerboard Reservation Navajo on a grand theft charge. He arrived late — but not very late — and her kidding about his watch being on Navajo time lacked its usual vigor. She looked absolutely used up, he thought. Beautiful but tired, and maybe the fatigue explained the diminution of the usual spark, of the delight he usually sensed in her when she first saw him. Or maybe it was because he was weary himself. Anyway, just being with her, seeing her across the table, cheered him. He took her hand.

"Janet, you work too hard," Chee said. "You should marry me and let me take you away from all this."

"I intend to marry you," she said, rewarding him with a weary smile. "You keep forgetting that. But all you do is keep making more work for me. Arresting these poor innocent people."

"That sounds to me like you won

71

today," Chee said. "Charmed the jury again?"

"It didn't take any charm. This time it wouldn't have been reasonable to have even a reasonable doubt. His brother-in-law did it and the state cops totally screwed up the investigation."

"Do you have to go right back to Window Rock tomorrow? Why not take a day off? Tell 'em you are doing the post-trial paperwork. Maybe preparing a false arrest suit or something."

"Ah, Jim," she said. "I have to drive down there tonight."

"Tonight! That's crazy. That's more than two hours on a dangerous road," he said. "You're tired. Get some sleep. What's the hurry?"

She looked apologetic. Shrugged. "No choice, Jim. I'd love to stay over. Can't do it. Duty calls."

"Ah, come on," Chee said. "Duty can wait."

Janet squeezed his hand. "Really," she said. "I have to go to Washington. On a bunch of legal stuff with Justice and the Bureau of Indian Affairs. I have to be there day after tomorrow ready to argue." She shrugged, made a wry face. "So I have to pack tonight and drive to

Albuquerque tomorrow to catch my plane."

Chee picked up the menu, said, "Like I've been telling you, you work way too hard." He tried to keep it out, but the disappointment again showed in his voice.

"And as I told you, it's the fault of you policemen," she said, smiling her tired smile. "Arresting too many innocent people."

"I haven't had much luck at arresting people lately," he said. "I can't even catch any guilty ones."

The Carriage Inn had printed a handsome menu on which nothing changed but the prices. Variety was provided by the cooks, who came and went. Chee decided to presume that the current one was adept at preparing Mexican foods.

"Why not try the chile relleños?"

Janet grimaced. "That's what you said last time. This time I'm trying the fish."

"Too far from the ocean for fish," Chee said. But now he remembered that his last time here the cook had converted the relleños to something like leather. Maybe he'd order the chicken-fried steak.

"It's trout," Janet said. "A local fish. The waiter told me they steal 'em out of the fish hatchery ponds."

"Okay then," Chee said. "Trout for me, too."

"You look totally worn-out," she said. "Is Captain Largo getting to be too much for you?"

"I spent the day with a redneck New Mexico brand inspector," Chee said. "We drove all the way up to Mancos with him talking every inch of the way. Then back again, him still talking."

"About what? Cows?"

"People. Mr. Finch works on the theory that you catch cattle rustlers by knowing everything about everybody who owns cattle. I guess it's a pretty good system, but then he passed all that information along to me. You want to know anything about anybody who raises cows in the Four Corners area? Or hauls them? Or runs feedlots? Just ask me."

"Finch?" she said. "I've run into him twice in court." She shook her head, smiling.

"Who won?"

"He did. Both times."

"Oh, well," Chee said. "It's too bad,

but sometimes justice triumphs over you public defenders. Were your clients guilty?"

"Probably. They said they weren't. But this Finch guy is smart."

Chee did not want to talk about Finch.

"You know, Janet," he said. "Sometime we need to talk about . . ."

She put down the menu and looked at him over her glasses. "Sometime, but not tonight. What took you and Mr. Finch to Mancos?"

No. Not tonight, Chee thought. They would just go over the same ground. She'd say that if the police were doing their jobs properly there really wasn't a conflict of interest if a public defender was the wife of a cop. And he'd say, yeah, but what if the cop had arrested the very guy she was defending and was a witness? What if she were cross-examining her own husband as a hostile witness? And she'd fall back on her Stanford Law School lecture notes and tell him that all she wanted to extract from anyone was the exact truth. And he'd say, but sometimes the lawyer isn't after quite 100 percent of the truth, and she'd say that some evidence can't be admitted, and he'd say, as an attorney it would be easy for her to get a job with a private firm, and she'd remind him he'd turned down an offer from the Arizona Department of Public Safety and was a cinch for a job with the Bureau of Indian Affairs law-and-order division if he would take it. And he'd say, that would mean leaving the reservation, and she'd say, why not? Did he want to spend his life here? And that would open a new can of worms. No. Tonight he'd let her change the subject.

The waiter came. Janet ordered a glass of white wine. Chee had coffee.

"I went to Mancos to tell a widow that we'd found her husband's skeleton," Chee said. "Mr. Finch went along because it gave him an excuse to contemplate the cows in the lady's feedlot."

"All you found were dry bones? Her husband must have been away a lot. I'll bet he was a policeman," she said, and laughed.

Chee let that pass.

"Was it the skeleton they spotted up on Ship Rock about Halloween?" she asked, sounding mildly repentant.

Chee nodded. "He turned out to be a guy named Harold Breedlove. He owned a big ranch near Mancos."

"Breedlove," Janet said. "That sounds familiar." The waiter came — a lanky, rawboned Navajo who listened attentively to Janet's questions about the wine and seemed to understand them no better than did Chee. He would ask the cook. About the trout he was on familiar ground. "Very fresh," he said, and hurried off.

Janet was looking thoughtful. "Breedlove," she said, and shook her head. "I remember the paper said there was no identification on him. So how'd you get him identified? Dental chart?"

"Joe Leaphorn had a hunch," Chee said.

"The legend-in-his-own-time lieutenant? I thought he'd retired."

"He did," Chee said. "But he remembered a missing person case he'd worked on way back. This guy who disappeared was a mountain climber and an inheritance was involved, and —"

"Hey," Janet said. "Breedlove. I remember now."

Remember what? Chee thought. And why? This had happened long before Janet had joined the DNA, and become a resident reservation Navajo instead of one in name only, and entered his life, and made him happy. His expression had a question in it.

"From when I was with Granger-hyphen-Smith in Albuquerque. Just out of law school," she said. "The firm represented the Breedlove family. They had public land grazing leases, some mineral rights deals with the Jicarilla Apaches, some water rights arrangements with the Utes." She threw out her hands to signify an endless variety of concerns. "There were some dealings with the Navajo Nation, too. Anyway, I remember the widow was having the husband declared legally dead so she could inherit from him. The family wanted that looked into."

She stopped, looking slightly abashed. Picked up the menu again. "I'll definitely have the trout," she said.

"Were they suspicious?" Chee asked.

"I presume so," she said, still looking at the menu. "I remember it did look funny. The guy inherits a trust and two or three days later he vanishes. Vanishes under what you'd have to consider unusual circumstances."

The waiter came. Chee watched Janet order trout, watched the waiter admire her. A classy lady, Janet. From what

Chee had learned about law firms as a cop, lawyers didn't chat about their clients' business to rookie interns. It was unethical. Or at least unprofessional.

He knew the answer but he asked it anyway. "Did you work on it? The looking into it?"

"Not directly," Janet said. She sipped her water.

Chee looked at her.

She flushed slightly. "The Breedlove Corporation was John McDermott's client. His job," she said. "I guess because he handled all things Indian for the firm. And the Breedlove family had all these tribal connections."

"Did you find anything?"

"I guess not," Janet said. "I don't remember the family having us intervene in the case."

"The family?" Chee said. "Do you remember who, specifically?"

"I don't," she said. "John was dealing with an attorney in New York. I guess he was representing the rest of the Breedloves. Or maybe the family corporation. Or whatever." She shrugged. "What did you think of Finch, aside from him being so talkative?"

John, Chee thought. John. Professor John McDermott. Her old mentor at Stanford. The man who had hired her at Albuquerque when he went into private practice there, and took her to Washington when he transferred, and made her his mistress, used her, and broke her heart.

"I wonder what made them suspicious?" Chee said. "Aside from the circumstances."

"I don't know," Janet said.

Their trout arrived. Rainbows, neatly split, neatly placed on a bed of wild rice. Flanked by small carrots and boiled new potatoes. Janet broke off a tiny piece of trout and ate it.

Beautiful, Chee thought. The perfect skin, the oval face, the dark eyes that expressed so much. He found himself wishing he was a poet, a singer of ballads. Chee knew a lot of songs but they were the chants the shaman sings at the curing ceremonials, recounting the deeds of the spirits. No one had taught him how to sing to someone as beautiful as this.

He ate a bite of trout.

"If I had been driving a patrol car yesterday instead of my old pickup," he said, "I could have given a speeding ticket to a guy driving a white Porsche convertible. Really flying. But I was driving my truck."

"Wow," Janet said, looking delighted. "My favorite car. I have a fantasy about tooling around Paris in one of those. With the top down."

Maybe she looked happy because he was changing the subject. Moving away from unhappy ground. But to Chee the trout now seemed to have no taste at all.

7

Joe Leaphorn, uneasily conscious that he was now a mere civilian, had given himself three excuses for calling on Hosteen Nez and thereby butting into police business.

First, he'd come to like the old man way back when he was picking his brain in the Breedlove missing person case. Thus going to see him while Nez was recuperating from being shot was a friendly thing to do. Second, Canyon de Chelly wasn't much out of his way, since he was going to Flagstaff anyway. Third, a trip into the canyon never failed to lift Joe Leaphorn's spirits.

Lately they had needed a lift. Most of the things he'd yearned to do when retirement allowed it had now been done — at least once. He was bored. He was lonely. The little house he and Emma had shared so many years had never recovered from the emptiness her death had left in every room. That was worse now without the job to distract him. Maybe he was oversensitive, but he felt like an intruder down at the police headquarters. When he dropped in to chat with old friends he often found them busy. Just as he had always been. And he was a mere civilian now, no longer one of the little band of brothers.

Good excuses or not, Leaphorn had been a policeman too long to go unprepared. He took his GMC Jimmy with the four-wheel drive required in the canyon both by National Park Service rules and by the uncertain bottom up Chinle Wash. He had stopped at the grocery in Ganado and bought a case of assorted soda pop flavors, two pounds of bacon, a pound of coffee, a large can of peaches, and a loaf of bread. Only then did he head for Chinle.

Once there, he made another stop at the district Tribal Police office to make sure his visit wouldn't tread on the toes of the investigating officer. He found Sergeant Addison Deke at his desk. They chatted about family matters and mutual friends and finally got around to the shooting of Amos Nez.

Deke shook his head, produced a wry grin. "The people around here have that one all solved for us," he said. "They say old Nez was tipping us off about who was breaking into tourists' cars up on the canyon lookout points. So the burglars got mad at him and shot him."

"That makes sense," Leaphorn said. Which it did, even though he could tell from Deke's face that it wasn't true.

"Nez hadn't told us a damn thing, of course," Deke said. "And when we asked him about the rumor, it pissed him off. He was insulted that his neighbors would even think such a thing."

Leaphorn chuckled. Car break-ins at several of the Navajo Nation's more popular tourist attractions were a chronic headache for the Tribal Police. They usually involved one or two hard-up families whose boys considered the salable items left in tourist cars a legitimate harvest — like wild asparagus, rabbits, and sand plums. Their neighbors disapproved, but it wasn't the sort of thing one would get a boy in trouble over.

Leaphorn's next stop was seven-tenths of a mile up the rim road from the White House Ruins overlook — the point from which the sniper had shot Nez. Leaphorn pulled his Jimmy off into the grass at the spot where Deke had told him they'd found six newly fired 30.06 cartridges. Here the layer of tough igneous rock had broken into a jumble of room-sized boulders, giving the sniper a place to watch and wait out of sight from the road. He looked directly down and across the canyon floor. Nez would have been riding his horse along the track across the sandy bottom of the wash. Not a difficult shot in terms of distance for one who knew how to use a rifle, but shooting down at that angle would require some careful adjustment of the sights to avoid an overshot. Whoever shot Nez knew what he was doing.

The next stop was at the Canyon de Chelly park office on the way in. He chatted with the rangers there and picked up the local gossip. Relative to Hosteen Nez, the speculation was exactly what Leaphorn had heard from Deke. The old man had been shot because he was tipping the cops on the car break-ins. How about enemies? No one could imagine that, and they knew him well. Nez was a kindly man, a traditional who helped his family and was generous with his neighbors. He loved jokes. Always in good humor. Everybody liked him. He'd guided in the canyon for years and he could even handle the tourists who wanted to get drunk without making them angry. Always contributed something to help out with the ceremonials when somebody was having a curing sing.

How about eccentricities? Gambling? Grazing rights problems? Any odd behavior? Well, yes. Nez's mother-in-law lived with him, which was a direct violation of the taboo against such conduct. But Nez rationalized that. He said he and old lady Benally had been good friends for years before he'd met her daughter. They'd talked it over and decided that when the Holy People taught that a son-in-law seeing his mother-in-law caused insanity, blindness, and other maladies, they meant that this happened when the two didn't like each other. Anyway, old lady Benally was still going strong in her nineties and Nez was not blind and didn't seem to be any crazier than anyone else.

Indeed, Nez seemed to be feeling pretty good when Leaphorn found him.

"Pretty good," he said, "considering the shape I'm in." And when Leaphorn laughed at that, he added, "But if I'd known I was going to live so damn long, I'd have taken better care of myself."

Nez was sprawled in a wired-together overstuffed recliner, his head almost against the red sandstone wall of a cul-de-sac behind his hogan. The early afternoon sun beat down upon him. Warmth radiated from the cliff behind him, the sky overhead was almost navy blue, and the air was cool and fresh, and smelled of autumn's last cutting of alfalfa hay from a field up the canyon. Nothing in the scene, except for the cast on the Nez legs and the bandages on his neck and chest, reminded Leaphorn of a hospital room.

Leaphorn had introduced himself in the traditional Navajo fashion, identifying his parents and their clans. "I wonder if you remember me," he said. "I'm the policeman who talked to you three times a long time ago when the man you'd been guiding disappeared."

"Sure," Nez said. "You kept coming back. Acting like you'd forgot something to ask me, and then asking me everything all over again."

"Well, I was pretty forgetful."

"Glad to hear that," Nez said. "I thought you figured I was maybe lying to you a little bit and if you asked me often enough I'd forget and tell the truth."

This notion didn't seem to bother Nez. He motioned Leaphorn to sit on the boulder beside his chair.

"Now you want to talk to me about who'd want to shoot me. I tell you one thing right now. It wasn't no car burglars. That's a lot of lies they're saying about me."

Leaphorn nodded. "That's right," he said. "The police at Chinle told me you weren't helping them catch those people."

Nez seemed pleased at that. He nodded.

"But you know, maybe the car burglars don't know that," Leaphorn said. "Maybe they think you're telling on 'em."

Nez shook his head. "No," he said. "They know better. They're my kinfolks."

"You picked a good place to get some sunshine here," Leaphorn said. "Lots of heat off the cliff. Out of the wind. And —"

Nez laughed. "And nobody can get a shot at me here. Not from the rim anyway."

"I noticed that," Leaphorn said.

"I figured you had."

"I read the police report," Leaphorn said, and recited it to Nez. "That about right?"

"That's it," Nez said. "The son of a bitch just kept shooting. After I sort of crawled under the horse, he hit the horse twice more." Nez whacked his hand against the cast. "Thump. Thump."

"Sounds like he wanted to kill you," Leaphorn said.

"I thought maybe he just didn't like my horse," Nez said. "He was a pretty sorry horse. Liked to bite people."

"The last time I came to see you it was also bad news," Leaphorn said. "You think there could be any connection?"

"Connection?" Nez said. He looked genuinely surprised. "No. I didn't think of that." But he thought now, staring at Leaphorn, frowning. "Connection," he repeated. "How could there be? What for?"

Leaphorn shrugged. "I don't know. It was just a thought. Did anybody tell you our missing man from way back then has turned up?"

"No," Nez said, looking delighted. "I didn't know that. After a month or so I figured he must be dead. Didn't make

89

any sense to leave that pretty woman that way."

"You were right. He was dead. We just found his bones," Leaphorn said, and watched Nez, waiting for the question. But no question came.

"I thought so," Nez said. "Been dead a long time, too, I bet."

"Probably more than ten years," Leaphorn said.

"Yeah," Nez said. He shook his head, said, "Crazy bastard," and looked sad.

Leaphorn waited.

"I liked him," Nez said. "He was a good man. Funny. Lots of jokes."

"Are you going to play games with me like you did eleven years ago, or you going to tell me what you know about this? Like why you think he was crazy and why you thought he'd been dead all this time."

"I don't tell on people," Nez said. "There's already plenty of trouble without that."

"There won't be any more trouble for Harold Breedlove," Leaphorn said. "But from the look of all those bandages, there's been some trouble for you."

Nez considered that. Then he considered Leaphorn.

"Tell me if you found him on Ship Rock," Nez said. "Was he climbing Tse' Bit' a'i'?"

Absolutely nothing Amos Nez could have said would have surprised Leaphorn more than that. He spent a few moments re-collecting his wits.

"That's right," he said finally. "Somebody spotted his skeleton down below the peak. How the hell did you know?"

Nez shrugged.

"Did Breedlove tell you he was going there?"

"He told me."

"When?"

Nez hesitated again. "He's dead?"

"Dead."

"When I was guiding them," Nez said. "We were way up Canyon del Muerto. His woman, Mrs. Breedlove, she'd gone up a little ways around the corner. To urinate, I guess it was. Breedlove, he'd been talking about climbing the cliff there." He gestured upward. "You been up there. It's straight up. Worse than that. Some places the top hangs over. I said nobody could do it. He said he could. He told me some places he'd climbed up in Colorado. He started talking then about all the things he wanted to do while he was still young and now he was already thirty years old and he hadn't done them. And then he said —" Nez cut it off, looking at Leaphorn.

"I'm not a policeman anymore," he said. "I'm retired, like you. I just want to know what the hell happened to the man."

"Maybe I should have told you then," Nez said.

"Yeah. Maybe you should have," Leaphorn said. "Why didn't you?"

"Wasn't any reason to," Nez said. "He said he wasn't going to do it until spring came. Said now it was too close to winter. He said not to talk about it because his wife wanted him to stop climbing."

"Did Mrs. Breedlove hear him?"

"She was off taking a leak," Nez said. "He said he thought maybe he'd do it all by himself. Said nobody had ever done that."

"Did you think he meant it? Did he sound serious?"

"Sounded serious, yes. But I thought he was just bragging. White men do that a lot."

"He didn't say where he was going?"

"His wife came back then. He shut up about it."

"No, I mean did he say anything about where he was going to go that evening? After you came in out of the canyon."

"I remember they had some friends coming to see them. They were going to eat together."

"Not drinking, was he?"

"Not drinking," Nez said. "I don't let my tourists drink. It's against the law."

"So he said he was going to climb Tse' Bit' a'i' the following spring," Leaphorn said. "Is that the way you remember it?"

"That's what he said."

They sat a while, engulfed by sunlight, cool air, and silence. A raven planed down from the rim, circled around a cottonwood, landed on a Russian olive across the canyon floor, and perched, waiting for them to die.

Nez extracted a pack of cigarettes from his shirt, offered one to Leaphorn, and lit one for himself.

"Like to smoke while I'm thinking," he said.

"I used to do that too," Leaphorn said. "But my wife talked me into quitting."

"They'll do that if you're not careful," Nez said.

"Thinking about what?"

"Thinking about why he told me that. You know, maybe he figured I'd say something and his woman would hear it and stop him." Nez exhaled a cloud of blue smoke. "And he wanted somebody to stop him. Or when spring came and he slipped off to climb it by himself, he thought maybe he'd fall off and get killed and if nobody knew where he was nobody would find his body. And he didn't want to be up there dead and all alone."

"And you think he figured you'd hear about him disappearing and you'd tell people where to find him?" Leaphorn asked.

"Maybe," Nez said, and shrugged.

"It didn't work."

"Because he was already missing," Nez said. "Where was he all those months between when he goes away from his wife here, and when he climbed our Rock with Wings?"

Leaphorn grinned. "That's what I was hoping you'd know something about. Did he say anything that gave you ideas about where he was going after he left here? Who he was meeting?"

Nez shook his head. "That's a long

time to stay away from that good woman," Nez said. "Way too long, I think. I guess you policemen haven't found out where he was?"

"No," Leaphorn said. "We don't have the slightest idea."

8

A mild prelude to winter had come quietly during the night, slipping across the Arizona border, covering Chee's house trailer with about five inches of wet whiteness. It caused him to shift his pickup into four-wheel drive to make the climb from his site under the San Juan River cottonwoods up the slope to the highway. But the first snow of winter is a cheering sight for natives of the high, dry Four Corners country. It's especially cheering for those doing Chee's criminal investigation division's job. The snow was making extra work for the troopers out on the highways, but for the detectives it dampened down the crime rate.

Lieutenant Jim Chee's good humor even survived the sight of the stack of folders Jenifer had dumped on his desk. The note atop them said: "Cap. Largo wants to talk to you right away about the one on top but I don't think he'll be in before noon because with this snow he'll have to get some feed out to his cows."

On the table of organization, Jenifer

was Chee's employee, the secretary of his criminal investigation unit. But Jenifer had been hired by Captain Largo a long time ago and had seen lieutenants come and go. Chee understood that as far as Jenifer was concerned he was still on probation. But the friendly tone of the note suggested she was thinking he might meet her standards.

"Hah!" he said, grinning. But that faded away before he finished working through the folders. The top one concerned the theft of two more Angus calves from a woman named Roanhorse who had a grazing lease west of Red Rock. The ones in the middle involved a drunken brawl at a girl dance at the Lukachukai chapter house, in which shots were fired and the shooter fled in a pickup, not his own; a request for a transfer from this office by Officer Bernadette (Bernie) Manuelito, the rookie trainee Chee had inherited with the job; a report of drug use and purported gang activity around Hogback, and so forth. Plus, of course, forms to be filled out on mileage, maintenance, and gasoline usage by patrol vehicles, and a reminder that he hadn't submitted vacation schedules for his office.

The final folder held a citizen's complaint that he was being harassed by Officer Manuelito. What remained of Chee's high spirits evaporated as he read it.

The form was signed by Roderick Diamonte. Mr. Diamonte alleged that Officer Manuelito was parking her Tribal Police car at the access road to his place of business at Hogback, stopping his customers on trumped-up traffic violations, and using what Diamonte called "various sneaky tricks" in an effort to violate their constitutional protection against illegal searches. He asked that Officer Manuelito be ordered to desist from this harassment and be reprimanded.

Diamonte? Yes, indeed. Chee remembered the name from the days when he had been a patrolman assigned here. Diamonte operated a bar on the margin of reservation land and was one of the first people to come to mind when something lucrative and illegal was going on. Still, he had his rights.

Chee buzzed Jenifer and asked if Manuelito was in. She was out on patrol.

"Would you call her? Tell her I want

to talk to her when she comes in. Please." Chee had learned early on that Jenifer's response time shortened when an order became a request.

"Right," Jenifer said. "I thought you'd want to talk to her. I guess you know who that Diamonte is, don't you?"

"I remember him," Chee said.

"And you had a call," Jenifer said. "From Janet Pete in Washington. She left a number."

Someday when he was better established Chee intended to talk to his secretary about her practice of deciding which calls to tell him about when. Calls from Janet tended to get low priority. Maybe that was because Jenifer had the typical cop attitude about defense lawyers. Or maybe not.

He called the number.

"Jim," she said. "Ah, Jim. It's good to hear your voice."

"And yours," he said. "You called to tell me you're headed out to National Airport. Flying home. You want me to pick you up at the Farmington Airport?"

"Don't I wish," she said. "But I'm stuck here a little longer. How about you? The job getting any easier? And did you get a snowstorm? The weather girl always stands in front of the Four Corners when she's giving us the news, but it looked like a front was pushing across from the west."

They talked about the weather for a moment, talked about love, talked about wedding plans. Chee didn't ask her about the Justice Department and Bureau of Indian Affairs business that had called her away. It was one of several little zones of silence that develop when a cop and a defense lawyer are dating.

And then Janet said: "Anything new developing on the Fallen Man business?"

"Fallen Man?" Chee hadn't been giving that any thought. It was a closed case. A missing person found. A corpse identified. Officially an accidental death. Officially none of his business. A curious affair, true, but the world of a police lieutenant was full of such oddities and he had too much pressing stuff on his desk to give it any time.

"No. Nothing new." Chee wanted to say, "He's in the dead file," but he was a little too traditional for that. Death is not a subject for Navajo humor.

"Do you know if anyone ever climbed

up there — I mean after the rescue party brought the bones down — to see if they could find any evidence of funny stuff?"

Chee thought about that. And about Janet's interest in it.

"You know," she continued, talking into his silence. "Was there any suggestion that it might not have been an accident? Or that somebody was up there with him and just didn't report it?"

"No," Chee said. "Anyway, we didn't send anyone up." He found himself feeling defensive. "The only apparent motive would be the widow wanting his money, and she waited five years before getting him declared legally dead. And had an ironclad alibi. And —" But Chee stopped. Irked. Why explain all this? She already knew it. They'd talked about it the last time he'd seen her. At dinner in Farmington.

"Why —" he began, but she was already talking. A new subject. She'd gone to a dinner concert at the Library of Congress last night, some fifteenth-century music played on the fifteenth-century instruments. Very interesting. The French ambassador was there — and his wife. You should have seen her dress. Wow. And so it went.

When the call was over, Chee picked up the Manuelito file again. But he held it unopened while he thought about Janet's interest in the Fallen Man. And about how a dinner concert at the Library of Congress must have been by invitation only. Or restricted to major donors to some fund or other. Super exclusive. In fact he had no idea the Library of Congress even produced such events, no idea how he could wangle an invitation if he'd wanted to go, no idea how Janet had come to be there.

Well, yes, he did have an idea about that. Of course. Janet had friends in Washington. From those days when she had worked there as what she called "the House Indian" of Dalman, MacArthur, White and Hertzog, Attorneys at Law. One of those friends had been John McDermott. Her ex-lover and exploiter. From whom Janet had fled.

Chee escaped from that unhappy thought into the problem presented by Officer Bernadette Manuelito.

The Navajo culture that had produced Acting Lieutenant Jim Chee had taught him the power of words and of thought. Western metaphysicians might argue that language and imagination are products of reality. But in their own migrations out of Mongolia and over the icy Bering Strait, the Navajos brought with them a much older Asian philosophy. Thoughts, and words that spring from them, bend the individual's reality. To speak of death is to invite it. To think of sorrow is to produce it. He would think of his duties instead of his love.

Chee flipped open the Manuelito folder. He read through it, wondering why he could have ever believed he wanted an administrative post. That brought him back to Janet. He'd wanted the promotion to impress her, to make himself eligible, to narrow the gap between the child of the urban privileged class and the child of the isolated sheep camp. Thus he had made a thoroughly non-Navajo decision based on an utterly non-Navajo way of thinking. He put down the Manuelito file and buzzed Jenifer.

Officer Manuelito, it seemed, had come in early, and called in about nine saying she was working on the cattle-rustling problem. Chee allowed himself a rare expletive. What the hell was she doing about cattle theft? She was supposed to be finding witnesses to a homicide at a wild party.

"Would you ask the dispatcher to contact her, please, and ask her to come in?" Chee said.

"Want 'em to tell her why?" Jenifer asked.

"Just tell her I want to talk to her," Chee said, forgetting to say please.

But what would he say to Officer Manuelito? He'd have time to decide that by the time she got to the office. It would keep him from thinking about what might have provoked Janet's curiosity about Harold Breedlove, late of the Breedlove family that had been a client of John McDermott.

9

As it happened, Officer Manuelito didn't get to the office.

"She says she's stuck," Jenifer reported. "She went out Route 5010 south of Rattlesnake and turned off on that dirt track that skirts around the west side of Ship Rock. Then she slid off into a ditch." This amused Jenifer, who chuckled. "I'll see if I can get somebody to go pull her out."

"I think I'll just take care of it myself," Chee said. "But thanks anyway."

He pulled on his jacket. What the devil was Manuelito doing out in that empty landscape by the Rock with Wings? He'd told her to work her way down a list of people who might be willing to talk about gang membership at Shiprock High School, not practicing her skill at driving in mud.

Just getting out of the parking lot demonstrated to Chee how Manuelito could manage to get stuck. The overnight storm had drifted eastward, leaving the town of Shiprock under a cloudless sky. The temperature was already well above freezing and the sun was making short work of the snow. But even after he shifted into four-wheel drive, Chee's truck did some wheel-spinning. The ditches beside the highway were already carrying runoff water and a cloud of white steam swirled over the asphalt where the moisture was evaporating.

Navajo Route 5010, according to the road map, was "improved." Which meant it was graded now and then and in theory at least had a gravel surface. On a busy day, probably six or eight vehicles would use it. This morning, Officer Manuelito's patrol car had been the first to leave its tracks in the snow and Chee's pickup was number two. Chee noted approvingly that she had made a slow and careful left turn off of 5010 onto an unnumbered access road that led toward Ship Rock — thereby leaving no skid marks. He made the same turn, felt his rear wheels slipping, corrected, and eased the truck gingerly down the road.

All muscles were tense, all senses alert. He was enjoying testing his skill against the slick road surface. Enjoying the clean, cold air in his lungs, the gray-and-white patterns of soft snow on sage and salt bush and chamisa, enjoying the beauty, the vast emptiness, and a silence broken only by the sound of his truck's engine and its tires in the mud. The immense basalt monolith of Ship Rock towered beside him, its west face still untouched by the warming sun and thus still coated with its whitewash of snow. The Fallen Man must have prayed for that sort of moisture before his thirst killed him on that lonely ledge.

Then the truck topped a hillock, and there was Officer Bernadette Manuelito, a tiny figure standing beside her stuck patrol car, representing an unsolved administrative problem, the end of joy, and a reminder of how good life had been when he was just a patrolman. Ah, well, there was a bright side. Even from here he could see that Manuelito had stuck her car so thoroughly that there would be no hope of towing it out with his vehicle. He'd simply give her a ride back to the office and send out a tow truck.

Officer Manuelito had seemed to Lieutenant Jim Chee to be both unusually pretty and unusually young to be wearing a Navajo Tribal Police uniform.

This morning she wouldn't have made that impression. She looked tired and disheveled and at least her age, which Chee knew from her personnel records was twenty-six years. She also looked surly. He leaned across the pickup seat and opened the door for her.

"Tough luck," he said. "Get your stuff out of it, and the weapons, and lock it up. We'll send out a tow truck to get it when the mud dries."

Officer Manuelito had prepared an explanation of how this happened and would not be deterred.

"The snow covered up a little wash, there. Drifted it full so you couldn't see it. And . . ."

"It could happen to anybody," Chee said. "Let's go."

"You didn't bring a tow chain?"

"I did bring a tow chain," Chee said. "But look at it. There's no traction now. It's clay and it's too soft."

"You have four-wheel drive," she said.

"I know," Chee said, feeling in no mood to debate this. "But that just means you dig yourself in by spinning four wheels instead of two. I couldn't budge it. Get your stuff and get in."

Officer Manuelito brushed a lock of

hair off her forehead, leaving a streak of gray mud. Her lips parted with a response, then closed. "Yes, sir," she said.

That was all she said. Chee backed the pickup to a rocky place, turned it, and slipped and slid his way back to 5010 in leaden silence. Back on the gravel, he said:

"Did you know that Diamonte filed a complaint against you? Charged you with harassment."

Officer Manuelito was staring out the windshield. "No," she said. "But I knew he said he was going to."

"Yep," Chee said. "He did. Said you were hanging around. Bothering his customers."

"His dope buyers."

"Some of them, probably," Chee said.

Manuelito stared relentlessly out of the windshield.

"What were you doing?" Chee asked.

"You mean besides harassing his customers?"

"Besides that," Chee said, thinking that the very first thing he would do when they got back to the office was approve this woman's transfer to anywhere. Preferably to Tuba City, which was about as far as he could get her from Shiprock. He glanced at her, waiting for a reply. She was still focused on the windshield.

"You know what he runs out there?" she said.

"I know what he used to do when I was assigned here before," Chee said. "In those days he wholesaled booze to the reservation bootleggers, fenced stolen property, handled some marijuana. Things like that. Now I understand he's branched out into more serious dope."

"That's right," she said. "He still supplies the creeps who push pot and now he's selling the worse stuff too."

"That's what I always heard," Chee said. "And most recently from Teddy Begayaye. The kid Begayaye picked up at the community college last week named Diamonte as his source for coke. But then he changed his mind and decided he just couldn't remember where he got it."

"I know Diamonte's selling it."

"So you bring in your evidence. We take it to the captain, he takes it to the federal prosecutors, or maybe the San Juan County cops, and we put the bastard in jail."

"Sure," Manuelito said.

"But we don't go out there, with no evidence, and harass his customers. There's a law against it."

Chee sensed that she was no longer staring at the windshield. She was looking at him.

"I heard that you did," she said. "When you were a cop here before."

Chee felt his face flushing. "Who told you that?"

"Captain Largo told us when we were in recruit training."

The son of a bitch, Chee thought.

"Largo was using me as a bad example?"

"He didn't say who did it. But I asked around. People said it was you."

"It just about got me kicked out of the police," Chee said. "The same thing could happen to you."

"I heard it got the place shut down, too," Manuelito said.

"Yeah, and about the time I got off suspension, he was going full blast again."

"Still . . ." Manuelito said. And let the thought trail off.

"Don't say 'still.' You stay away from there. It's Begayaye's job, looking into the dope situation. If you run across anything useful, tell Teddy. Or tell me. Don't go freelancing around."

"Yes, sir," Manuelito said, sounding very formal.

"I mean it," Chee said. "I'll put a letter in your file reporting these instructions."

"Yes, sir," Manuelito said.

"Now. What's this transfer request about? What's wrong with Shiprock? And where do you want to go?"

"I don't care. Anywhere."

That surprised Chee. He'd guessed Manuelito wanted to be closer to a boyfriend somewhere. Or that her mother was sick. Something like that. But now he remembered that she was from Red Rock. By Big Rez standards, Shiprock was conveniently close to her family.

"Is there something about Shiprock you don't like?"

That question produced a long silence, and finally:

"I just want to get away from here."

"Why?"

"It's a personal reason," she said. "I don't have to say why, do I? It's not in the personnel rules."

"I guess not," Chee said. "Anyway, I'll approve it."

"Thank you," Manuelito said.

"That's no guarantee you'll get it, though. You know how it works. Largo may kill it. And there has to be the right kind of opening somewhere. You'll have to be patient."

Officer Manuelito was pointing out the window. "Did you notice that?" she asked.

All Chee saw was the grassland rolling away toward the great dark shape of Ship Rock.

"I mean the fence," she said. "There where that wash runs down into the borrow ditch. Notice the posts."

Chee noticed the posts, two of which were leaning sharply. He stopped the pickup.

"Somebody dug at the base of the posts," she said. "Loosened them so you could pull them up."

"And lay the fence down?"

"More likely raise it up," she said. "Then you could drive cows down the wash and right under it."

"Do you know whose grazing lease this is?"

"Yes, sir," she said. "A man named Maryboy has it."

"Has he lost any cattle?"

113

"I don't know. Not lately, anyway. At least I haven't seen a report on it."

Chee climbed out of the truck, plodded through the snow, and tried the posts. They lifted easily but the snow made it impossible to determine exactly why. He thought about Zorro, Mr. Finch's favorite cow thief.

Manuelito was standing beside him.

"See?" she said.

"When did you notice this?"

"I don't know," Officer Manuelito said. "Just a few days ago."

"If I remember right, just a few days ago — and today too — you were supposed to be running down that list of people at that dance. Looking for anyone willing to tell us about gang membership. About what they saw. Who'd tell us who had the gun. Who shot it. That sort of thing. Is that right? That was number one on the list you were handed after the staff meeting."

"Yes, sir," Officer Manuelito said, proving she could sound meek if she wanted to. She was looking down at her hands.

"Do any of those possible witnesses live out here?"

"Well, not exactly. The Roanhorse

couple is on the list. They live over near Burnham."

"Near Burnham?" The Burnham trading post was way to hell south of here. Down Highway 666.

"I sort of detoured over this way," Manuelito explained uneasily. "We had that report that Lucy Sam had lost some cattle, and I knew the captain was after you about catching somebody and putting a stop to that and —"

"How did you know that?"

Now Manuelito's face was a little flushed. "Well," she said. "You know how people talk about things."

Yes, Chee knew about that.

"Are you telling me you just drove out here blind? What were you looking for?"

"Well," she said. "I was just sort of looking."

Chee waited. "Just sort of looking?"

"Well," she said. "I remembered my grandfather telling me about Hosteen Sam. That was Lucy's father. About him hating it when white people came out here to climb Ship Rock. They would park out there, over that little rise there by the foot of the cliff. He would write down their license number or what the car looked like and when he went into town he would go by the police station and try to get the police to arrest them for trespassing. So when I was assigned here, and one of the problems worrying the captain was people stealing cattle, I came out here to ask Hosteen Sam if he would keep track of strange pickups and trucks for us."

"Pretty good idea," Chee said. "What did he say?"

"He was dead. Died last year. But his daughter said she would do it for me and I gave her a little notebook for it, but she said she had the one her father had used. So, anyway, I thought I would just make a little detour by there and see if she had written down anything for us."

"Quite a little detour," Chee said. "I'd say about sixty miles or so. Had she?"

"I don't know. I noticed some other posts leaning over and I decided to pull off and see if they had been cut off or dug up or anything else funny. And then I got stuck."

It was a clever idea, Chee was thinking. He should have thought of it himself. He'd see if he could find some people to keep a similar eye on things up near the Ute reservation, and over

116

on the Checkerboard. Wherever people were losing cattle. Who could he get? But he was distracted from that thought. His feet, buried to the ankles in the melting snow, were complaining about the cold. And the sun had now risen far enough to illuminate a different set of snowfields high above them on Ship Rock. They reflected a dazzling white light.

Officer Manuelito was watching him. "Beautiful, isn't it?" she said. "Tse' Bit' a'i'. It never seems to look the same."

"I remember noticing that when I was a little boy and I was staying for a while with an aunt over near Toadlena," Chee said. "I thought it was alive."

Officer Manuelito was staring at it. "Beautiful," she said, and shuddered. "I wonder what he was doing up there. All alone."

"The Fallen Man?"

"Deejay doesn't think he fell. He said no bones were broken and if you'd fallen down that cliff it would break something. Deejay thinks he was climbing with somebody and they just stranded him there."

"Who knows?" Chee said. "Anyway, it's not in the books as anything but an accidental death. No evidence of foul play. We don't have to worry about it." Chee's feet were telling him that his boots were leaking. Leaking ice water. "Let's go," he said, heading back for his truck.

Officer Manuelito was still standing there, staring up at the cliffs towering above her.

"They say Monster Slayer couldn't get down either. When he climbed up to the top and killed the Winged Monster he couldn't get down."

"Come on," Chee said. He climbed into the truck and started the engine, thinking that you'd have a better chance if you were a spirit like Monster Slayer. When spirits scream for help other spirits hear them. Spider Woman had heard and came to the rescue. But Harold Breedlove could have called forever with nothing but the ravens to hear him. The stuff of bad dreams.

They drove in silence.

Then Officer Manuelito said, "To be trapped up there. I try not to even think about it. It would give me nightmares."

"What?" Chee said, who hadn't been listening because by then he was working his way around a nightmare of his own. He was trying to think of another reason Janet Pete might have asked him about the Fallen Man affair. He wanted to find a reason that didn't involve John McDermott and his law firm representing the Breedlove family. Maybe it was the oddity of the skeleton on the mountain that provoked her question. He always came back to that. But then he'd find himself speculating on who had taken Janet to that concert and he'd think of John McDermott again.

10

The first thing Joe Leaphorn noticed when he came through the door was his breakfast dishes awaiting attention in the sink. It was a bad habit and it demanded correction. No more of this sinking into slipshod widower ways. Then he noticed the red light blinking atop his telephone answering machine. The indicator declared he'd received two calls today — pretty close to a post-retirement record. He took a step toward the telephone.

But no. First things first. He detoured into the kitchen, washed his cereal bowl, saucer, and spoon, dried them, and put them in their place on the dish rack. Then he sat in his recliner, put his boots on the footstool, picked up the telephone, and pushed the button.

The first call was from his auto insurance dealer, informing him that if he'd take a defensive driving course he could get a discount on his liability rates. He punched the button again.

"Mr. Leaphorn," the voice said. "This is John McDermott. I am an attorney and our firm has represented the interests of the Edgar Breedlove family for many years. I remember that you investigated the disappearance of Harold Breedlove several years ago when you were a member of the Navajo Tribal Police. Would you be kind enough to call me, collect, and discuss whether you might be willing to help the family complete its own investigation of his death?"

McDermott had left an Albuquerque number. Leaphorn dialed it.

"Oh, yes," the secretary said. "He was hoping you'd call."

After the "thank you for calling," McDermott didn't linger long over formalities.

"We would like you to get right onto this for us," he said. "If you're available, our usual rate is twenty-five dollars an hour, plus your expenses."

"You mentioned completing the investigation," Leaphorn said. "Does that mean you have some question about the identification of the skeleton?"

"There is a question concerning just about everything," McDermott said. "It is a very peculiar case."

"Could you be more specific? I need a better idea of what you'd like to find out."

"This isn't the sort of thing we can discuss over the telephone," McDermott said. "Nor is it the sort of thing I can talk about until I know whether you will accept a retainer." He produced a chuckle. "Family business, you know."

Leaphorn discovered he was allowing himself to be irritated by the tone of this — not a weakness he tolerated. And he was curious. He produced a chuckle of his own.

"From what I remember of the Breedlove disappearance, I don't see how I could help you. Would you like me to recommend someone?"

"No. No," McDermott said. "We'd like to use you."

"But what sort of information would I be looking for?" Leaphorn asked. "I was trying to find out what happened to the man. Why he didn't come back to Canyon de Chelly that evening. Where he went. What happened to him. And of course the important thing was what happened to him. We know that now, if the identification of the skeleton is correct. The rest of it doesn't seem to matter."

McDermott spent a few moments deciding how to respond.

"The family would like to establish who was up there with him," he said.

Now this was getting a bit more interesting. "They've learned someone was up there when he fell? How did they learn that?"

"A mere physical fact. We've talked to rock climbers who know that mountain. They say you couldn't do it alone, not to the point where they found the skeleton. They say Harold Breedlove didn't have the skills, the experience, to have done it."

Leaphorn waited but McDermott had nothing to add.

"The implication, then, is that someone went up with him. When he fell, they abandoned him and didn't report it. Is that what you're suggesting?"

"And why would they do that?" McDermott asked.

Leaphorn found himself grinning. Lawyers! The man didn't want to say it himself. Let the witness say it.

"Well, let's see then. They might do it if, for example, they had pushed him over. Given him a fatal shove. Watched him fall. Then they might forget to report it."

"Well, yes."

"And you're suggesting the family has some lead to who this forgetful person might be."

"No, I'm not suggesting anything."

"The only lead, then, is the list of those who might be motivated. If I can rely on my memory, the only one I knew of was the widow. The lady who would inherit. I presume she did inherit, didn't she? But perhaps there's a lot I didn't know. We didn't have a criminal case to work on, you know. We didn't — and still don't — have a felony to interest the Navajo Police or the Federal Bureau of Investigation. Just a missing person then. Now we have what is presumed to be an accidental death. There was never any proof that he hadn't simply —" Leaphorn paused, looked for a better way to phrase it, found none, and concluded, "Simply run away from wife and home."

"Greed is often the motivation in murder," McDermott said.

Murder, Leaphorn thought. It was the first time that word had been used.

"That's true. But if I am remembering what I was told at the time, there wasn't much to inherit except the ranch, and it was losing money. Unless there was some sort of nuptial agreement, she would have owned half of it anyway. Colorado law. The wife's community property. And if I remember what I learned then, Breedlove had already mortgaged it. Was there a motive beyond greed?"

McDermott let the question hang. "If you'll work with this, I'll discuss it with you in person."

"I always wondered if there was a nuptial agreement. But now I've heard that she owns the ranch."

"No nuptial agreement," McDermott said, reluctantly. "What do you think? If you don't like the hourly arrangement, we could make it a weekly rate. Multiply the twenty-five dollars by forty hours and make it a thousand a week."

A thousand a week, Leaphorn thought. A lot of money for a retired cop. And what would McDermott be charging his client?

"I tell you what I'll do," Leaphorn said. "I'll give it some thought. But I'll have to have some more specific information."

"Sleep on it, then," McDermott said. "I'm coming to Window Rock tomorrow anyway. Why don't we meet for lunch?"

Joe Leaphorn couldn't think of any reason not to do that. He wasn't doing anything else tomorrow. Or for the rest of the week, for that matter.

They set the date for one P.M. at the Navajo Inn. That allowed time for the lunch-hour crowd to thin and for McDermott to make the two-hundred-mile drive from Albuquerque. It also gave Leaphorn the morning hours to collect information on the telephone, talking to friends in the ranching business, a Denver banker, a cattle broker, learning all he could about the Lazy B ranch and the past history of the Breedloves.

That done, he drove down to the Inn and waited in the office lobby. A white Lexus pulled into the parking area and two men emerged: one tall and slender with graying blond hair, the other six inches shorter, dark-haired, sun-browned, with the heavy-shouldered, slim-waisted build of one who lifts weights and plays handball. Ten minutes early, but it was probably McDermott and who? An assistant, perhaps.

Leaphorn met them at the entrance, went through the introductions, and ushered them in to the quiet corner table he'd arranged to hold.

"Shaw," Leaphorn said. "George Shaw? Is that correct?"

"Right," the dark man said. "Hal Breedlove was my cousin. My best friend, too, for that matter. I was the executor of the estate when Elisa had him declared legally dead."

"A sad situation," Leaphorn said.

"Yes," Shaw said. "And strange."

"Why do you say that?" Leaphorn could think of a dozen ways Breedlove's death was strange. But which one would Mr. Shaw pick?

"Well," Shaw said. "Why wasn't the fall reported, for one thing?"

"You don't think he made the climb alone?"

"Of course not. He couldn't have," Shaw said. "I couldn't do it, and I was a grade or two better at rock climbing than Hal. Nobody could."

Leaphorn recommended the chicken enchilada, and they all ordered it. McDermott inquired whether Leaphorn had considered their offer. Leaphorn said he had. Would he accept, then? They'd like to get moving on it right away. Leaphorn said he needed some more information. Their orders arrived.

Delicious, thought Leaphorn, who had been dining mostly on his own cooking. McDermott ate thoughtfully. Shaw took a large bite, rich with green chile, and frowned at his fork.

"What sort of information?" McDermott asked.

"What am I looking for?" Leaphorn said.

"As I told you," McDermott said, "we can't be too specific. We just want to know that we have every bit of information that's available. We'd like to know why Harold Breedlove left Canyon de Chelly, and precisely when, and who he met and where they went. Anything that might concern his widow and her affairs at that time. We want to know everything that might cast light on this business." McDermott gave Leaphorn a small, deprecatory smile. "Everything," he said.

"My first question was what I would be looking for," Leaphorn said. "My second one is why? This must be expensive. If Mr. Shaw here is willing to pay me a thousand a week through your law firm, you will be charging him, what? The rate for an Albuquerque lawyer I know about used to be a hundred and ten dollars an hour. But that was long ago, and that was Albuquerque. Double it for a Washington firm? Would that be about right?"

"It isn't cheap," McDermott said.

"And maybe I find nothing useful at all. Probably you learn nothing. Tracks are cold after eleven years. But let us say that you learn the widow conspired to do away with her husband. I don't know for sure but I'd guess then she couldn't inherit. So the family gets the ranch back. What's it worth? Wonderful house, I hear, if someone rich wants to live in it way out there. Maybe a hundred head of cattle. I'm told there's still an old mortgage Harold's widow took out six years ago to pay off her husband's debts. How much could you get for that ranch?"

"It's a matter of justice," McDermott said. "I am not privy to the family's motives, but I presume they want some equity for Harold's death."

Leaphorn smiled.

Shaw had been sipping his coffee. He drained the cup and slammed it into the saucer with a clatter.

"We want to see Harold's killer hanged," he said. "Isn't that what they do out here? Hang 'em?"

"Not lately," Leaphorn said. "The mountain is on the New Mexico side of the reservation and New Mexico uses the gas chamber. But it would probably be federal jurisdiction. We Navajos don't have a death penalty and the federal government doesn't hang people." He signaled the waiter, had their coffee replenished, sipped his own, and put down the cup.

"If I take this job I don't want to be wasting my time," he said. "I would look for motives. An obvious one is inheritance of the ranch. That gives you two obvious suspects — the widow and her brother. But neither of them could have done it — at least not in the period right after Harold disappeared. The next possibility would be the widow's boyfriend, if she had one. So I would examine all that. Premeditated murder usually involves a lot of trouble and risk. I never knew of one that didn't grow out of a strong motivation."

Neither Shaw nor McDermott responded to that.

"Usually greed," Leaphorn said.

"Love," said Shaw. "Or lust."

"Which does not seem to have been

130

consummated, from what I know now," Leaphorn said. "The widow remained single. When I was investigating the disappearance years ago I snooped around a little looking for a boyfriend. I couldn't pick up any gossip that suggested a love triangle was involved."

"Easy enough to keep that quiet," Shaw said.

"Not out here it isn't," Leaphorn said. "I would be more interested in an economic motive." He looked at Shaw. "If this is a crime it's a white man's crime. No Navajo would kill anyone on that sacred mountain. I doubt if a Navajo would be disrespectful enough even to climb it. Among my people, murder tends to be motivated by whisky or sexual jealousy. Among white people, I've noticed crime is more likely to be motivated by money. So if I take the job, I'd be turning on my computer and tapping into the metal market statistics and price trends."

Shaw gave McDermott a sidewise glance, which McDermott didn't notice. He was staring at Leaphorn.

"Why?"

"Because the gossipers around Mancos say Edgar Breedlove bought the ranch more because his prospectors had found molybdenum deposits on it than for its grazing. They say the price of moly ore rose enough about ten or fifteen years ago to make development profitable. They say Harold, or the Breed-love family, or somebody, was negotiating for a mineral lease and the Mancos Chamber of Commerce had high hopes of a big mining payroll. But then Harold disappeared and before you know it the price was down again. I'd want to find out if any of that was true."

"I see," McDermott said. "Yes, it would have made the ranch more valuable and made the motive stronger."

"What the hell," Shaw said. "We were keeping quiet about it because news like that leaks out, it causes problems. With local politicians, with the tree-huggers, with everybody else."

"Okay," Leaphorn said. "I guess if I take this job, then I'm safe in figuring the ranch is worth a lot more than the grass growing on it."

"What do you say?" Shaw said, his voice impatient. "Can we count on you to do some digging for us?"

"I'll think about it," Leaphorn said. "I'll call your office."

"We'll be here a day or two," Shaw said. "And we're in a hurry. Why not a decision right now?"

A hurry, Leaphorn thought. After all these years. "I'll let you know tomorrow," he said. "But you haven't answered my question about the value of the ranch."

McDermott looked grim. "You'd be safe to assume it was worth killing for."

11

"Twisting the tail of a cow will encourage her to move forward," the text declared. "If the tail is held up over the back, it serves as a mild restraint. In both cases, the handler should hold the tail close to the base to avoid breaking it, and stand to the side to avoid being kicked."

The paragraph was at the top of the fourth-from-final page of a training manual supplied by the Navajo Nation for training brand inspectors of its Resource Enforcement Agency. Acting Lieutenant Jim Chee read it, put down the manual, and rubbed his eyes. He was not on the payroll of the tribe's REA. But since Captain Largo was forcing him to do its job he'd borrowed an REA brand inspector manual and was plowing his way through it. He'd covered the legal sections relating to grazing rights, trespass, brand registration, bills of sale, when and how livestock could be moved over the reservation boundary, and disease quarantine rules, and was now into advice about handling livestock without getting hurt. To Chee, who had been kicked by several horses but never by a cow, the advice seemed sound. Besides, it diverted him from the paperwork — vacation schedules, justifications for overtime pay, patrol car mileage reports, and so forth — that was awaiting action on his cluttered desk. He picked up the manual.

"The ear twitch can be used to divert attention from other parts of the body," the next paragraph began. "It should be used with care to avoid damage to the ear cartilage. To make the twitch, fasten a loop of cord or rope around the base of the horns. The rope is then carried around the ear and a half-hitch formed. The end of the rope is pulled to apply restraint."

Chee studied the adjoining illustration of a sleepy-looking cow wearing an ear twitch. Chee's childhood experience had been with sheep, on which an ear twitch wouldn't be needed. Still, he figured he could make one easily enough.

The next paragraph concerned a "rope casting harness" with which a person working alone could tie up a mature cow or bull without the risk of strangulation that was involved with usual bulldogging techniques. It looked easy, too, but required a lot of rope. Two pages to go and he'd be finished with this.

Then the telephone rang.

The voice on the telephone belonged to Officer Manuelito.

"Lieutenant," she said, "I've found something I think you should know about."

"Tell me," Chee said.

"Out near Ship Rock, that place where the fence posts had been dug out. You remember?"

"I remember."

"Well, the snow is gone now and you can see where before it snowed some-body had thrown out a bunch of hay."

"Ah," Chee said.

"Like they wanted to attract the cattle. Make them easy to get a rope on. To get 'em into a chute. Into your trailer."

"Manuelito," Chee said. "Have you finished interviewing that list of pos-sible witnesses in that shooting busi-ness?"

Silence. Finally, "Most of them. Some of them I'm still looking for."

"Do they live out near Ship Rock?"

"Well, no. But —"

"Don't say but," Leaphorn said. He shifted his weight in his chair, aware that his back hurt from too much sitting, aware that out in the natural world the sun was bright, the sky a dark blue, the chamisa had turned gold and the snakeweed a brilliant yellow. He sighed.

"Manuelito," he said. "Have you gone out to talk to the Sam woman about whether she's seen anything suspicious?"

"No, sir," Officer Manuelito said, sounding surprised. "You told me to —"

"Where are you calling from?"

"The Burnham trading post," she said. "The people there said they hadn't seen anything at the girl dance. But I think they did."

"Probably," Chee said. "They just didn't want to get the shooter into trouble. So come on in now, and buzz me when you get here, and we'll go out and see if Lucy Sam has seen anything interesting."

"Yes, sir," Officer Manuelito said, and she sounded like she thought that was a good idea. It seemed like a good idea to Chee, too. The tossing hay over the fence business sounded like Zorro's trademark as described by Finch, and that sounded like an opportunity to beat that arrogant bastard at his own game.

Officer Manuelito looked better today. Her uniform was tidy, hair black as a raven's wing and neatly combed, and no mud on her face. But she still displayed a slight tendency toward bossiness.

"Turn up there," she ordered, pointing to the road that led toward Ship Rock, "and I'll show you the hay."

Chee remembered very well the location of the loosened fence posts, but the beauty of the morning had turned him amiable. With Manuelito, he would work on correcting one fault at a time, leaving this one for a rainy day. He turned as ordered, parked when told to park, and followed her over to the fence. With the snow cover now evaporated, it was easy to see that the dirt had been dug away from the posts. It was also easy to see, scattered among the sage, juniper, and rabbit brush, what was left of several bales of alfalfa after the cattle had dined.

"Did you tell Delmar Yazzie about this?" Chee asked.

Officer Manuelito looked puzzled. "Yazzie?"

"Yazzie," Chee said. "The resource-enforcement ranger who works out of Shiprock. Mr. Yazzie is the man responsible for keeping people from stealing cattle."

Officer Manuelito looked flustered. "No, sir," she said. "I thought we could sort of stake this place out. Keep an eye on it, you know. Whoever is putting out this hay bait will be back and once he gets the cows used to coming here, he'll —"

"He'll rig himself up a sort of chute," Chee said, "and back his trailer in here, and drive a few of 'em on it, and . . ."

Chee paused. Her flustered look had been replaced by the smile of youthful enthusiasm. But now Chee's impatient tone had caused the smile to go away.

Acting Lieutenant Chee had intended to tell Officer Manuelito some of what he'd learned in digesting the brand inspector training manual. If they did indeed catch the cattle thief and managed to get a conviction, the absolute maximum penalty for his crime would be a fine "not to exceed $100" and a jail term "not to exceed six months." That's what it said in section 1356 of subchapter six of chapter seven of the Livestock Inspection and Control Manual. Reading that section just after Manuelito's call had fueled Chee's urge to get out of the office and into the sunlight. But why was he venting his bad mood on this rookie cop? Even interrupting her to do it — an inexcusable rudeness for any Navajo. It wasn't her fault, it was Captain Largo's. And besides, Finch had hurt his pride. He wanted to deflate that pompous jerk by catching Finch's Zorro before Finch got him. Manuelito looked like a valuable help in that project.

Chee swallowed, cleared his throat. ". . . and then we'd have an easy conviction," he concluded.

Officer Manuelito's expression had become unreadable. A hard lady to mislead.

"And put a stop to one cow thief," he added, conscious of how lame it sounded. "Well, let's go. Let's see if anyone's at home at the Sam place."

The Rural Electrification Administration had run a power line across the empty landscape off in the direction of the Chuska Mountains, which took it within a few miles of the Sam place, and the Navajo Communication Company had followed by linking such inhabited spots as Rattlesnake and Red Rock to the world with its own telephone lines. But the Sam outfit had either been too far off the route to make a connection feasible, or the Sam family had opted to preserve its privacy. Thus the fence posts that lined the dirt track leading to the Sam hogan were not draped with telephone wire, and thus there had been no way for Jim Chee to warn Ms. Sam of the impending visit.

But as he geared down into low to creep over the cattle guard and onto the track leading into the Sam grazing lease, he noticed the old boot hanging on the gate post was right side up. Someone must be home.

"I hope someone's here," Officer Manuelito said.

"They are," Chee said. He nodded toward the boot.

Officer Manuelito frowned, not understanding.

"The boot's turned up," Chee said. "When you're leaving, and nobody's going to be home, you turn the boot upside down. Empty. Nobody home. That saves your visitor from driving all the way up to the hogan."

"Oh," Manuelito said. "I didn't know that. We lived over near Keams Canyon before Mom moved to Red Rock."

She sounded impressed. Chee became aware that he was showing off. And enjoying it. He nodded, said: "Yep. You probably had a different signal over there." And thought it would be embarrassing now if nobody was home. The trouble with cattle guard signaling was that people forgot to stop and change the boot.

But Lucy Sam's pickup was resting in front of her double-wide mobile home and Lucy Sam was peering out of the screen door at them. Chee let the patrol car roll to a stop amid a flock of startled chickens. They waited, giving Ms. Sam the time required to prepare herself for receiving visitors. It also gave Chee time to inspect the place.

The mobile home was one of the flimsier models but it had been placed solidly on a base of concrete blocks to keep the wind from blowing under it. A small satellite dish sat on its roof, helping a row of old tires hold down the aluminum panels as well as bringing in a television signal. Beside this insubstantial residence stood the Sam hogan, solidly built of sandstone slabs with its door facing properly eastward. Chee's practiced eyes could tell that it had been built to the specifications prescribed for the People by Changing Woman, their giver of laws. Beyond the hogan was a hay shed with a plank holding pen for cattle, a windmill with attendant water tank, and, on top of the shed, a small wind generator, its fan blades spinning in the morning breeze. Down the slope a rusty and long-deceased Ford F100 pickup rested on blocks with its wheels missing. Farther down stood an outhouse. Beyond this untidy clutter of rural living, the view stretched away forever.

It reminded Chee of a professor he'd had once at the University of New Mexico who had done a research project on how Navajos place their hogans. The answer seemed to Chee glaringly obvious. A Navajo, like a rancher anywhere, would need access to water, to grazing, to a road, and above all a soul-healing view of — in the words of one of the curing chants — "beauty all around you."

The Sam family had put beauty first. They had picked the very crest of the high grassy ridge between Red Wash and Little Ship Rock Wash. To the west the morning sun lit the pink and orange wilderness of erosion that gave the Red Rock community its name. Beyond that the blue-green mass of the Carrizo Mountains rose. Far to the north in Colorado, the Roman nose shape of Sleeping Ute Mountain dominated, and west of that was the always-changing pattern of lights and shadows that marked the edge of Utah's canyon country. But look eastward, and all of this was overpowered by the dark monolith of the Rock with Wings towering over the rolling grassland. Only five or six million years old, the geologists said, but in Chee's mythology it had been there since God created time or, depending on the version one preferred, had flown in fairly recently carrying the first Navajo clans down from the north.

Lucy Sam reappeared at her doorway, the signal that she was ready to receive her visitors. She had started a coffeepot brewing on her propane stove, put on a blouse of dark blue velveteen, and donned her silver and turquoise jewelry in their honor. Now they went through

144

the polite formalities of traditional Navajo greetings, seated themselves beside the Sam table, and waited while Ms. Sam extracted what she called her "rustler book" from a cabinet stacked with magazines and papers.

Chee considered himself fairly adept at guessing the ages of males and fairly poor with females. Ms. Sam he thought must be in her late sixties — give or take five or ten years. She did her hair bound up in the traditional style, wore the voluminous long skirt demanded by traditional modesty, and had a television set on a corner table tuned to a morning talk show. It was one of the sleazier ones — a handsome young woman named Ricki something or other probing into the sexual misconduct, misfortune, hatreds, and misery of a row of retarded-looking guests, to the amusement of the studio audience. But Chee was distracted from this spectacle by what was sharing table space with the television set.

It was a telescope mounted on a short tripod and aimed through the window at the world outside. Chee recognized it as a spotting scope — the sort the marksmanship instructor had peered through on the police recruit firing range to tell him how far he'd missed the bull's-eye. This one looked like an older, bulkier model, probably an artillery observer's range-finding scope and probably bought in an army surplus store.

Ms. Sam had placed her book, a black ledger that looked even older than the scope, on the table. She settled a pair of bifocals on her nose and opened it.

"I haven't seen much since you asked me to be watching," she said to Officer Manuelito. "I mean I haven't seen much that you'd want to arrest somebody for." She looked over the bifocals at Chee, grinning. "Not unless you want to arrest that lady that used to work at the Red Rock trading post for fooling with somebody else's husband."

Officer Manuelito was grinning too. Chee apparently looked blank, because Ms. Sam pointed past the telescope and out the window.

"Way over there toward Rock with Wings," she explained. "There's a nice little place down there. Live spring there and cottonwood trees. I was sort of looking around through the telescope to see if any trucks were parked anywhere and I see the lady's little red car just driving up toward the trees. And then in a minute, here comes Bennie Smiley's pickup truck. Then, quite a little bit later, the truck comes out over the hill again, and then four or five minutes, here comes the little red car."

She nodded to Chee, decided he was hopeless, and looked at Manuelito. "It was about an hour," she added, which caused Officer Manuelito's smile to widen.

"Bennie," she said. "I'll be darned."

"Yes," Ms. Sam said.

"I know Bennie," Officer Manuelito said. "He used to be my oldest sister's boyfriend. She liked him but then she found out he was born to the Streams Come Together clan. That's too close to our 'born to' clan for us."

Ms. Sam shook her head, made a disapproving sound. But she was still smiling.

"That lady with the red car," Manuelito said. "I wonder if I know her, too. Is that Mrs. —"

Chee cleared his throat.

"I wonder if you noticed any pickups, anything you could haul a load of hay in, stopped over there on the road past the Rattlesnake pumping station. Probably a day or so before the snow." He glanced at Officer Manuelito, tried to read her expression, decided she was either slightly abashed for gossiping instead of tending to police business, or irritated because he'd interrupted her. Probably the latter.

Ms. Sam was thumbing through the ledger, saying, "Let's see now. Wasn't it Monday night it started snowing?" She thumbed past another page, tapped the paper with a finger. "Big fifth-wheel truck parked there beside Route 33. Dark blue, and the trailer he was pulling was partly red and partly white, like somebody was painting it and didn't get it finished. Had Arizona plates. But that was eight days before it snowed."

"That sounds like my uncle's truck," Manuelito said. "He lives over there at Sanostee."

Ms. Sam said she thought it had looked familiar. And, no, she hadn't noticed any strange trucks the days just before the storm, but then she'd gone into Farmington to buy groceries and was gone one day. She read off the four other entries she'd made since getting Manuelito's request. One sounded like Dick Finch's truck with its bulky camper. None of the others would mean anything unless and until some sort of pattern developed. Pattern! That made him think of the days he'd worked for Leaphorn. Leaphorn was always looking for patterns.

"How did you know it was an Arizona license?" Chee asked. "The telescope?"

"Take a look," Ms. Sam said, and waved at the scope.

Chee did, twiddling the adjustment dial. The mountain jumped at him. Huge. He focused on a slab of basalt fringed with mountain oak. "Wow," Chee said. "Quite a scope."

He turned it, brought in the point where Navajo Route 33 cuts through the Chinese Wall of stone that wanders southward from the volcano. A school bus was rolling down the asphalt, heading for Red Rock after taking kids on their fifty-mile ride into high school at Shiprock.

"We bought it for him, long time ago when he started getting sick," Ms. Sam said — using the Navajo words that avoided alluding directly to the name of the dead. "I saw it in that big pawnshop on Railroad Avenue in Gallup. Then he could sit there and watch the world and keep track of his mountain."

She produced a deprecatory chuckle, as if Chee might think this odd. "Every day he'd write down what he saw. You know. Like which pairs of kestrels were coming back to the same nests. And where the red-tailed hawks were hunting. Which kids were spray-painting stuff on that old water tank down there, or climbing the windmill. That sort of thing."

She sighed, gestured at the talk show. "Better than this stuff. He loved his mountain. Watching it kept him happy."

"I heard he used to come down to Shiprock, to the police station, and report people trespassing and climbing Tse' Bit' a'i'," Chee said. "Is that right?"

"He wanted them arrested," she said. "He said it was wrong, those white people climbing a mountain that was sacred. He said if he was younger and had some money he would go back East and climb up the front of that big cathedral in New York." Ms. Sam laughed. "See how they liked that."

"What sort of things did he write in the book?" Chee asked, thinking of Lieutenant Leaphorn and feeling a twinge of excitement. "Could I see it?"

"All sorts of things," she said, and handed it to him. "He was in the marines. One of the code talkers, and he liked to do things the way they did in the marines."

The entries were dated with the numbers of day, month, and year, and the first one was 25/7/89. After the date Hosteen Sam had written in a tiny, neat missionary-school hand that he had gone into Farmington that day and bought this book to replace the old one, which was full. The next entry was dated 26/7/89. After that Sam had written: "Redtail hawks nesting. Sold two rams to D. Nez."

Chee closed the book. What was the date Breedlove had vanished? Oh, yes.

He handed Ms. Sam the ledger.

"Do you have an earlier book?"

"Two of them," she said. "He started writing more after he got really sick. Had more time then." She took two ledgers down from the top of the cabinet where she stored canned goods and handed them to Chee. "It was something that kills the nerves. Sometimes he would feel pretty good but he was getting paralyzed."

"I've heard of it," Manuelito said. "They say there's no cure."

"We had a sing for him," Ms. Sam said. "A Yeibichai. He got better for a little while."

Chee found the page with the day of Hal Breedlove's disappearance and scanned the dates that followed. He found crows migrating, news of a coyote family, mention of an oil field service truck, but absolutely nothing to indicate that Breedlove or anyone else had come to climb Hosteen Sam's sacred mountain.

Disappointing. Well, anyway, he would think about this. And he'd tell Lieutenant Leaphorn about the book. That thought surprised him. Why tell Leaphorn? The man was a civilian now. It was none of his business. He didn't exactly like Leaphorn. Or he hadn't thought he did. Was it respect? The man was smarter than anybody Chee had ever met. Damn sure smarter than Acting Lieutenant Jim Chee. And maybe that was why he didn't exactly like him.

12

For the first time in his life that meta-
phor whites use about money burning
a hole in your pocket had taken on
meaning for Joe Leaphorn. The heat
had been caused by a check for twenty
thousand dollars made out to him
against an account of the Breedlove
Corporation. Leaphorn had endorsed it
and exchanged it for a deposit slip to
an account in his name in the Mancos
Security Bank. Now the deposit slip
resided uneasily in his wallet as he
waited for Mrs. Cecilia Rivera to finish
dealing with a customer and talk to
him. Which she did, right now.

Leaphorn rose, pulled back a chair for
her at the lobby table where she had
deposited him earlier. "Sorry," she said.
"I don't like to keep a new customer
waiting." She sat, examined him briefly,
and got right to the point. "What did
you want to ask me about?"

"First," Leaphorn said, "I want to tell
you what I'm doing here. Opening this
account and all."

"I wondered about that," Mrs. Rivera
said. "I noticed your address was Win-

dow Rock, Arizona. I thought maybe you were going into some line of business up here." That came out as a question.

"Did you notice who the check was drawn against?" Leaphorn asked. Of course she would have. It was a very small bank in a very small town. The Breedlove name would be famous here, and Leaphorn had seen the teller discussing the deposit with Mrs. Rivera. But he wanted to make sure.

"The Breedloves," Mrs. Rivera said, studying his face. "It's been a few years since we've seen a Breedlove check but I never heard of one bouncing. Hal's widow banked here for a little while after he — after he disappeared. But then she quit us."

Mrs. Rivera was in her mid-seventies, Leaphorn guessed, thin and sun-wrinkled. Her bright black eyes examined him through the top half of her bifocals with frank curiosity.

"I'm working for them now," Leaphorn said. "For the Breedloves." He waited.

Mrs. Rivera drew in a long breath. "Doing what?" she asked. "Would it be something to do with that moly mine project?"

"It may be that," Leaphorn said. "To tell the truth, I don't know. I'm a retired policeman." He extracted his identification case and showed it to her. "Years ago when Hal Breedlove disappeared, I was the detective working that case." He produced a deprecatory expression. "Obviously I didn't have much success with it, because it took about eleven years to find him, and then it was by accident. But anyway, the family seems to have remembered."

"Yes," Mrs. Rivera said. "Young Hal did like to climb up onto the mountains." A dim smile appeared. "From what I read in the *Farmington Times*, I guess he needed more studying on how to climb down off of them."

Leaphorn rewarded this with a chuckle.

"In my experience," he said, "bankers are like doctors and lawyers and ministers. Their business depends a lot on keeping confidences." He looked at her, awaiting confirmation of this bit of misinformation. Leaphorn had always found bankers wonderful sources of information.

"Well, yes," she said. "Lot of business secrets come floating around when you're negotiating loans."

"Are you willing to handle another one?"

"Another secret?" Mrs. Rivera's expression became avid. She nodded.

And so Lieutenant Joe Leaphorn, retired, laid his cards on the table. More or less. It was a tactic he'd used for years — based on his theory that most humans prefer exchanging information to giving it away. He'd tried to teach Jim Chee that rule, which was: Tell somebody something interesting and they'll try to top it. So now he was going to tell Mrs. Rivera everything he knew about the affair of Hal Breedlove, who had been by Four Corners standards her former neighbor and was her onetime customer. In return he expected Mrs. Rivera to tell him something she knew about Hal Breedlove, and his ranch, and his business. Which was why he had opened this account here. Which was what he had decided to do yesterday when, after long seconds of hesitation, he had accepted the check he had never expected to receive.

They had met again yesterday at the Navajo Inn — Leaphorn, McDermott, and George Shaw.

"If I take this job," Leaphorn had said,

"I will require a substantial retainer." He kept his eyes on Shaw's face.

"Substantial?" said McDermott. "How sub—"

"How much?" asked Shaw.

How much, indeed, Leaphorn thought. He had decided he would mention a price too large for them to pay, but not ludicrously overdone. Twenty thousand dollars, he had decided. They would make a counteroffer. Perhaps two thousand. Two weeks pay in advance. He would drop finally to, say, ten thousand. They would counter. And finally he would establish how important this affair was to Shaw.

"Twenty thousand dollars," Leaphorn said.

McDermott had snorted, said, "Be serious. We can't —"

But George Shaw had reached into his inside coat pocket and extracted a checkbook and a pen.

"From what I've heard about you we won't need to lawyer this," he said. "The twenty thousand will be payment in full, including any expenses you incur, for twenty weeks of your time or until you develop the information we need to settle this business. Is that acceptable?"

Leaphorn hadn't intended to accept anything — certainly not to associate himself with these two men. He didn't need money. Or want it. But Shaw was writing the check now, face grim and intent. Which told Leaphorn there was much more involved here than he'd expected.

Shaw had torn out the check, handed it to him. A little piece of the puzzle that had stuck in Leaphorn's mind for eleven years — that had been revived by the shooting of Hosteen Nez — had clicked into place. Unreadable yet, but it shed a dim light on the effort to kill Nez. If twenty thousand dollars could be tossed away like this, millions more than that must be somehow involved. That told him hardly anything. Just a hint that Nez might still be, to use that white expression, "worth killing." Or for Shaw, perhaps worth keeping alive.

He had held the check a moment, a little embarrassed, trying to think of what to say as he returned it. He knew now that he would try again to find a way to solve this old puzzle, but for himself and not for these men. He extended the check to Shaw, said, "I'm sorry. I don't think —"

Then he had seen how useful that check could be. It would give him a Breedlove connection. He wasn't a policeman any longer. This would give him the key he'd need to unlock doors.

And this morning, in this small, old-fashioned bank lobby, Leaphorn was using it.

"This is sort of hard to explain," he told Mrs. Rivera. "What I'm trying to do for the Breedlove family is vague. They want me to find out everything about the disappearance of Hal Breedlove and about his death on Ship Rock."

Mrs. Rivera leaned forward. "They don't think it was an accident?"

"They don't exactly say that. But it was a pretty peculiar business. You remember it?"

"I remember it very well," Mrs. Rivera said, with a wry laugh. "The Breedlove boy did his banking here — like the ranch always had. He was my customer and he was four payments behind on a note. We'd sent him notices. Twice, I believe it was. And the next thing you know, he's vanished."

Mrs. Rivera laughed. "That's the sort of thing a banker remembers a long, long time."

"How was it secured? I understand he didn't get title to the ranch until his birthday — just before he disappeared."

Mrs. Rivera leaned back now and folded her arms. "Well, now," she said. "I don't think we want to get into that. That's private business."

"No harm me asking, though," Leaphorn said. "It's a habit policemen get into. Let me tell you what I know, and then you decide if you know anything you would be free to add that might be helpful."

"That sounds fair enough," she said. "You talk. I'll listen."

And she did. Nodding now and then, sometimes indicating surprise, enjoying being an insider on an investigation. Sometimes indicating agreement as Leaphorn explained a theory, shaking her head in disapproval when he told her how little information Shaw and McDermott had given him to work on. As Leaphorn had hoped, Mrs. Rivera had become a partner.

"But you know how lawyers are," he said. "And Shaw's a lawyer, too. I checked on it. He specializes in corporate tax cases. Anyway, they sure didn't give me much to work with."

"I don't know what I can add," she said. "Hal was a spendthrift, I know that. Always buying expensive toys. Snowmobiles, fancy cars. He'd bought himself a — can't think of the name — one of those handmade Italian cars, for example. A Ferrari, however you pronounce that. Cost a fortune and then he drove it over these old back roads and tore it up. He'd worked out some sort of deal with the trust and got a mortgage on the ranch. But then when they sold cattle in the fall and the money went into the ranch account he'd spend it right out of there instead of paying his debts."

She paused, searching for something to add. "Hal always had Sally get him first-class tickets when he flew — Sally has Mancos Travel — and first class costs an arm and a leg."

"And coach class gets there almost as quick," Leaphorn said.

Mrs. Rivera nodded. "Even when they went places together Sally had her instructions to put Hal into first class and Demott in coach. Now what do you think of that?"

Leaphorn shook his head.

"Well, I think it's insulting," Mrs. Rivera said.

"Could have been Demott's idea," Leaphorn said.

"I don't think so," Mrs. Rivera said. "Sally told —" She cut that off.

"I talked to Demott when I was investigating Breedlove's disappearance," Leaphorn said. "He seemed like a solid citizen."

"Well, yes. I guess so. But he's a strange one, too." She chuckled. "I guess maybe we all get a little odd. Living up here with mountains all around us, you know."

"Strange," Leaphorn said. "How?"

Mrs. Rivera looked slightly embarrassed. She shrugged. "Well, he's a bachelor for one thing. But I guess there's a lot of bachelors around here. And he's sort of a halfway tree-hugger. Or so people say. We have some of those around here, too, but they're mostly move-ins from California or back East. Not the kind of people who ever had to worry about feeding kids or working for a living."

"Tree-hugger? How'd he get that reputation?" Leaphorn was thinking of a favorite nephew, a tree-hugger who'd gotten himself arrested leading a noisy protest at a tribal council meeting, trying to stop a logging operation in the Chuskas. In Leaphorn's opinion his nephew had been on the right side of that controversy.

"Well, I don't know," Mrs. Rivera said. "But they say Eldon was why they didn't do that moly operation. Up there in the edge of the San Juan National Forest."

Leaphorn said, "Oh. What happened?"

"It was years ago. I think the spring after Hal went missing. We weren't in on the deal, of course. This bank is way too little for the multimillion-dollar things like that. A bank up in Denver was involved I think. And I think the mining company was MCA, the Moly Corp. Anyway, the way it was told around here, there was some sort of contract drawn up, a mineral lease involving Breedlove land up the canyon, and then at first the widow was going to handle it, but Hal legally was still alive and she didn't want to file the necessary papers to have the courts say he was dead. So that tied it up. People say she stalled on that because Demott was against it. Demott's her brother, you know. But to tell the truth, I think it was her own idea. She's loved that place since she was a tot. Grew up on it, you know."

"I don't know much about their background," Leaphorn said.

"Well, it used to be the Double D ranch. Demott's daddy owned it. The price of beef was way down in the thirties. Lot of ranches around here went at sheriff's auction, including that one. Old Edgar Breedlove bought it, and he kept the old man on as foreman. Old Breedlove didn't care a thing about ranching. One of his prospectors had found the moly deposit up the headwaters of Cache Creek and that's what he wanted. But anyway, Eldon and Elisa grew up on the place."

"Why didn't he mine the molybdenum?" Leaphorn asked.

"War broke out and I guess he couldn't get the right kind of priority to get the manpower or the equipment." She laughed. "Then when the war ended, the price of the ore fell. Stayed down for years and then went shooting up. Then Hal got himself lost and that tied it all up once again."

"And by the time she had Breedlove declared dead, the price of ore had gone down. Is that right?"

"Right," Mrs. Rivera said. And looked thoughtful.

"And now it's up again," Leaphorn said.

"That's just what I was thinking."

"You think that might be why the Breedlove Corporation would pay me the twenty thousand?"

She looked over her glasses at him. "That's an unkind thought," she said, "but I confess it occurred to me."

"Even though Hal's widow owns the place now?"

"She owns it, unless they can prove she had something to do with killing him. We had our lawyer look into that. She wanted to extend a mortgage on the place." She looked mildly apologetic. "Can't take chances, you know, with your investors' money."

"Did you extend the mortgage?"

Mrs. Rivera folded her arms again. But finally she said, "Well, yes, we did."

Leaphorn grinned. "Could I guess then that you don't think she had anything to do with killing Breedlove? Or anyway, nobody is ever going to prove it?"

"I just own a piece of this bank," Mrs.

Rivera said. "There's people I'm responsible to. So I'd have to agree with you. I thought the loan was safe enough."

"Still do?"

She nodded, remembering. Then shook her head.

"When it happened, I mean when he just disappeared like that, I had my doubts. I always thought Elisa was a fine young lady. Good family. Raised right. She used to help take care of her grandmother when the old lady had the cancer. But you know, it sure did look suspicious. Hal inherits the Lazy B and then the very same week — or pretty close to that, anyway — he's gone. So you start thinking she might of had herself another man somewhere and — well, you know."

"That's what I thought, too," Leaphorn said. "What do you think now?"

"I was wrong," she said.

"You sound certain," Leaphorn said.

"You live in Window Rock," she said. "That's a little town like Mancos. You think some widow woman there with a rich husband lost somewhere could have something going with a boyfriend and everybody wouldn't know about it?"

Leaphorn laughed. "I'm a widower,"

he said. "And I met this nice lady from Flagstaff on some police work I was doing. The very first time I had lunch with her, when I got back to the office they were planning my wedding."

"It's the same way out here," Mrs. Rivera said. "About the time everybody around here decided that Hal was gone for good, they started marrying Elisa off to the Castro boy."

Leaphorn smiled. "You know," he said, "we cops tend to get too high an opinion of ourselves. When I was up here asking around after Hal disappeared I went away thinking there wasn't a boyfriend in the background."

"You got here too quick," Mrs. Rivera said. "Here at Mancos we let the body get cold before the talking starts."

"I guess nothing came of that romance," Leaphorn said. "At least she's still a widow."

"From what I heard, it wasn't from lack of Tommy Castro's trying. About the time she got out of high school everybody took for granted they were a pair. Then Hal showed up." Mrs. Rivera shrugged, expression rueful. "They made a kind of foursome for a while."

"Four?"

"Well, sometimes it was five of 'em. This George Shaw, he'd come out with Hal sometimes and Eldon would go. He and Castro were the old heads, the coaches. They'd go elk hunting together. Camping. Rock climbing. Growing up with her dad raising her, and then her big brother, Elisa was quite a tomboy."

"What broke up the group? Was it the country boy couldn't compete with the big-city glamour?"

"Oh, I guess that was some of it," she said. "But Eldon had a falling-out with Tommy. They're too much alike. Both bull-headed."

Leaphorn digested that. Emma's big brother hadn't liked him, either, but that hadn't bothered Emma. "Do you know what happened?"

"I heard Eldon thought Tommy was out of line making a play for his little sister. She was just out of high school. Eight or ten years between 'em, I guess."

"So Elisa was willing to let big brother monitor her love life," Leaphorn said. "I don't hear about that happening much these days."

"Me neither," Mrs. Rivera said, and

laughed. "But you know," she said, suddenly dead serious, "Elisa is an unusual person. Her mother died when she was about in the second grade, but Elisa takes after her. Has a heart big as a pumpkin and a cast-iron backbone, just like her mother. When old man Demott was losing the ranch it was Elisa's mama who held everything together. Got her husband out of the bars, and out of jail a time or two. One of those people who are aways there in the background looking out for other people. You know?"

Mrs. Rivera paused at this to see what Leaphorn thought of it. Leaphorn, not sure of where this was leading, just nodded.

"So there Elisa was after Hal was out of the picture. Tommy was beginning to court her again, and Eldon wanted to run him off. They even got into a yelling match down at the High Country Inn. So there's Elisa with two men to take care of — and knowing how she is I have a theory about that." She paused again. "It's just a theory."

"I'd like to hear it," Leaphorn said.

"I think she loved them both," Mrs. Rivera said. "But if she married the

Castro boy, what in the wide world was Eldon going to do? It was her ranch now. Eldon loved it but he wouldn't stay around and work for Tommy, and Tommy wouldn't want him to." She sighed. "If we had a Shakespeare around here, they could have made a tragedy out of it."

"So this Castro was a rock climber, too," Leaphorn said. "Does he still live here?"

"If you got gas down at the Texaco station you might have seen him. That's his garage."

"What do you think? Did this affection for Castro linger on after she married Hal?"

"If it did, she didn't let it show." She thought about that awhile, looked sad, shook her head. "Far as you could tell being an outsider, she was the loyal wife. I couldn't see much to love in Hal myself but every woman's different about that and Elisa was the sort who — the more that was wrong with a man, the more she'd stand behind him. She mourned for him. Matter of fact, I think she still does. You hardly ever see her looking happy."

"How about her brother, then? You

said he was sort of strange."

She shrugged. "Well, he liked to climb up cliffs. To me, that's strange."

"Somebody said he taught Hal the sport."

"That's not quite the way it was. After old Edgar got the place away from Demott's daddy, Hal and Shaw would come out in the summers. Shaw had been climbing already. So he didn't need much teaching. And Demott and Castro were already into climbing some when they had time. Eldon was about six or eight years older than Hal and more of an athlete. From what I heard he was the best of the bunch."

A customer came in and the cool smell of autumn and the sound of laughter followed him through the doorway from the street. Leaphorn could think of just one more pertinent question.

"You mentioned Hal Breedlove had overdue note payments when he disappeared. How'd that get paid off?"

It was the sort of bank business question he wasn't sure she would answer. Neither was she. But finally she shook her head and laughed.

"Well, you sort of guessed right about not having it secured the way we should have. Old family, and all. So we weren't pressing. But we'd sold off another loan to a Denver bank. Made it to a feedlot operator who liked to go off to Vegas and try to beat the blackjack tables. With people like that you make sure you have it secured. Wrote it on sixty-two head of bred heifers he had grazing up in a Forest Service lease. The Denver people foreclosed on it and they called us for help on claiming the property."

She laughed. "Those Denver people had sixty-two head of cows out in the mountains grazing on a Forest Service lease and not an idea in the world about what to do with them. So I told 'em Eldon Demott might round them up for 'em and truck them over to Durango to the auction barn. And he did."

"He got paid enough for that to pay off Breedlove's note?"

She laughed again. "Not directly. But I mentioned we made the loan on bred heifers. So we sold the Denver bank a mortgage on sixty-two head, but when Demott went to get 'em, they weren't pregnant anymore. They were mama cows."

She paused, wanting to see if Leaphorn understood the implications of this. Leaphorn said: "Ah, yes. He didn't get back from Las Vegas to brand 'em."

"Ah, yes, is right," Mrs. Rivera said. "In fact he didn't get back at all. The sheriff has a warrant out for him. So there was Eldon with sixty-two cows loaded up and all those calves left over. They were all still slicks. Not any of 'em branded yet. Nobody in the world had title to 'em. Nobody owned 'em but the Lord in heaven."

"Enough to pay off the note?"

"He might've had a little bit left over," she said, and looked at Leaphorn over her glasses. "Wait a minute now," she said. "Don't you get any wrong ideas. I don't actually know what in the world happened to those calves. And I've been talking way too much and it's time to get some work done."

Back at his car, Leaphorn fished his cellular telephone from the glove compartment, dialed his Window Rock number, and punched in the proper code to retrieve any messages accumulated by his answering machine. The first call was from George Shaw, asking if he had anything to report and saying he could be reached at room 23, Navajo Inn. The second call was from Sergeant

Addison Deke at the Chinle police station.

"Better give me a call, Joe," Deke said. "It probably doesn't amount to anything but you asked me to sort of keep an eye on Amos Nez and you might like to hear about this."

Leaphorn didn't check on whether there was a third call. He dialed the Arizona area code and Chinle police department number. Yes, Sergeant Deke was in.

He sounded apologetic. "Probably nothing, Joe," he said. "Probably wasting your time. But after we talked, I told the boys to keep it in their minds that whoever shot Nez might try it again. You know, keep an eye out. Be looking." Deke hesitated.

Leaphorn, who almost never allowed impatience to show, said, "What did they see?"

"Nothing, actually. But Tazbah Lovejoy came in this morning — I don't think you know him. He's a young fellow out of recruit training two years ago. Anyway Tazbah told me he'd run into one of those Resource Enforcement Agency rangers having coffee, and this guy was telling him about seeing a poacher up on the rim of Canyon del Muerto yesterday."

Sergeant Deke hesitated again. This time Leaphorn gave him a moment to organize his thoughts.

"The ranger told Tazbah he was checking on some illegal firewood cutting, and he stopped at that turnout overlook down into del Muerto. Wanted to take a leak. He was getting that done, standing there, looking out across the canyon, and he kept seeing reflections off something or other across the canyon. No road over there, you know, and he wondered about it. So he went to his truck and got his binoculars to see what he could see. There was a fellow over there with binoculars. The reflections turned out to be coming off the lenses, I guess. Anyway, he had a rifle, too."

"Deer hunter, maybe," Leaphorn said.

Deke laughed. "Joe," he said. "How long's it been since you've been deer hunting? That'd be out on that tongue of the plateau between del Muerto and Black Rock Canyon. Nobody's seen a deer over there since God knows when."

"Maybe it was an Anglo deer hunter then. Did he get a good look at him?"

"I don't think so. The ranger thought

175

it was funny. Hunter over there and nothing to hunt. But I guess he was going to call it attempted poaching, or conspiracy to poach. So he drove back up to Wheatfields campground and tried to get back in there as far as he could on that old washed-out track. But he gave up on it."

"Did he get a good enough look to say man or woman?"

"I asked Tazbah and he said the ranger didn't know for sure. He said they were thinking man, on grounds a woman wouldn't be stupid enough to go hunting where there wasn't anything to shoot at. I thought you'd like to know about it because it was just up the canyon a half mile or so from where that sniper shot old Amos."

"Which would put it just about right over the Nez place," Leaphorn said.

"Exactly," Deke said. "You could jump right down on his roof."

13

Acting Lieutenant Jim Chee was parked at sunrise on the access road to Beclabito Day School because he wanted to talk to Officer Teddy Begayaye at a private place. Officer Begayaye would be driving to the office from his home at Tec Nos Pos. Chee wanted to tell him that vacation schedules were being posted today, that he was getting the Thanksgiving week vacation time he had asked for. He wanted Begayaye to provide him some sort of justification (beyond his twelve years of seniority) for approving it. Another member of Chee's criminal investigation squad wanted the same days off, namely, Officer Manuelito. She had applied for them first, and Chee wanted to give her some reason (beyond her total lack of seniority) why she didn't get it — thereby avoiding friction in the department. Thus Chee had parked where Begayaye could see him instead of hiding his patrol car behind the day school sign in hope of nabbing a speeder.

But now Chee wasn't thinking of vacation schedules. He was thinking of the date he had tonight with Janet Pete, back from whatever law business had taken her to Washington. Janet shared an apartment at Gallup with Louise Guard, another of the DNA lawyers. Chee had hopes that Louise, as much as he liked her, would be away somewhere for the evening (or, better, had found herself another apartment). He wanted to show Janet a videotape he'd borrowed of a traditional Navajo wedding. She had more or less agreed, with qualifications, that they would do the ceremony the Navajo way and that he could pick the *haatalii* to perform it. But she clearly had her doubts about it. Janet's mother had something more socially correct in mind. However, if he lucked out and Ms. Guard actually had shoved off for somewhere, he would hold the videotape for another evening. He and Janet hadn't seen each other for a week and there were better ways to occupy the evening.

The vehicle rolling down U.S. 64 toward him was a camper truck, dirty and plastered with tourist stickers. Dick Finch's vehicle. It slowed to a crawl, with Finch making a series of hand signals. Most of them were meaningless to Chee, but one of them said "follow me."

Chee started his engine and followed, driving eastward on 64 with Finch speeding. Chee topped the ridge. Finch's truck had already disappeared, but a plume of dust hanging over the dirt road that led past the Rattlesnake pump station betrayed it. Chee made the left turn into the dust — thinking how quickly this arid climate could replace wet snow with blowable dirt. Just out of sight of the highway the camper was parked, with Finch standing beside it.

Finch walked over, smiling that smile of his. Lots of white teeth.

"Good morning," Chee said.

"Captain Largo wants us to work together," Finch said. "So do my people. Get along with the Navajos, they tell me. And the Utes and the Zunis, Arizona State Police, the county mounties, and everybody. Good policy, don't you think?"

"Why not?" Chee said.

"Well, there might be a reason why not," Finch said, still smiling, waiting for Chee to say "Like what?" Chee just looked at him until Finch tired of the game.

"For example, somebody's been taking a little load of heifers now and then off that grazing lease west of your Ship Rock mountain. They're owned by an old codger who lives over near Toadlena. He rents grass from a fella named Maryboy, and his livestock is all mixed up with Maryboy's and nobody keeps track of the cattle."

Finch waited again. So did Chee. What Finch was telling him so far was common enough. People who had grazing leases let other people use them for a fee. One of the problems of catching cattle thieves was the animals might be gone a month before anyone noticed. Finally Chee said: "What's your point?"

"Point is, as we say, I've got reason to believe that the fella picking up these animals is this fella I've been trying to nail. He comes back to the mountain about every six months or so and picks up a load. Does the same thing over around Bloomfield, and Whitehorse Lake, and Burnham, and other places. When I catch him, a lot of this stealing stops. My job gets easier. So a couple of months ago, I found where he got the last ones he took from that Ship Rock pasture. The son of a bitch was throwing hay over a fence at a place where he could back his truck in. Chumming them up like he was a fisherman. I imagine he'd blow his horn when he threw the hay over. Cows are curious. Worse than cats. They'd come to see about it. And they've got good memories. Do it about twice, and when they hear a horn they think of good alfalfa hay. Come running."

Finch laughed. Chee knew exactly where this was leading.

"Manuelito spotted that hay, too," Chee said. "She noticed how the fence posts had been dug up there, loosened so they can be pulled up. She took me out to show me."

"I saw you," Finch said. "Watched you through my binoculars from about two miles away. Trouble is, our cow thief was probably watching, too. He's baited that place three times now. No use wasting any more hay. It's time to collect his cows."

Finch stared at Chee, his smile still genial. Chee felt his face flushing, which seemed to be the reaction Finch was awaiting.

"But he ain't going to do it now, is he? You can bet your ass he's got a set of binoculars every bit as good as mine, and he's careful. He sees a police car parked there. Sees a couple of cops tromping around. He's gone and he won't be back and a lot of my hard work is down the goddamn tube."

"This suggests something to me," Chee said.

"I hoped it would. I hoped it would make you want to learn a little more about this business before you start practicing it."

"Actually it suggests that you screwed up. You had about four hours of talking to me on that ride up to Mancos, with me listening all the way. You told me about this Zorro you're trying to catch — and I guess this is him. But you totally forgot to tell me about this trap you were going to spring so we could coordinate. How could you forget something like that?"

Finch's face had also become a little redder through its windburn. The smile had gone away. He stared at Chee. Looked down at his boots. When he looked up he was grinning.

"Touché! I got a bad habit of underestimating folks. You say that woman cop with you noticed the fence posts had been dug loose. I missed that. Good-looking lady, too. You give her my congratulations, will you. Tell her any old time she wants to work alongside of me, or under me either, she's more than welcome."

Chee nodded, started his engine.

"Hold it just a minute," Finch said, his smile looking slightly more genuine. "I didn't stop you just to start an argument. Wondered if I could get you to be a witness for something."

Chee left the motor running. "For what?"

"There's five Angus calves at a feedlot over by Kirtland. Looks like they were branded through a wet gunnysack, like the wise guys do it, but they're still so fresh they haven't even scabbed over yet. And the fellow that signed the bill of sale hasn't got any mother cows. He claimed he sold 'em off — which we can check on. On the other hand, a fellow named Bramlett is short five Angus calves off some leased pasture. I'm going over and see if there's five wet cows there. If there is I call the feedlot and they bring the calves over and I turn on my video camera and get a tape of the mama cows saying hello to their missing calves. Letting 'em nurse, all that."

"So what do you need me for?"

"It'd be a mostly Navajo jury, and the cow thief — he's a Navajo," Finch said. "Be good to have a Navajo cop on the witness stand."

Chee looked at his watch. By now Teddy Begayaye would be at the office celebrating getting his requested vacation time, and Manuelito would be sore about it. Too late for any preventive medicine there. But he had, after all, ruined Finch's trap. Besides, it would give him another hour away from the office and something positive for a change to report to Captain Largo on the cow-theft front.

"I'll follow you," Chee said, "and if you speed, you get a ticket."

Finch sped, but kept it within the Navajo Tribal Police tolerance zone. He parked beside the fence at the holding pasture at just about nine A.M. It was bottomland here, a pasture irrigated by a ditch from the San Juan River, and it held maybe two hundred head of Angus — young cows and their calves — last spring's crop but still nursing.

Chee parked as Finch was climbing the fence, snagging his jeans on the barbed wire.

"I think I saw a wet one already," he shouted, pointing into the herd, which now was moving uneasily away. "You stay back by your car."

Wet one? Chee thought. He'd been raised with sheep, not cows. But "wet" must be what you called a cow with a painfully full udder. A cow whose nursing calf was missing. Finch had been right about cow memories. Their memory connected men on foot with being roped, bulldogged, and branded. They were scattering away from Finch. So the question was, how was Finch going to locate five such cows in that milling herd and know he hadn't just counted the same cow five times?

Finch picked himself a spot free of cow manure, dropped to his knees, and rolled over on his back. He folded his arms under his head and lay motionless. The cows, which had shied fearfully away from him, stopped their nervous milling. They stared at Finch. He yawned, squirmed into a more comfortable position. A heifer, head and ears stretched forward, moved a cautious step toward him. Others followed, noses pointed, ears forward. The calves, with no memory of branding to inhibit them, were first. By eleven minutes after nine, Finch was surrounded by a ring of Angus cattle, sniffing and staring.

As for Finch, only his head was moving, and he made an udder inspection. He arose, creating a panic, and walked through the scattering herd, already dialing his portable telephone, talking into it as he climbed the fence. He closed it, walked up to Chee's window.

"Five wet ones," he said. "They're going to bring the calves right out. I'm going to videotape it, but it'd help if you'd stick around so you can testify. You know, tell the jury that the calves ran right up to their mamas and started nursing, and their mamas let 'em do it."

"That was pretty damn clever," Chee said.

"I told you about cows being curious," Finch said. "They're scared of a man standing up. Lay down and they say, 'What the hell's going on here?' and come on over to take a look." He brushed off his jeans. "Drawback is you're likely to get manure all over yourself."

"Well, it's a lot quicker than chasing them all over the pasture, trying to get a look."

Finch was enjoying this approval.

"You know where I learned that trick? I was in the dentist's office at Farmington waiting to get a root canal. Picked up a *New Yorker* magazine and there was an article in there about a Nevada brand inspector name of Chris Collis. It was a trick he used. I called him and asked him if it really worked. He said sure."

Finch fished his video camera out of the truck cab, fiddled with it. Chee radioed his office, reported his location, collected his messages. One was from Joe Leaphorn. It was brief.

A truck from the feedlot arrived bearing two men and five terrified Angus calves. Each was ear-tagged with its number and released into the pasture. Each ran, bawling, in search of its mother, found her, underwent a maternal inspection, was approved and allowed to nurse while Finch videotaped the happy reunions.

But Chee wasn't paying as much attention as he might have been. While Finch was counting turgid udders,

Chee had checked with his office. Leaphorn wanted to talk to him again about the Fallen Man. He said he was working for the Breedlove family now.

14

The question nagging at Jim Chee wasn't the sort he wanted to explore on the Tribal Police radio band. He stopped at the Hogback trading post, dropped a quarter in the pay phone, and called the number Leaphorn had left. It proved to be the Anasazi Inn in Farmington, but the front desk said Leaphorn had checked out. Chee dropped in another quarter and called his own office. Jenifer answered. Yes, Leaphorn had called again. He said he was on his way back from Farmington to Window Rock and he would drop by and try to catch Chee at his office.

Chee got there about five minutes faster than the speed limit allowed. Leaphorn's car was in the parking lot. The man himself was perched, ramrod straight, on a chair in the waiting room, reading yesterday's copy of *Navajo Times*.

"If you have a couple of minutes, I want to pass on some information," Leaphorn said. "Otherwise, I can catch you when you have some time."

"I have time," Chee said, and ushered

him into his office.

Leaphorn sat. "I'll be brief. I've taken a retainer from the Breedlove Corporation. Actually, it's really the family, I guess. They want me to sort of reinvestigate the disappearance of Hal Breedlove." He paused, awaited a reaction. If he was reading Chee's studiously blank expression properly, the young man didn't like the arrangement.

"So it's official business for you now," Chee said. "At least unofficially official."

"Right," Leaphorn said. "I wanted you to know that because I may be bothering you now and then. With questions." He paused again.

"Is that it?" Chee asked. If it was, he had some questions of his own.

"There's something else I wanted to tell you. I think it's pretty clear the family thinks Hal was murdered. If they have any evidence of that they're not telling me. Maybe it's just that they want it to be murder. And they want to be able to prove it. They want to regain title to the ranch."

"Oh," Chee said. "Did they tell you that?"

Leaphorn hesitated, his expression quizzical. What the devil was bothering

Chee? "I was thinking that would be the most likely motive," he said. "What do you think?"

Chee nodded noncommittally.

"Can you tell me who you made the deal with?" he asked.

"You mean the individual?" Leaphorn said. "I think private detectives are supposed to have a thing about client confidentiality, but I haven't learned to think like a private eye. Never will. This is my one and only venture. George Shaw handed me my check." He laughed, and told Chee how he'd outsmarted himself, trying to learn how big a deal this was for the Breedlove Corporation.

"So Hal's cousin signed the check, but the lawyer with him, you remember his name?"

"McDermott," Leaphorn said. "John McDermott. He's the lawyer handling it. He called me and arranged the meeting. Works for a Washington firm, but I think he used to have an office in Albuquerque. And —" He stopped, aware of Chee's expression. "You know this guy?"

"Indirectly," Chee said. "He was sort of an Indian affairs specialist for an Albuquerque firm. I think he represented Peabody Coal when they were negotiating one of the coal contracts with us, and a couple of pipeline companies dealing with the Jicarillas. Then he moved to Washington and is doing the same thing on that level. I think it's with the same law firm."

Leaphorn looked surprised. "You know a lot more about him than I do," he said. "How's his reputation? It okay?"

"As a lawyer? I guess so. He used to be a professor."

"He struck me as arrogant. Is that your impression?"

Chee shrugged. "I don't know him. I just know a little about him."

"Well, he didn't make a good first impression."

"Could you tell me when he called you? I mean made the first contact."

The question obviously surprised Leaphorn. "Let's see," he said. "Two or three days ago."

"Was it last Tuesday?"

"Tuesday? Let's see. Yeah. It was a call on my answering machine. I returned it."

"Morning or afternoon?"

"I don't know. It could have been

either one. But it's still on the record-
ing. I think I could find out."

"I'd appreciate that," Chee said.

"Will do," Leaphorn said, and paused.
"I'm trying to place the date. That would
have been about the day after you got
the skeleton identified. Right?"

Chee sighed. "Lieutenant Leaphorn,"
he said, "you already know just what
I'm thinking, don't you?"

"Well, I'd guess you're wondering how
that lawyer found out so quickly that
the skeleton had turned out to be somebody so important to his client. No an-
nouncement had been made. Nothing
in the papers until a day or so later and
I don't think it ever made the national
news. Just a little story around here,
and about three paragraphs in the *Albuquerque Journal*, and a little bit more
in the *Rocky Mountain News*."

"That's what I'm thinking," Chee said.

"But you're ahead of me on something
else. I don't know why it's important."

"You couldn't guess," Chee said. "It's
something personal."

"Oh," Leaphorn said. He ducked his
head, shook it, and said, "Oh," again.
Sad, now. And then he looked up. "You
know, they could have had this thing

staked out, though. An important client. Maybe they had some law firm out here retained to tip them off if anything turned up that would bear in any way at all on this son-and-heir being missing. They knew he was a mountain climber. So when an unidentified body turns up . . ." He shrugged. "Who knows how law firms operate?" he said, not believing it himself.

"Sure," Chee said. "Anything's possible."

Leaphorn was leaving, hat in hand, but he stopped in the doorway and turned.

"One other thing that might bear on all this," he said. He told Chee of Sergeant Deke's account of the man with the binoculars and the rifle on the canyon rim. "Deke said he's going up the canyon and warn Nez that somebody may still be trying to kill him. I hope we can figure this out before they do it."

Chee sat for a moment looking at the closed door, thinking of Leaphorn, thinking of Janet Pete, of John McDermott back in New Mexico. Was he back in her life? Apparently he was. For the first time, the Fallen Man became more than an abstract tragedy in Chee's mind. He buzzed Jenifer.

"I'm taking off now for Gallup," he said. "If Largo needs me — if anybody calls — tell them I'll be back tomorrow."

"Hey," Jenifer said, "you have two meetings on the calendar for this afternoon. The security man from the community college and Captain Largo was —"

"Call them and tell them I had to cancel," Chee said, forgetting to say please, and forgetting to say thanks when he hung up. Captain Largo wouldn't like this. But then he didn't particularly like Captain Largo and he sure as hell didn't like being an acting lieutenant.

15

Louise Guard's Ford Escort was not in the driveway of the little house she shared with Janet Pete in Gallup. Good news, but not as good as it would have seemed when Jim Chee was feeling better about life. This evening his mood had been swinging back and forth between a sort of grim anger at the world that Janet occupied and self-contempt for his own immature attitude. It hadn't taken long for Chee, who was good at self-analysis, to determine that his problem was mostly jealousy. Maybe it was 90 percent jealousy. But even so, that left 10 percent or so that seemed legitimate.

He gave the door of his pickup the hard slam required to shut it and walked up the pathway with the videotape of the traditional wedding clutched in one hand and the other holding a pot of some sort of autumn-blooming flowers he'd bought for her at Gallup Best Blossoms. It wasn't a very impressive floral display, but what could you expect in November?

"Ah, Jim," Janet said, and greeted

him with such a huge and enthusiastic hug that it left him helpless — tape in one hand and flowerpot in the other. It also left him feeling guilty. What the devil was wrong with him? Janet was beautiful. Janet was sweet. She loved him. She was wearing a set of designer jeans that fit her perfectly and a blouse of something that shimmered. Her black hair was done in a new fashion he'd been observing on the nighttime soap opera shows. It made her look young and jaunty and like someone the muscular actor in the tank top would be laughing with at the fancy party in a Coca-Cola commercial.

"I'd almost forgotten how beautiful you are," Chee said. "Just back from Washington, you should be looking tired."

Janet was in the kitchen by then, watering whatever it was he'd brought her, opening the refrigerator and fixing something for them.

"It wasn't tiresome," she shouted. "It was lots of fun. The people in the BIA were on their very best behavior, and the people over at Justice were reasonable for a change. And there was time to see a show some German artist had going in the National Gallery. It was really interesting stuff. Partly sculpture and partly drawings. And then there was the concert I told you about. The one in the Library of Congress hall. It was partly Mozart. Really great."

Yes. The concert. He'd thought about that before. Maybe too much. In Washington and at the Library of Congress it wouldn't be a public event. It would be exclusive. Some sort of high-society fund-raiser. Shaking down the social set for some worthy literacy cause, probably. Almost certainly it would be by invitation only. Or just members and guests for the big-money patrons of library projects. She'd mentioned some ambassador being there. He had thought, once, that John McDermott might have taken her. But that was crazy. She detested the man. He had taken advantage of the leverage a distinguished professor has over his students. He'd seduced Janet. He'd taken her to Albuquerque as his live-in intern, had taken her to Washington as his token Indian. She had come back to New Mexico ashamed and broken-hearted when she realized what he was doing. There were a dozen ways McDermott could have learned the Fallen Man had been identified. Leaphorn, as usual, was right. McDermott's firm probably had connections with lawyers in New Mexico. Of course they would. They would be working with Arizona and New Mexico law firms on Indian business. Anyway, he damn sure wasn't going to bring it up. It would be insulting.

From the kitchen the sound of something clattering, the smell of coffee. Chee inspected the room around him. Nothing different that he could see except for something or other on the mantle over the gas-log fireplace. It was made of thin stainless steel tubing combined with shaped Plexiglas in three or four colors held together by what seemed to be a mixture of aluminum wiring and thread. Most peculiar. In fact, weird. Chee grinned at it. Something Louise had found somewhere. A conversation piece. Louise haunted garage sales, and in Gallup, garage sales were always offering odd harvests.

Janet emerged with a cup of coffee for him — fragile china on a thin-as-paper saucer — and a crystal goblet of wine for herself. She snuggled onto the sofa beside him, clicked glass against cup, smiled at him, and said, "To your capture of a whole squadron of cattle rustlers, your promotion to commander in chief of the Navajo police, chief honcho of the Federal Bureau of Ineptitude, and international boss of Interpol."

"You forgot my busting up the Shiprock graffiti vandals and election as sheriff of San Juan County and bureaucrat in chief of the Drug Enforcement Agency."

"All that, too," Janet said, raised her glass again, and sipped. She picked up the videocassette and inspected it. "What's this?"

"Remember?" Chee said. "My paternal uncle's niece was having a traditional wedding at their place north of Little Water. I got him to get me a copy of the videotape they had made."

Janet turned it over and inspected the back, which was just as black and blank as the other side. "You want me to look at it?"

"Sure," Chee said, his good feelings fading fast. "Remember? We talked about that." They had argued a little, actually. About cultures, and traditions, and all that. It wasn't that Janet was opposed, but her mother wanted a huge ceremony in an Episcopal cathedral in Baltimore. And Janet had agreed, or so he thought, that they would do both. "You said you had never been to a regular Navajo wedding with a shaman and the entire ceremony. I thought you'd be interested."

"Louise described it to me," Janet said, and put the videotape on the coffee table in a way that made Chee want to change the subject. Suddenly Louise's peculiar purchase seemed useful.

"I see Louise has been sailing the garage sales again. Quite an acquisition there," he said, nodding toward the thing. He laughed. "Louise is a wonderful lady, but I wonder about her taste sometimes."

Janet had no comment.

Chee said: "What's it for?" And waited, and belatedly understood that he should have kept his stupid mouth shut.

"It's called 'Technic Inversion Number Three, Side View,' " Janet said.

"Remarkable," Chee said. "Very interesting."

"I found it in the Kremont Gallery,"

Janet said, glum. "The artist is a man named Egon Kuzluzski. The critic at the *Washington Post* called him the most innovative sculptor of the decade. An artist who finds beauty and meaning in the technology which is submerging modern culture."

"Very complex," Chee said. "And the colors . . ." He couldn't think of a way to finish the sentence.

"I really thought you would like it," Janet said. "I'm sorry you don't."

"I do," Chee said, but he knew it was too late for that. "Well, not really. But I think it takes time to understand something that's so innovative. And then tastes vary, of course."

Janet didn't respond to that.

"It's the reason they have horse races," Chee said, and attempted a chuckle. "Differences of opinion, you know."

"I ran into something interesting in Washington," Janet said, in a fairly obvious effort to cut off this discussion. "I think it was why everybody was so cooperative with our proposals. Crime on Indian reservations has become very chic inside the Beltway. Everybody had read up on narcotics invading Indian territory, and Indian gang problems,

Indian graffiti, Indian homicides, child abuse, the whole schmear. All very popular with the Beltway intelligentsia. We have finally made it into the halls of the mighty."

"I guess that would fall into the bad news, good news category," Chee said, grinning with relief at being let off the hook.

"Whatever you call it, it means everybody is looking for our expertise these days."

Chee's grin faded. "You got a job offer?"

"I didn't mean me. But one of the top assistants in BIA Law and Order wanted to let me know they're recruiting experienced reservation cops with the right kind of credentials for Civil Service, and I heard the same thing over at Justice." She smiled at him. "At Justice they actually asked me to be a talent scout for them, and when they told me what they wanted it sounded like they were describing you." She patted him on the leg. "I told 'em I'd already signed you up."

"Thank God for that," Chee said. "I did time in Washington a couple of times, remember? At the FBI academy for their training course, and once on

an investigation." He shuddered, remembering. At the academy he had
been the tolerated rube, one of "them."
But they would, naturally, look on
Janet as one of "us." It was a fact he'd
have to find a way to deal with.

Janet removed her hand.

"Really, Jim, Washington's a nice
place. It's cleaner than most cities, and
something beautiful every place you
look and there's always —"

"Beautiful what? Buildings? Monu-
ments? There's too much smog, too
much noise, too much traffic, too damn
many people everywhere. You can't see
the stars at night. Too cloudy to see the
sunset." He shook his head.

"There's the breeze coming in off the
Potomac," Janet said. "And the clean
salty smell of the bay, and seafood
fresh from the ocean and good wine.
In April, the cherry blossoms, and the
green, green hills, and the great art
galleries, and theater, and music." She
paused, waved her hands, overcome by
the enormous glories of Washington's
culture. "And the pay scales are about
double what either one of us can make
here — especially in the Justice Department."

"Working in the J. Edgar Hoover Building," Chee said. "That'd be a real kick. That old blackmailer should have been doing about twenty years for misuse of public records, but they named the building after him. At least it's an appropriately ugly building."

Janet let that one lie, sipped her wine, reminded Chee his coffee was getting cold. He tested it. She was right.

"Jim," she said, "that concert was absolutely thrilling. It was the Philadelphia Orchestra. The annual Founders Society affair. The First Lady was there, and all sorts of diplomats — all white tie and the best jewels dug out of the safety-deposit boxes. And Mozart. You like Mozart."

"I like a lot of Mozart," Chee said.

He took a deep breath. "It was one of those members-only things, I guess," he said. "Members and guests."

"Right," she said, smiling at him. "I was mingling with the crème de la crème."

"I'll bet your old law firm is a member," Chee said. "Probably a big donor."

"You betcha," Janet said, still smiling. Then she realized where Chee was headed. The smile went away.

"You're going to ask me who took me," she said.

"No, I'm not."

"I was a guest of John McDermott," she said.

Chee sat silent and motionless. He had known it, but he still didn't want to believe it.

"Does that bother you?"

"No," Chee said. "I guess not. Should it?"

"It shouldn't," she said. "After all, we go way back. He was my teacher. And then I worked with him."

He was looking at her. Wondering what to say. She flushed. "What are you thinking?" she said.

"I'm thinking I had it all wrong. I thought you detested the man for the way he treated you. The way he used you."

She looked away. "I did for a while. I was angry."

"But not now? No longer angry?"

"The Navajo way," she said. "You're supposed to get yourself back into harmony with the way the world is."

"Did you know he's out here again?"
She nodded.

"Did you know he's hired Joe Leaphorn to look into that Fallen Man business?"

"He told me he was going to try," she said.

"I wondered how he learned about the skeleton being identified as Harold Breedlove," Chee said. "It wasn't the sort of story that would have hit the *Washington Post*."

"No," she said.

"Did you tell him?"

"Why not?" she said, staring at him. "Why the hell not?"

"Well, I don't know. The man you're going to marry is on the telephone reminding you he loves you. And you ask him about a case he's working on, and so he sort of violates police protocol and tells you the skeleton has been identified." He stopped. This wasn't fair. He'd held this anger in for too many hours. He had heard his voice, thick with emotion.

She was still staring at him, face grim, waiting for him to continue.

"So?" she said. "Go on."

"So I'm not exactly sure what happened next. Did you call him right away and tell him what you'd learned?"

She didn't respond to that. But she edged a bit away from him on the sofa.

"One more question and then I'll drop

it. Did that son of a bitch ask you to get that information out of me? In other words, I want to know whether he —"

Janet was on her feet.

"I think you'd better go now," she said.

He got up. His anger had drained away now. He simply felt tired and sick.

"Just one more thing I'd like to know," he said. "It would tell me something about just how important this business is to the Breedlove Corporation. In other words if you'd told him about the skeleton being found up there when you first got to Washington, it might naturally have reminded McDermott of Hal Breedlove disappearing. And he'd want to know who the skeleton belonged to. But if it was already on his mind even before that, if he brought it up instead of you, then it would mean a higher level of — it would mean they already —"

"Go away," Janet said. She handed him the videotape. "And take this with you."

He took the tape.

"Janet," he said. "Did you recommend that he hire Leaphorn to work for him?"

He asked that before he noticed the angry tears in Janet's eyes. She didn't answer and he didn't expect her to.

16

December came to the Four Corners but winter lingered up in the Utah mountains. It had buried the Wasatch Range under three feet and ventured far enough south to give Colorado's San Juans a snowcap. But the brief post-Halloween storm that had whitened the slopes of Ship Rock and the Chuskas proved to be a false threat. It was dry again across the Navajo Nation — skies dark blue, mornings cool, sun dazzling. The south end of the Colorado Plateau was enjoying that typically beautiful autumn weather that makes the inevitable first blizzard such a dangerous surprise.

Beautiful or not, Jim Chee was keeping himself far too busy to enjoy it — even if his glum mood would have allowed it. He had learned that he could handle administrative duties if he tried hard enough, and that he would never, ever enjoy them. For the first time in his life, he felt no sense of pleasure as he went to work. But the work got done. He made progress. The vacation schedules were established in a way that produced no serious discontent among the officers who worked with him. A system had been devised whereby whatever policemen who happened to be in the Hogback neighborhood would drop in on Diamonte's establishment for a friendly chat. This happened several times a week, thus keeping Diamonte careful and his customers uneasy without giving him any solid grounds for complaint. As a by-product, it had also produced a couple of arrests of young fellows who had been ignoring fugitive warrants.

On top of that, his budget for next year was about half finished and a plan had been drafted for keeping better track of gasoline usage and patrol car maintenance. This had produced an unusual (indeed, unprecedented in the experience of Acting Lieutenant Jim Chee) smile on the face of Captain Largo. Even Officer Bernadette Manuelito seemed to be responding to this new efficiency in Chee's criminal investigation domain.

This came about after the word reached the ear of Captain Largo (and very shortly thereafter the ear of Acting Lieutenant Chee) that Mr. Finch had nailed a pair of cattle-stealing brothers so thoroughly that they had actually admitted not just rustling five un-weaned calves but also about six or seven other such larcenies from the New Mexico side of Chee's jurisdiction. So overwhelming was the evidence, the captain said, that they had plea-bargained themselves into jail at Aztec.

"Well, good," Chee had said.

"Well, goddammit," Largo replied, "why can't we nail some of those bastards ourselves?"

Largo's imperial "we" had actually meant him, Chee realized. He also realized, before this uncomfortable conversation ended, that Finch had revealed to Largo not only Chee's ignorance of heifer curiosity but how he and Officer Manuelito had screwed up Finch's trap out by Ship Rock. Chee had walked down the hall away from this meeting with several resolutions strongly formed. He would catch Finch's favorite cow thief before Finch could get his hands on him. Having beaten Finch at Finch's game, he would resign his role as acting lieutenant and go back to being a real policeman. There would be no more trying to be a bureaucrat to impress Janet. And to accomplish the first phase of this program he would shift Manuelito over to work on rustler cases — she and Largo being the only ones in the Shiprock District who took it seriously.

Officer Bernadette Manuelito responded to this shift in duties by withdrawing her request for a transfer. At least, that was Jim Chee's presumption. Jenifer had another notion. She had noticed that the frequent calls between the lady lawyer in Window Rock and the acting lieutenant in Shiprock had abruptly ceased. Jenifer was very good at keeping the Shiprock District criminal investigation office running smoothly because she made it her business to know what the hell was going on. She made a couple of calls to old friends in the small world of law enforcement down at Window Rock. Yes, indeed. The pretty lawyer had been observed shedding tears while in conversation with a lady friend in her car. She had also been seen having dinner at the Navajo Inn with that good-looking lawyer from Washington. Things, it seemed, were in flux. Having learned this, it was Jenifer's theory that Officer

Manuelito would learn of it too — not as directly perhaps, or as fast, but she would learn of it.

Whatever her motives, Manuelito seemed to like her new duties. She stood in front of Chee's desk, looking excited, but not about rustling.

"That's what I said," she said. "They showed up at old Mr. Maryboy's place last night. They told him they wanted trespass permission on his grazing lease. They wanted to climb Ship Rock."

"And it was George Shaw and John McDermott?" Chee said.

"Yes, sir," Officer Manuelito said. "That's what they told him. They paid him a hundred dollars and said if they did any damage they'd pay him for that."

"My God," Chee said. "You mean those two lawyers are going to climb Ship Rock?"

"Old man Maryboy said the little one had climbed it before. Years ago. He said most of the white people just sneaked in and climbed it, but George Shaw had come to his house to get permission. He remembered that. How polite Shaw had been. But this time

Shaw said they were bringing a team of climbers."

"So the tall one with the mustache probably isn't going up," Chee said, wondering if he sounded disappointed. But should he be disappointed? Would having McDermott fall off a cliff solve his problem with Janet? He didn't think so.

"They didn't say why they were going up there, I guess," Chee said.

"No, sir. I asked him about that. Mr. Maryboy said they didn't tell him why." She laughed, showing very pretty white teeth. "He said why do white men do anything? He said he knew a white fellow once who was trying to get a patent on a cordless bungee jumper."

Chee rewarded that with a chuckle. The way he'd heard it, it was a string-less yo-yo, but Maryboy had revised it to fit mountain climbers.

"But what I wanted to tell you about was business," Officer Manuelito said. "Mr. Maryboy told me he was missing four steers."

"Maryboy," Chee said. "Let's see. He has —"

"Yes, sir," she said. "That's his lease where we found the loose fence posts.

Where somebody was throwing the hay over the fence. I went by his place to tell him about that. I was going to give him a notebook and ask him to keep track of strange trucks and trailers. He said I was a little late, but he took the notebook and said he'd help."

"Did he say how late?" Maryboy hadn't reported a cattle theft. Chee was sure of that. He checked on everything involving rustling every day. "Did he say why he hadn't reported the loss?"

"He said he missed 'em sometime last spring. He was selling off steers and came up short. And he said he didn't report it because he didn't think it would do any good. He said when it happened before, a couple of times, he went in and told us about it but he never did get his animals back."

That was one of the frustrations Chee had been learning to live with in dealing with rustling. People didn't keep track of their cattle. They turned them out to graze, and if they had a big grazing lease and reliable water maybe they'd only see them three or four times a year. Maybe only at calving time and branding time. And if you did see them, maybe you wouldn't notice if you were short a couple. Chee had spent his boyhood with sheep. He could tell an Angus from a Hereford but beyond that one cow looked a lot like every other cow. He could understand how you wouldn't miss a couple, and if you did, what could you do about it? Maybe the coyotes had got 'em, or maybe it was the little green men coming down in flying saucers. Whatever, you weren't going to get 'em back.

"So we put an *X* on our map and mark it 'unreported,' " Chee said, "which doesn't help much."

"It might," Officer Manuelito said. "Later on."

Chee was extracting their map from his desk drawer. He kept it out of sight on the theory that everyone in the office except Manuelito would think this project was silly. Or, worse, they would think he was trying to copy Joe Leaphorn's famous map. Everybody in the Tribal Police seemed to know about that and the Legendary Lieutenant's use of it to exercise his theory that everything fell into a pattern, every effect had its cause, and so forth.

The map was a U.S. Geological Survey

quadrangle chart large enough in scale to show every arroyo, hogan, windmill, and culvert. Chee pushed his in basket aside, rolled it out and penned a tiny blue ? on the Maryboy grazing lease with a tiny 3 beside it. Beside that he marked in the date the loss had been discovered.

Officer Manuelito looked at it and said: "A blue three?"

"Signifies unreported possible thefts," Leaphorn said. "Three of them." He waved his hand around the map, indicating a scattering of such designations. "I've been adding them as we learn about them."

"Good idea," Manuelito said. "And add an X there, too. Maryboy is going to be a lookout for us." She pulled up a chair, sat, leaned her elbows on the desk, and studied the chart.

Chee added the X. The map now had maybe a score of those, each marking the home of a volunteer equipped with a notebook and ballpoint pen. Chee had bought the supplies with his own money, preferring that to trying to explain this system to Largo. If it worked, which today didn't seem likely to Chee, he would decide whether to ask for a reimbursement of his twenty-seven-dollar outlay.

"Funny how this is already working out," Manuelito said. "I thought it would take months."

"What do you mean?"

"I mean the patterns you talked about," she said. "How those single-animal thefts tend to fall around the middle of the month."

Chee looked. Indeed, most of the *1s* that marked single-theft sites were followed by midmonth dates. And a high percentage of those midmonth dates were clustered along the reservation border. But what did that signify? He said: "Yeah."

"I don't think we should concentrate on those," she said, still staring thoughtfully at the map. "But if you want me to, I could check with the bars and liquor stores around Farmington and try to work up a list of guys who come in about the middle of the month with a fresh supply of money." She shook her head. "It wouldn't prove anything, but it would give us a list of people to look out for."

About halfway through this monologue, Chee's brain caught up with

Manuelito's thinking. The Navajo Nation relief checks arrived about the first of the month. Every reservation cop knew that the heavy workload produced by the need to arrest drunks tended to ease off in the second week when the liquor addicts had used up their cash. He visualized a dried-out drunk driving past a pasture and seeing a five-hundred-dollar cow staring through the fence at him. How could the man resist? And why hadn't he thought of that?

He thought of it now. Weeks compiling the list, weeks spent cross-checking, sorting, coming up finally with four or five cases, getting maybe two convictions resulting in hundred-dollar fines, which would be suspended, and thirty-day sentences, which would be converted to probation. Meanwhile, serious crime would continue to flourish.

"I think instead we'll sort those out and set them aside. Let's concentrate on solving the multiple thefts," Chee said.

"There's a pattern there, too, I think," Officer Manuelito said. "Am I right?"

Chee had noticed this one himself. The multiple thefts tended to show up in empty country — from grazing leases like Maryboy's where the owner might not see his herd for a month or so. They talked about that, which led them back to their growing list of rustler-watchers, which led them back to Lucy Sam.

"You looked through her telescope," Manuelito said. "Did you notice she could see that place where the fence posts were loose?"

Chee shook his head. He had been looking at the mountain. Thinking of the Fallen Man stranded on the cliff up there, calling for help.

"You could," Manuelito said. "I looked."

"I think I should go talk to her," Chee said. But he wasn't thinking of rustling when he said it. He was wondering what Lucy Sam's father might have seen all those years ago when Hal Breedlove had huddled on that little shelf waiting to die.

17

The sound of *bang, bang, bang, thud, thud* stopped Joe Leaphorn in his tracks. It came from somewhere up Cache Creek, nearby, just around the bend and beyond a stream-side stand of aspens. But it stopped him just for a moment. He smiled, thinking he'd spent too many years as a cop with a pistol on his hip, and moved up the path. The aspen trunks were wearing their winter white now, their leaves forming a yellow blanket on the ground around them. And through the barren branches Leaphorn could see Eldon De-mott, bending over something, back muscles straining.

Doing what? Leaphorn stopped again and watched. Demott was stretching barbed wire over what seemed to be a section of aspen trunk. And now, with more banging, stapling the wire to the wood.

Something to do with a fence, he guessed. Here a cable had been stretched between ponderosas on opposite sides of the stream, and the fence seemed to be suspended from that.

Leaphorn shouted, "Hello!"

It took Demott just a moment to recognize him but he did even before Leaphorn reminded him.

"Yeah," Demott said. "I remember. But no uniform now. Are you still with the Tribal Police?"

"They put me out to pasture," Leaphorn said. "I retired at the end of June."

"Well, what brings you all this way up the Cache? It wouldn't have something to do with finally finding Hal, would it? After all these years?"

"That's a good guess," Leaphorn said. "Breedlove's family hired me to go over the whole business again. They want me to see if I overlooked anything. See if I could find out where he went when he left your sister at Canyon de Chelly. See if anything new turned up the past ten years or so."

"That's interesting," Demott said. He retrieved his hammer. "Let me get done with this." He secured the wire with two more staples, straightened his back, and stretched.

"I'm trying to rig up something to solve a problem here," he explained. "The damned cows come to drink here, and then they move downstream a little ways — or their calves do — and they come out on the wrong side of the fence. We call it a water gap. Is that the term you use?"

"We don't get enough water down in the low country where I was raised to need 'em much," Leaphorn said.

"In the mountains, it's the snowmelt. The creek gets up, washes the brush down, it catches on the fence and builds up until it makes a dam out of it, and the dam backs up the water until the pressure tears out the fence," Demott said. "It's the same story every spring. And then you got cattle up and down the creek, ruining the stream banks, getting erosion started and everything silted up."

It was cool up here, probably a mile and a half above sea level, but Demott was sweating. He wiped his brow on his shirtsleeve.

"The way it's supposed to work, it's kinda like a drawbridge. You make a section of fence across the creek and just hang it from that cable with a dry log holding the bottom down. When the flood comes down, the log floats. That lifts the wire, the brush sails right by under it, and when the runoff season's over, the log drops back into place and you've got a fence again."

"It sounds pretty foolproof," Leaphorn said, thinking that it might work with snowmelt, but runoff from a male rain roaring down the side of a mesa would knock it into the next county and take the cable with it, and the trees, too. "Or maybe I should say cowproof."

Demott looked skeptical. "Actually, it just works until too much stuff catches on the log," he said. "Anyway, it's worth trying." He sat on a boulder, wiped his face again.

"What can I tell you?"

"I don't know," Leaphorn said. "But we wrote off this thing with your brother-in-law almost eleven years ago. It was just another adult missing person case. Another skip-out without a clue to where or why. So there's been a lot of time for you to get a letter, or hear some gossip, or find out that somebody who knew him had seen him playing the slots in Las Vegas. Something like that. There's no crime involved, so you wouldn't have had any reason to tell us about it."

Demott was wiping mud off the side

of his hand on his pant leg. "I can tell you why they hired you," he said.

Leaphorn waited.

"They want this place back."

"I thought they might," Leaphorn said. "I couldn't think of another reason."

"The sons-a-bitches," Demott said. "They want to lease out the mineral rights. Or more likely, just sell the whole outfit to a mining company and let 'em wreck it all."

"That's the idea I got from the bank lady at Mancos."

"Did she tell the plan? They'd do an open pit operation on the molybdenum deposits up there." Demott pointed up Cache Creek, past the clusters of white-barked aspens, past the stately forest of ponderosa, into the dark green wilderness of firs. "Rip it all out," he said, "and then . . ."

The emotion in Demott's voice stopped him. He took a deep breath and sat for a moment, looking down at his hands.

Leaphorn waited. Demott had more than this to say. He wanted to hear it.

Demott gave Leaphorn a sidewise glance. "Have you seen the Red River canyon in New Mexico? Up north of Taos?"

"I've seen it," Leaphorn said.

"You seen it before and after?"

"I haven't been there for years," Leaphorn said. "I remember a beautiful trout stream, maybe a little bigger than your creek here, winding through a narrow valley. Steeper than this one. High mountains on both sides. Beautiful place."

"They ripped the top right off of one of those mountains," Demott said. "Left a great whitish heap of crushed stone miles long. And the holding ponds they built to catch the effluent spill over and that nasty stuff pours down into Red River. They use cyanide in some sort of solution to free up the metal and that kills trout and everything else."

"I haven't been up there for years," Leaphorn said.

"Cyanide," Demott repeated. "Mixed with sludge. That's what we'd have pouring down Cache Creek if the Breedlove Corporation had its way. That slimy white silt brewed with cyanide."

Leaphorn didn't comment on that. He spent a few minutes letting Demott get used to him being there, listening to the music of Cache Creek bubbling over its

226

rocky floor, watching a puffy white cloud just barely making it over the ridge upstream. It was dragging its bottom through the tips of the fir trees, leaving rags of mist behind. A beautiful day, a beautiful place. A cedar waxwing flew by. It perched in the aspens across the creek and watched them, chirping bird comments.

Demott was watching him too, still absently picking at the resin and dirt on his left hand. "Well, enough of that," he said. "I don't know what to tell you. I got no letters and neither did Elisa. If she had, I would have known it. We're a family that don't keep secrets, not from one another. And we didn't hear anything, either. Nothing."

"You'd think there'd be rumors," Leaphorn said. "You know how people are."

"I do," Demott said. "I thought it was strange, too. I'm sure there must have been a lot of talk about it up at Mancos and around. Hal disappearing was the most exciting thing that happened around here in years. I'm sure some people would say Elisa killed her husband so she could get the ranch, or she had a secret boyfriend do it, or I killed him so the ranch would come back into the Demott family."

"Yeah," Leaphorn said. "I'd think that would be the natural kind of speculation, considering the circumstances. But you didn't hear any of that kind of talk?"

Demott looked shocked. "Why, they wouldn't say things like that around me. Or Elisa either, of course. And you know, the funny thing was Elisa loved Hal, and I think folks around here understood that."

"How about you? What did you think of him?"

"Oh, I got pretty sick of Hal," Demott said. "I won't lie about it. He was a pain in the butt. But you know in a lot of ways I liked him. He had a good heart, and he was good for Elisa. Treated her like a quality lady, and that's what she is. And it made you feel sad, you know. I think he could have amounted to something if he'd been raised right."

Demott despaired of getting the hand suitably clean by rubbing at it. He got up, squatted by the stream, and washed it.

"I'm not sure I know what you mean," Leaphorn said. "What went wrong?"

Finished with his ablutions, Demott resumed his seat and thought about how to tell this.

"Hard to put it exactly," he said. "But when he was just a kid his folks would send him out here and we'd get him on a horse, and he'd do his share of work just like everybody else. Made a good enough hand, for a youngster. When we was baling hay, or moving the cows or anything, he'd do the twelve-hour day right along with us. And when the work was laid by, he'd go rock climbing with me and Elisa. In fact he got good at it before she did." Demott exhaled hugely, shook his head.

No mention of Tommy Castro. "Just the three of you?" Leaphorn asked.

Demott hesitated. "Pretty much."

"Tommy Castro didn't go along?"

Demott flushed. "Where'd you hear about him?"

Leaphorn shrugged.

Demott drew in a deep breath. "Castro and I were friends in high school and, yeah, he and I climbed together some. But then when Elisa got big enough to learn and she'd come along, Tommy began to make a move on her. I told him she was way too young and to knock it off. I put a stop to that."

"He still climb?"

"I have no idea," Demott said. "I stay away from him. He stays away from me."

"No problem with Hal, though."

"He was more her age and more her type, even though he was citified and born with the old silver spoon." Demott thought about that. "You know," he said, "I think he really did love this place as much as we did. He'd talk about getting his family to leave it to him as his part of the estate. Had it all figured out on paper. It wasn't worth near as much as the share he'd get otherwise, but it was what he wanted. That's what he'd say. Prettiest place on earth, and he'd make it better. Improve the stream where it was eroding. Plant out some ponderosa seedlings where we had a fire kill. Keep the herd down to where there wouldn't be any more overgrazing."

"I didn't see much sign of overgrazing now," Leaphorn said.

"Not now, you don't. But before Hal's daddy died he always wanted this place to carry a lot more livestock than the grass could stand. He was always putting the pressure on my dad, and after dad passed away, putting it on me. As a matter of fact he was threatening to fire me if I didn't get the income up to where he thought it ought to be."

"You think he would have done it?"

"We never will know," Demott said. "I wasn't going to overgraze this place, that's for damn sure. But just in time Breedlove had his big heart attack and passed away." He chuckled. "Elisa credited it to the power of my prayers."

Leaphorn waited. And waited. But Demott was in no hurry to interrupt his memories. A breeze came down the stream, cool and fresh, rustling the leaves behind Leaphorn and humming the little song that breezes sing in the firs.

"It's a mighty pretty day," Demott said finally. "But blink your eyes twice and winter will be coming over the mountain."

"You were going to tell me what went wrong with Hal," Leaphorn said.

"I got no license to practice psychiatry," Demott said. He hesitated just a moment, but Leaphorn knew it was coming. It was something Demott wanted to talk about — and probably had for a long, long time.

"Or theology, either," he continued. "If

that's the word for it. Anyway, you know how the story goes in our Genesis. God created Adam and gave him absolutely everything he could want, to see if he could handle it and still be obedient and do the right thing. He couldn't. So he fell from grace."

Demott glanced at Leaphorn to see if he was following.

"Got kicked out of paradise," Demott said.

"Sure," Leaphorn said. "I remember it." It wasn't quite the way he'd always heard it, but he could see the point Demott might make with his version.

"Old Breedlove put Hal in paradise," Demott said. "Gave him everything. Prep school with the other rich kids, Dartmouth with the children of the ruling class — absolutely the very goddamn best that you can buy with money. If I was a preacher I'd say Hal's daddy spent a ton of money teaching his boy to worship Mammon — however you pronounce that. Anyway, it means making a god out of things you can buy." He paused, gave Leaphorn a questioning glance.

"We have some of the same philosophy in our own Genesis story," Leaphorn said. "First Man calls evil 'the way to make money.' Besides, I took a comparative religion course when I was a student at Arizona State. Made an A in it."

"Okay," Demott said. "Sorry. Anyway, when Hal was about a senior or so he flew into Mancos one summer in his own little airplane. Wanted us to grade out a landing strip for it near the house. I figured out how much it would cost, but his daddy wouldn't come up with the money. They got into a big argument over it. Hal had already been arguing with him about taking better care of this place, putting money in instead of taking it all out. I think it was about then that the old man got pissed off. He decided he'd give Hal the ranch and nothing else and let him see if he could live off it."

"Figuring he couldn't?"

"Yep," Hal said. "And of course the old man was right. Anyhow Breedlove eased up on the pressure for profits some and I got to put in a lot of fencing we needed to protect a couple of the sensitive pastures and get some equipment in there for some erosion control along the Cache. Elisa and Hal got married after that. Everything going smooth. But that didn't last long. Hal took Elisa to Europe. Decided he just had to have himself a Ferrari. Great car for our kind of roads. But he bought it. And other stuff. Borrowed money. Before long we weren't bringing in enough from selling our surplus hay and the beef to cover his expenses. So he went to see the old man."

At this point Demott's voice was thickening. He paused, rubbed his shirtsleeve across his forehead. "Warm for this time of year," he said.

"Yeah," Leaphorn said, thinking it was a cool, dry sixty degrees or so even with the breeze gone.

"Anyway, he came back empty. Hal didn't have much to say but I believe they must have had a big family fight. I know for sure he tried to borrow from George — that's George Shaw, his cousin who used to come out and climb with us — and George must have turned him down too. I think the family must have told him they were going ahead with the moly strip mine deal, and to hell with him."

"But they didn't," Leaphorn said. "Why not?"

"I think it was because the old man had his heart attack a little bit after that. When he passed away it hung everything up in probate court for a while. This ranch was in trust for Hal. He didn't get it until he turned thirty, but of course the family didn't control it anymore. That's sort of where it stood for a while."

Demott paused. He inspected his newly washed hand. Leaphorn was thinking too, about this friction between Hal and his family and what it might imply.

"When I had my visit with Mrs. Rivera at the bank," Leaphorn said, "she told me things were starting to brew on the moly mine development again just before Hal disappeared. But this time she thought it was going to be a deal with a different mining company. She didn't think the family corporation was involved."

Demott lost interest in his hand.

"She tell you that?"

"That's what she said. She said a Denver bank was involved in the deal somehow. It was way too big an operation for her little bank to handle the money end of it."

"With Mrs. Rivera in business we don't really need a newspaper around here," Demott said.

"So I was thinking that if the family told Hal they were going to run right over him, maybe he decided he'd screw them instead. He'd make his own deal and cut them out."

"I think that's probably about the way it was," Demott said. "I know his lawyer told him all he had to do was slow things down in court long enough to get to his birthday. Then he'd have clear title and he could do what he wanted. That's what Elisa wanted him to do. But Hal was a fella who just could not wait. There were things he wanted to buy. Things he wanted to do. Places he hadn't seen yet. And he'd borrowed a lot of money he had to pay back."

Demott produced a bitter-sounding laugh. "Elisa didn't know about that. She didn't know he could use the ranch as collateral when he didn't own it yet. Came as quite a shock. But he had his lawyer work out some sort of deal which put up some sort of overriding interest in the place as a guarantee."

"Lot of money?"

"Quite a bit. He'd gotten rid of that

little plane he had and made a down payment on a bigger one. After he disappeared we let them take the plane back but we had to pay back the loan."

With that, Demott rose and collected his tools. "Back to work," he said. "Sorry I didn't know anything that would help you."

"One more question. Or maybe two," Leaphorn said. "Are you still climbing?"

"Too old for it," he said. "What's that in the Bible about it? About when you get to be a man you put aside the ways of the boy. Something like that."

"How good was Hal?"

"He was pretty good but he was reckless. He took more chances than I like. But he had all the skills. If he'd put his mind to it he could have been a dandy."

"Could he have climbed Ship Rock alone?"

Demott looked thoughtful. "I thought about that a lot ever since Elisa identified his skeleton. I didn't think so at first, but I don't know. I wouldn't even try it myself. But Hal . . ." He shook his head. "If he wanted something, he just had to have it."

"George Shaw went out to the Maryboy place the other day and got permission for a climb," Leaphorn said. "Next day or two. Any idea what he thinks might be found up there?"

"George is going to climb it?" Demott's tone was incredulous and his expression shocked. "Where'd you hear that?"

"All I know is that he told me he paid Maryboy a hundred dollars for trespass rights. Maybe he'll get somebody to climb it but I think he meant he was going up himself."

"What the hell for?"

Leaphorn didn't answer that. He gave Demott some time to answer it himself.

"Oh," Demott said. "The son of a bitch."

"I would imagine he thinks maybe somebody gave Hal a little push."

"Yeah," Demott said. "Either he thinks I did it, and I left something behind that would prove it — and he could use that to void Elisa's inheritance — or he did it himself and he remembers that he left something up there that would nail him and he wants to go get it."

Leaphorn shrugged. "As good a guess as any."

Demott put down his tools.

"When Elisa came back from having the bones cremated she told me none of them had been broken," he said. "Some of them were disconnected, you know. That could have been done in a fall, or maybe the turkey vultures pulled 'em apart. They're strong enough to do that, I guess. Anyway, I hope it was a fall, and he didn't just get hung up there to starve to death for water. He could have been a damn good man."

"I never knew him," Leaphorn said. "To me he was just somebody to hunt for and never find."

"Well, he was a good, kind boy," Demott said. "Big-hearted." He picked up his tools again. "You know, when the cop came up to show Elisa Hal's stuff I saw that folder he had with him. He had it labeled 'Fallen Man.' I thought, Yes, that described Hal. The old man gave him paradise and it wasn't enough for him."

18

Lucy Sam had seemed glad to see Chee.

"I think they're going to be climbing up Tse' Bit' a'i' again," she told Chee. "I saw a big car drive down the road toward Hosteen Maryboy's place two days ago, and it stayed a long time, and when I saw it coming back from there, I drove over there to see how he was doing and he told me about it."

"I heard about it, too," Chee said, thinking how hard it was to keep secrets in empty country.

"The man paid Hosteen Maryboy a hundred dollars," she said, and shook her head. "I don't think we should let them climb up there, even for a thousand dollars."

"I don't think so either," Chee said. "They have plenty of their own mountains to play around on."

"The one who lived here before," Lucy Sam said, using the Navajo circumlocution to avoid saying the name of the dead, "he'd say that it would be like us Navajos climbing all over that big church in Rome, or getting up on top of the Wailing Wall, or crawling all over that place where the Islamic prophet went up to heaven."

"It's disrespectful," Chee agreed, and with that subject out of the way he shifted the conversation to cattle theft.

Had Hosteen Maryboy mentioned to her that he'd lost some more cattle? He had, and he was angry about it. There would have been enough money in those cows to make the last payments on his pickup truck.

Had Ms. Sam seen anything suspicious since the last time he'd been here? She didn't think so.

Could he look at the ledger where she kept her notes? Certainly. She would get it for him.

Lucy Sam extracted the book from its desk drawer and handed it to Chee.

"I kept it just the same way," she said, tapping the page. "I put down the date and the time right here at the edge and then I write down what I see."

As he leafed backward through the ledger, Chee saw that Lucy Sam wrote down a lot more than that. She made a sort of daily journal out of it, much as her father had done. And she had not just copied her father's system, she also followed his Franciscan padres' writing style — small, neat lettering in small, neat lines — which had become sort of a trademark of generations of those Navajos educated at St. Michael's School west of Window Rock. It was easily legible and wasted neither paper nor ink. But readable or not, Chee found nothing in it very helpful.

He skipped back to the date when he and Officer Manuelito had visited the site of the loose fence posts. They had rated an entry, right after Lucy Sam's notation that "Yazzie came. Said he would bring some firewood" and just before "Turkey buzzards are back." Between those Lucy had written, "Police car stuck on road under Tse' Bit' a'i'. Truck driver helps." Then, down the page a bit: "Tow truck gets police car." The last entry before the tow truck note reported, "That camper truck stopped. Driver looked around."

That camper truck? Chee felt his face flush with remembered embarrassment. That would have been Finch checking to see how thoroughly they had sprung his Zorro trap. He worked his way forward through the pages, learning more about kestrels, migrating grosbeaks, a local family of coyotes, and other Colorado Plateau fauna than he wanted to know. He also gained some insights into Lucy Sam's loneliness, but nothing that he could see would be useful to Acting Lieutenant Chee in his role as rustler hunter. If Zorro had come back to collect a load of Maryboy's cows from the place he'd left the hay, he'd done it when Lucy Sam wasn't looking.

But she was looking quite a lot. There was a mention of a "very muddy" white pickup towing a horse trailer on the dirt road that skirted Ship Rock, but no mention of it stopping. Chee made a mental note to check on that. About a dozen other vehicles had come in view of Lucy Sam's spotting scope, none of them potential rustlers. They included a Federal Express delivery truck, which must have been lost, another mention of Finch's camper truck, and three pickups that she had identified with the names of local-area owners.

So what was useful about that? It told him that if Manuelito's network of watchers would pay off at all, it would require patience, and probably years, to establish suspicious-looking patterns. And it told him that Mr. Finch looked upon him as a competitor in his hunt for the so-called Zorro. Finch wanted him to write off Maryboy's loose-fence-posts location, but Finch hadn't written it off himself. He was keeping his eye on the spot. That produced another thought. Maryboy had been losing cattle before. Had either Lucy Sam or her father noticed anything interesting in the past? Specifically, had they ever previously noticed that white truck pulling its horse trailer? He would page back through the book and check on that when he had time. And he would also look through the back pages for school buses. He'd noticed a Lucy Sam mention of a school bus stuck on that same dirt road, and the road wasn't on a bus route. She had also mentioned "that camper truck" being parked almost all day at the base of the mountain the year before. Her note said "Climbing our mountain?"

Chee put down the ledger. Lucy Sam had gone out to feed her chickens and he could see her now in her sheep pen inspecting a young goat that had managed to entangle itself in her fence. He found himself imagining Janet Pete in that role and himself in old man Sam's wheelchair. It didn't scan. The white Porsche roared in and rescued her. But that wasn't fair. He was being racist. He had been thinking like a racist ever since he'd met Janet and fallen in love with her. He had been thinking that because her name was Pete, because her father was Navajo, her blood somehow would have taught her the ways of the *Dine* and made her one of them. But only your culture taught you values, and the culture that had formed Janet was blue-blooded, white, Ivy League, chic, irreligious, old-rich Maryland. And that made it just about as opposite as it could get from the traditional values of his people, which made wealth a symbol for selfishness, and had caused a friend of his to deliberately stop winning rodeo competitions because he was getting unhealthily famous and therefore out of harmony.

Well, to hell with that. He got up, refocused the spotting scope, and found the place where the posts had been loosened. That road probably carried no more than a dozen vehicles a week — none at all when the weather was wet. It was empty today, and there was no sign of anything around Mr. Finch's Zorro trap. Beyond it in the pasture he counted eighteen cows and calves, a mixture of Herefords and Angus, and three horses. He scanned across the Maryboy grassland to the base of Ship Rock and focused on the place where Lucy Sam had told him the climbing parties liked to launch their great adventures. Nothing there now but sage, chamisa, and a red-tailed hawk looking for her lunch.

Chee sat down again and picked up the oldest ledger. On his last visit he'd checked the entries on the days following Breedlove's disappearance but only with a casual glance. This time he'd be thorough.

Lucy Sam came in, washed her hands, and looked at him while she dried them.

"Something wrong?"

"Disappointed," Chee said. "So many details. This will take forever."

"He didn't have anything else to do," Lucy Sam said, voice apologetic. "After he got that sickness with his nerves, all he could do after that was get himself into his wheelchair. He couldn't go anyplace, he'd just sit there in the chair and sometimes he would read, or listen to the radio. And then he would watch through his telescope and keep his notes."

And he kept them very well, Chee noticed. Unfortunately they didn't seem to include what he wanted to find.

The date Hal Breedlove vanished came about midpoint in the old ledger. In Hosteen Sam's eyes it had been a windy day, cool, crows beginning to gather as they did when summer ended, flying in great, disorganized twilight flocks past Ship Rock to their roosting places in the San Juan River woods. Three oil field service trucks came down the road toward Red Rock and turned toward the Rattlesnake field. Some high clouds appeared but there had been no promise of rain.

The next day's entry was longer, devoted largely to the antics of four yearling coyotes who seemed to be trying to learn how to hunt in the prairie dog town down the slope. Interesting, but not what Chee was hoping for.

An hour and dozens of pages later, he closed the ledger, rubbed his eyes, and sighed.

"You want some lunch?" Lucy Sam

asked, which was just the question Chee had been hoping to hear. Lucy had been there at the stove across the kitchen from him, cutting up onions, stirring, answering his questions about abbreviations he couldn't read or points he didn't understand, and the smell of mutton stew had gradually permeated the room and his senses — making this foolish search seem far less important than his hunger.

"Please," he said. "That smells just like the stew my mother used to make."

"Probably is the same," Lucy said. "Everybody has to use the same stuff — mutton, onions, potatoes, can of tomatoes, salt, pepper." She shrugged.

Like his mother's stew, it was delicious. He told Lucy what he was looking for — about the disappearance of Hal Breedlove and then his skeleton turning up on the mountain. He was looking for some idea of when Hal Breedlove returned to make his fatal climb.

"You find anything?"

"I think I learned that the man didn't come right back here after running away from his wife in Canyon de Chelly. At least there was no mention of anybody climbing."

"There would have been," she said. "How far did you get?"

"Just through the first eight weeks after he disappeared. It's going to take forever."

"You know, they always do it the same way. They start climbing just at dawn, maybe before. That's because they want to get down before dark, and because there's some places where that black rock gets terribly hot when the afternoon sun shines on it. So all you got to do is take a look at the first thing written down each day. He would always do the same every morning. He would get up at dawn and roll his wheelchair to the door. Then he would sing the song to Dawn Boy and bless the morning with his pollen. Next he would take a look at his mountain. If there was anything parked there where the climbers always left their cars, it would be the first thing he wrote down."

"I'll try that, then," he said.

On the page at which Chee reopened the ledger the first entry was marked 9/15/85, which was several pages and eight days too early. He glanced at the first line. Something about a kestrel catching a meadowlark. He paged forward, checking Lucy's advice by scanning down the first notes after dates.

Now he was at 9/18/85 — halfway down the page. The first line read, "Climbers. Funny looking green van where climbers park. Three people going up. If Lucy gets back from Albuquerque I will get her to go into Shiprock and tell the police."

Chee checked the date again. September 18, 1985. That would be five days before Hal Breedlove disappeared from the Canyon de Chelly. He scanned quickly down the page, looking for other mentions of the climbers. He found two more on the same day.

The first said: "They are more than half way up now, creeping along under a cliff — like bugs on a wall." And the second: "The headlights turned on on the fancy green car, and the inside lights. I see them putting away their gear. Gone now, and the police did not come. I told Maryboy he should not let anyone climb Tse' Bit' a'i' but he did not listen to me."

Lucy was washing dishes in a pan of water on the table by the stove, watching him while she worked. He took the ledger to her, pointed to the entry.

"Do you remember this?" Chee asked. "It would have been about eleven years ago. Three people came to climb Ship Rock in some sort of green van. Your father wanted you to go tell the police but you had gone to Albuquerque."

Lucy Sam put on her glasses and read.

"Now why did I take the bus to Albuquerque?" she asked herself. "Yes," she answered. "Irma was having her baby there. Little Alice. Now she's eleven. And when I came home he was excited about those climbers. And angry. He wanted me to take him to see Hosteen Maryboy about it. And I took him over there, and they argued about it. I remember that."

"Did he say anything about the climbers?"

"He said they were a little bit slow. It was after dark when they got back to the car."

"Anything about the car?"

"The car?" She looked thoughtful. "I remember he hadn't seen one like it before. He said it was ugly, clumsy looking, square like a box. It was green and it had a ski rack on top."

Chee closed the ledger and handed it

to Lucy, trying to remember how Joe Leaphorn had described the car Hal Breedlove had abandoned after he had abandoned his wife. It was a recreational vehicle, green, something foreign-made. Yes. A Land-Rover. That would fit old man Sam's description of square and ugly.

"Thank you," he said to Lucy Sam. "I have to go now and see what Hosteen Maryboy can remember."

19

The sunset had flared out behind Beautiful Mountain when Chee's patrol car bounced over Lucy Sam's cattle guard and gained the pavement. In the darkening twilight his headlights did little good and Chee almost missed the unmarked turnoff. That put him on the dirt track that led southward toward Rol Hai Rock, Table Mesa, and the infinity of empty country between these massive old buttes and the Chuska range.

Lucy Sam had told him: "Watch your odometer and in about eight miles from the turnoff place you come to the top of a ridge and you can see Maryboy's place off to the left maybe a mile."

"It'll be dark," Chee said. "Is the turnoff marked?"

"There's a little wash there, and a big cottonwood where you turn," she said. "It's the only tree out there, and Maryboy keeps a ghost light burning at his hogan. You can't miss it."

"Okay," Chee said, wishing she hadn't added that 'can't miss it' phrase. Those were the landmarks he always missed.

"There's a couple of places with deep sand where you cross arroyos. If you're going too slow, you might get stuck. But it's a pretty good road in dry weather."

Chee had been over this track a time or two when duty called, and did not consider it pretty good. It was bad. Too bad to warrant even one of those dim lines that were drawn on the official road map with an "unimproved" label and a footnoted warning. But Chee drove it a little faster than common sense dictated. He was excited. That boxy green vehicle must have been Hal Breedlove's boxy green Land-Rover — the same car he'd seen at the Lazy B. One of those three men who climbed out of it must have been Breedlove. Why not suspect that one of the other two was the man who had called Breedlove at the Thunderbird Lodge three or four days later and lured him away from his wife to oblivion? He would get a description from Maryboy if the old man could provide one. And he might be able to because those who live lonely lives where fellow humans are scarce tend to remember strangers — especially those on the strange mission of risking their lives on Ship Rock. Whatever, he would learn all he could and then he would call Leaphorn.

For a reason he didn't even try to understand, sitting across a table from the Legendary Lieutenant and telling him all this seemed extremely important to Chee. He had thought he was angry at Leaphorn for signing up with John McDermott. But Leaphorn's clear black eyes would study him with approval. Leaphorn's dour expression would soften into a smile. Leaphorn would think awhile and then Leaphorn would tell him how this bit of information had solved a terrible puzzle.

The odometer had clicked off almost exactly the eight prescribed miles from the turnoff and the track was topping the ridge. The moon was not yet up, but the ragged black shape of the Chuskas to the right and the flat-topped bulk of Table Mesa to the left were outlined against a sky a-dazzle with stars. Ahead an ocean of darkness stretched toward the horizon. Then the track curved past a hummock of Mormon tea, and there shone the Maryboy ghost light, punctuating the night with a bright yellow spot.

Chee made the left turn past the cottonwood Lucy Sam had described into two sandy ruts separated by a grassy ridge. They led him along a shallow wash toward the light. The track dipped down a slope and the bright spot became just a glow. He heard a thud from somewhere a long ways off. More like a sudden clapping sound. But he was too busy driving for the moment to wonder what caused it. The track had veered down the bank of the wash, tilting his police car. It entered a dense tangle of chaparral, converted by his headlights into a tunnel of brightness. He emerged from that.

The ghost light was gone.

Chee frowned, puzzled. He decided it must be just out of sight behind the screen of brush he was driving past. The track emerged from the brush into flat grassland where nothing grew higher than the sage. Still no ghost light. Why not? Maryboy had turned it off, what else? Or the bulb had burned out. Out here, Maryboy wouldn't be on a Rural Electrification Administration power line. He'd be running a windmill generator and battery system. Perhaps the batteries had gone dead. Nonsense.

And yet the only reason one puts out a ghost light is because, for some reason, he believes he is threatened by the spirits of the dead. And if he believes that, why would he turn it off before Dawn Boy has restored harmony to the world? And why would he turn it off when he'd seen he had a visitor coming? Had Maryboy been expecting someone he would want to hide from?

Chee covered the last quarter mile slower than he would have had the light still been burning. His patrol car rolled past a plank stock pen with a loading ramp for cattle. His headlights reflected from the aluminum siding of a mobile home. Beyond it he could see the remains of a truck with its back wheels removed. Beyond that a fairly new pickup stood, and behind that, a small hogan, a small goat pen, a brush arbor, and two sheds. He parked a little further from the house than he would have normally and left the motor running a bit longer. And when he turned off the ignition he rolled down the window beside him and sat listening.

There was no light in the mobile home. Cold, dry December air poured through the truck window. It brought with it the smell of sage and dust, of dead leaves, of the goat pen. It brought the dead silence of a windless winter night. A dog emerged from one of the sheds, looking old, ragged, and tired. It limped toward his truck and stopped, the glare of his headlights reflecting from its eyes.

Chee leaned out of the window toward it. "Anybody home?" he asked. The dog turned and limped back into the shed. Chee switched off the car lights and waited, uneasy, for some sign of life from the house. Tapped his fingers on the steering wheel. Listened. From somewhere far away he heard the call of a burrowing owl hunting its prey. He thought. Someone turned off that damned ghost light. Therefore someone is here. I am absolutely not going back home and admit I came out here to talk to Maryboy and was too afraid of the dark to get out of the car.

Chee muttered an expletive, made sure that his official .38-caliber pistol was securely in its holster, took the flashlight from its rack, opened the car door, and got out — thankful for the policy that eliminated those dome lights that went on when the door opened. He stood beside the car, glad of the darkness, and shouted, "Hosteen Maryboy," and a greeting in Navajo. He identified himself by clan and family. He waited.

Only silence. But the sound of his own voice, loud and clear, had burst the bubble of his nervousness. He waited as long as politeness required, walked up to the entrance, climbed the two concrete block steps that led to the door, and tapped on the screen.

Nothing. He tapped again, harder this time. Again, no response. He tried the screen, swung it open. Tried the door. The knob turned easily in his hand.

"Hosteen Maryboy," Chee shouted. "You've got company." He listened. Nothing. And opened the door to total darkness. Flicked on his flash.

If time is measurable in such circumstances, it might have taken a few nanoseconds for Chee's flashlight beam to traverse this tiny room from end to end and find it unoccupied. But even while this was happening, his peripheral vision was telling him otherwise. He turned the flashlight downward.

The body lay on its back, feet toward the door, as if the man had come to answer a visitor's summons and then had been knocked directly backward.

In the moment that elapsed before Chee snapped off the flash and jumped into the darkness of the house he had reached several conclusions. The man had been shot near the center of the chest. He was probably, but not certainly, Mr. Maryboy. The claplike sound he had heard had been the fatal shot. Thus the shooter must be nearby. Having shot Maryboy, and seen Chee's headlights, he had switched off the ghost light. And, more to the immediate point, Acting Lieutenant Jim Chee was likely to get shot himself. He leaned against the wall beside the door, drew the pistol, cocked it, and made sure the safety was off.

Chee spent the next few minutes listening to the silence and thinking his situation through. Among the aromas that came from Hosteen Maryboy's kitchen he had picked up the acrid smell of burned gunpowder, confirming his guess that Maryboy had been shot only a few minutes ago. A frightening conclusion, it reinforced the evidence offered by the doused ghost light. The killer had not driven away. Chee would have met him on the access track. That he had walked away was possible but not likely. It would have meant abandoning his vehicle. Was it the pickup he'd noticed? Perhaps. But that was most likely Maryboy's. The killer, having seen him coming, would have had plenty of time to move his car but no way to drive out without meeting Chee on the track.

So what options did he have?

Chee squatted beside the body, felt for a pulse, and found none. The man was dead. That reduced the urgency a little. He could wait for daylight, which would even the odds. As it now stood the killer knew exactly where he was and he didn't have a clue. But waiting had a downside, too. It would occur to the killer sooner or later to fire a shot into the patrol car gas tank — or do something else to disable it. Then he could drive away unpursued. Or he might drain out some gasoline from any one of the vehicles, set this mobile home ablaze, and shoot Chee as he came out.

By now his eyes had adjusted to the darkness. Chee could easily see the windows. The starlight that came through them — dim as it was — allowed him to make out a chair, a couch, a table, and the door that led into the kitchen.

Could the killer be there? Or in the bedroom beyond it? Not likely. He sat against the wall, holding his breath, focusing every instinct on listening. He heard nothing. Still, he dreaded the thought of being shot in the back.

Chee picked up the flash, held it far from his body, pointed both his pistol and the flash at the kitchen doorway, and flicked it on. Nothing moved in the part of the room visible to him. He edged to the door, keeping the flash away from him. The kitchen was empty. And so, when he repeated that process, were the bedroom and the tiny bath behind it.

Back in the living room, Chee sat on the couch and made himself as comfortable as the circumstances permitted. He weighed the options, found no new ones, imagined dawn coming, imagined the sun rising, imagined waiting and waiting, imagined finally saying to hell with it and walking out to the patrol car. Then he would either be shot, or he wouldn't be. If he wasn't shot, he would have to get on the radio and report this affair to Captain Largo.

"When did this happen?" the captain would ask, and then, "Why did you wait all night to report it?" and then, "Are you telling me that you sat in the house all night because you were afraid to come out?" And the only answer to that would be "Yes, sir, that's what I did." And then, a little later, Janet Pete would be asking why he was being dismissed from the Navajo Tribal Police, and he would say — But would Janet care enough to ask? And did it matter anyway?

Something mattered. Chee got up, stood beside the door, looking and listening — impressed with how bright the night now seemed outside the lightless living room. But he saw nothing, and heard nothing. He pushed open the screen and, pistol in hand, dashed to the patrol car, pulled open the door and slid in — crouched low in the seat, grabbed the mike, started the engine.

The night dispatcher responded almost instantly. "Have a homicide at the Maryboy place," Chee said, "with the perpetrator still in the area. I need —"

The dispatcher remembered hearing the sound of two shots, closely spaced,

and of breaking glass, and something
she described as "scratching, squeak-
ing, and thumping." That was the end
of the message from Acting Lieutenant
Jim Chee.

20

At first Chee was conscious only of something uncomfortable covering much of his head and his left eye. Then the general numbness of the left side of his face registered on his consciousness and finally some fairly serious discomfort involving his left ribs. Then he heard two voices, both female, one belonging to Janet Pete. He managed to get his right eye in focus and there she was, holding his hand and saying something he couldn't understand. Thinking about it later, he thought it might have been "I told you so," or something to that effect.

When he awoke again, the only one in the room was Captain Largo, who was looking at him with a puzzled expression.

"What the hell happened out there?" Largo said. "What was going on?" And then, as if touched by some rare sentiment, he said, "How you feeling, Jim? The doctor tells us he thinks you're going to be all right."

Chee was awake enough to doubt that Largo expected an answer and gave himself a few moments to get oriented. He was in a hospital, obviously. Probably the Indian Health Service hospital at Gallup, but maybe Farmington. Obviously something bad had happened to him, but he didn't know what. Obviously again, it had something to do with his ribs, which were hurting now, and his face, which would be hurting when the numbness wore off. The captain could bring him up to date. And what day was it, anyway?

"What the hell happened?" Chee asked. "Car wreck?"

"Somebody shot you, goddammit," Largo said. "Do you know who it was?"

"Shot me? Why would somebody do that?" But even before he finished the sentence he began to remember. Hosteen Maryboy dead on the floor. Getting back into the patrol car. But it was very vague and dreamlike.

"They shot you twice through the door of the patrol car," Largo said. "It looked to Teddy Begayaye like you were driving away from the Maryboy place and the perpetrator fired two shots through the driver's-side door. Teddy found the empties. Thirty-eights by the looks of them, and of what they took out of you.

But you had the window rolled down, so the slugs had to get through that shatterproof glass after they punched through the metal. The doc said that probably saved you."

Chee was more or less awake now and didn't feel like anything had saved him. He felt terrible. He said, "Oh, yeah. I remember some of it now."

"You remember enough to tell me who shot you? And what the hell you were doing out at the Maryboy place in the middle of the night? And who shot Maryboy? And why they shot him? Could you give us a description? Let us know what the hell we're looking for — man, woman, or child?"

Chee got most of the way through answering most of those questions before whatever painkillers they had shot into him in the ambulance, and the emergency room, and the operating room, and since then cut in again and he started fading away. The nurse came in and was trying to shoo Largo out. But Chee was just awake enough to interrupt their argument. "Captain," he said, hearing his voice come out soft and slurry and about a half mile away. "I think this Maryboy homicide goes all the way back to that Hal Breedlove case Joe Leaphorn was working on eleven years ago. That Fallen Man business. That skeleton up on Ship Rock. I need to talk to Leaphorn about . . ."

The next time he rejoined the world of the living he did so more or less completely. The pain was real, but tolerable. A nurse was doing something with the flexible tubing to which he was connected. A handsome, middle-aged woman whose name tag said SANCHEZ, she smiled at him, asked him how he was doing and if there was anything she could do for him.

"How about a damage assessment?" Chee said. "A prognosis. A condition report. The captain said he thought I might live, but how about this left eye? And what's with the ribs?"

"The doctor will be in to see you pretty soon," the nurse said. "He's supposed to be the one to give the patient that sort of information."

"Why don't you do it?" Chee said. "I'm very, very interested."

"Oh, why not?" she said. She picked up the chart at the foot of his bed and scanned it. She frowned, made a disapproving clicking sound with her tongue.

"I don't like the sound of that," Chee said. "They're not going to decide I'm too banged up to be worth repairing?"

"We've got two misspelled words in this," she said. "They quit teaching doctors how to spell. But, no, I just wish I was as healthy as you are," she said. "I guess a body shop estimator would rate you as a moderately serious fender bender. Not bad enough to total you out, and just barely bad enough to cause the insurance company to send in its inspector and raise your premium rates."

"How about the eye?" Chee said. "It has a bandage over it."

"Because of" — she glanced down at the chart and read — " 'multiple superficial lacerations caused by glass fragments.' But from the looks of this, no damage was done where it might affect your vision. Maybe you'll have some bumpy shaving on that cheek for a while, and need to grow yourself about an inch of new eyebrow. But apparently no sight impairment."

"That's good to hear," Chee said. "How about the rest of me?"

She looked down at him sternly. "Now when the doctor comes in, you've got to act surprised. All right? Everything he tells you is news to you. And for God's sake don't argue with him. Don't be saying: 'That ain't what Florence Nightingale told me.' You understand?"

Chee understood. He listened. Two bullets involved. One apparently had struck the thick bone at the back of the skull a glancing blow, causing a scalp wound, heavy bleeding, and concussion. The other, apparently fired after he had fallen forward, came through the door. While the left side of his face was sprayed with debris, the slug was deflected into his left side, where it penetrated the muscles and cracked two ribs.

"I'd say you were pretty lucky," the nurse said, looking at him over the chart. "Except maybe in your choice of friends."

"Yeah," Chee said, wincing. "Does that chart show who sent me those flowers?"

There were two bunches of them, one a dazzling pot of some sort of fancy chrysanthemum and the other a bouquet of mixed blossoms.

The nurse extracted the card from the bouquet. "Want me to read it to you?"

"Please," Chee said.

"It says, 'Learn to duck,' and it's signed, 'Your Shiprock Rat Terriers.' "

"Be damned," Chee said, and felt himself flushing with pleasure.

"Friends of yours?"

"Yes, indeed," Chee said. "They really are."

"And the other card reads 'Get well quick, be more careful and we have to talk,' and it's signed 'Love, Janet.' " With that Nurse Sanchez left him to think about what it might mean.

The next visitor was a well-dressed young man named Elliott Lewis, whose tidy business suit and necktie proclaimed him a special agent of the Federal Bureau of Investigation. Nevertheless, he displayed his identification to Chee. His interest was in the wrongful death of Austin Maryboy, such felonious events on a federal reservation being under the jurisdiction of the Bureau. Chee told him what he knew, but not what he guessed. Lewis, in the best FBI tradition, told Chee absolutely nothing.

"This thing must have made some sort of splash in the papers," Chee said. "Am I right about that?"

Lewis was restoring his notebook and

tape recorder to his briefcase. "Why you say that?"

"Because the FBI got here early."

Lewis looked up from the housekeeping duties in his briefcase. He suppressed a grin and nodded. "It made the front page in the *Phoenix Gazette*, and the *Albuquerque Journal*, and the *Deseret News*," he said. "And I guess you could add the *Gallup Independent*, *Navajo Times*, *Farmington Times*, and the rest of 'em."

"How long you been assigned out here?" Chee asked.

"This is week three," Lewis said. "I'm fresh out of the academy but I've heard about our reputation for chasing the headlines. And you'll notice I've already got the names of the pertinent papers memorized."

Which left Chee regretting the barb. What was Lewis but another young cop trying to get along? Maybe the Bureau would teach him its famous arrogance. But it hadn't yet, and maybe with the old J. Edgar Hoover gang fading away, it was dropping the superman pose. Chee had worked with both kinds.

Lewis was also efficient. He asked the pertinent questions, which made it apparent that the theory of the crime appealing to the Bureau was a motive involving cattle theft — of which Maryboy was known to be a victim. Chee considered introducing mountain climbing into the conversation but decided against it. His head ached. Life was already too complicated. And how the devil could he explain it anyway? Lewis closed his notebook, switched off his tape recorder, and departed.

Chee turned his thoughts to the note Janet had signed. Remembering earlier notes, it sounded cool, considering the circumstances. Or was that his imagination? And there she was now, standing in the doorway, smiling at him, looking beautiful.

"You want a visitor?" she said. "They gave the fed first priority. I had to wait."

"Come in," he said, "and sit and talk to me."

She did. But en route to the chair, she bent over, found an unbandaged place, and kissed him thoroughly.

"Now I have two reasons to be mad at you," she said.

He waited.

"You almost got yourself killed," she said. "That's the worst thing. Lieutenants are supposed to send their troops out to get shot at. They're not supposed to get shot themselves."

"I know," he said. "I've got to work on it."

"And you insulted me," she added. "Are you recovered enough to talk about that?" No more banter now. The smile was gone.

"Did I?" Chee said.

"Don't you think so? You implied that I had tricked you. You pretty well said that I had used you to get information to pass along to John."

Chee didn't respond to that. "John," he was thinking. Not "McDermott," or "Mr. McDermott," but "John."

He shrugged. "I apologize, then," he said. "I think I misunderstood things. I had the impression the son of a bitch was your enemy. Everything I know about the man is what you told me. About how he had used you, taken advantage of his position. You the student and the hired hand. Him the famous professor and the boss. That made him your enemy, and anyone who treats you like that is my enemy."

She sat very still, hands folded in her lap, while he said all that. "Jim," she began, and then stopped, her lower lip between her teeth.

"I guess it shocked me," he said. "There I was, the naive romantic, thinking of myself as Sir Galahad saving the damsel from the dragon, and I find out the damsel is out partying with the dragon."

Janet Pete's complexion had become slightly pink.

"I agree with some of that," she said. "The part about you being naive. But I think we'd better talk about this later. When you're better. I shouldn't have brought it up now. I wasn't thinking. I'm sorry. I want you to hurry up and get well, and this isn't good for you."

"Okay," Chee said. "I'm sorry I hurt your feelings."

She stopped at the door. "I hope one really good thing will come out of this," she said. "I hope this being almost killed will cure you of being a policeman."

"What do you mean?" Chee said, knowing full well what she meant.

"I mean you could stay in law enforcement without carrying that damned gun, and doing that sort of work. You could take your pick of half a dozen jobs in —"

"In Washington," Chee said.

"Or elsewhere. There are dozens of offices. Dozens of agencies. In the BIA, the Justice Department. I heard of a wonderful opening in Miami. Something involving the Seminole agency."

Chee's head ached. He didn't feel well. He said, "Thanks for coming, Janet. Thanks for the flowers."

And then she was gone.

Chee drifted into a shallow sleep punctuated by uneasy dreams. He was awakened to take antibiotics and to have his temperature and vital signs checked. He dozed again, and was aroused to eat a bowl of lukewarm cream of mushroom soup, a portion of cherry Jell-O, and some banana-flavored yogurt. He was reminded that he was supposed to rise from his bed now and walk around the room for a while to get everything working properly. While dutifully doing that, he sensed a presence behind him.

Joe Leaphorn was standing in the doorway, his face wearing that expression of disapproval that Chee had learned to dread when he was the Legendary Lieutenant's assistant and gofer.

21

"Aren't you supposed to be in bed?" Leaphorn asked. He was wearing a plaid shirt and a Chicago Cubs baseball cap, but even that didn't minimize the effect. He still looked to Chee like the Legendary Lieutenant.

"I'm just doing what the doc told me to do," Chee said. "I'm getting used to walking so these ribs don't hurt." He was also getting used to looking at the image of himself in the mirror with one eye bandaged and the other one hideously black. But he wasn't admitting that to Leaphorn. In fact, he was disgusted with himself for explaining his conduct to Leaphorn. He should have told him to bug off. But he didn't. Instead he said, "Yes, sir. I'm being the model patient so they'll give me time off for good behavior."

"Well, I'm glad it's not as bad as I first heard it was," Leaphorn said, and helped himself to a chair. "I'd heard he almost killed you."

They dealt with all the facts of the incident then, quickly and efficiently — became two professionals talking about a crime. Chee eased himself back onto the bed. Leaphorn sat, holding his cap. His bristly short haircut was even grayer now than Chee had remembered.

"I'm not going to stay long," Leaphorn said. "They told me you're supposed to be resting. But I have something I wanted to tell you."

"I'm listening," Chee said, thinking, You also have something you want to ask me. But so what? That was the tried-and-true Leaphorn strategy. There was nothing underhanded about it.

Leaphorn cleared his throat. "You sure you don't want to get some rest?"

"To hell with resting," Chee said. "I want out of here and I think they may let me go this evening. The doc wants to change the bandages again and check everything."

"The quicker the better," Leaphorn said. "Hospitals are dangerous places."

Chee cut off his laugh just as it started. Leaphorn's wife had died in this very hospital, he remembered. A brain tumor removed. Everything went perfectly. The tumor was benign. But the staph infection that followed was lethal.

"Yes," he said. "I want to go home."

"I've done a little checking," Leaphorn said. He made an abashed gesture. "When you've been in the NTP as long as I was — and out of it just a little bit — then it seems people have trouble remembering you're just a civilian. That you're no longer official."

"Lieutenant," Chee said, and laughed. "I'm afraid you're always going to seem official to a lot of people. Including me."

Leaphorn looked vaguely embarrassed by that. "Well, anyway, things are going about the way you'd expect. It was a slim day for news, and the paper's made a pretty big thing out of it. That brings the feds hurrying right in. You've seen the newspapers, I guess?"

"No," Chee said, and pointed to his left eye. "I haven't been in very sharp focus until today. But I've seen the fed."

"Well, you can't be surprised they're on it. Big headlines. Slayer shoots policeman at the scene of the murder. No suspect. No motive. Big mystery. Big headlines. So the Bureau moves in right away without requiring the usual prodding. They found out that Maryboy had been having some livestock stolen. They found out you'd gone out there to check on rustling. So they're working that angle some . . ." Leaphorn paused, gave Chee a wry grin. "You know what I mean?"

Chee laughed. "Unless they've reformed since day before yesterday it means they're having my friends in the NTP at Shiprock working on it, and the Arizona Highway Patrol, and the New Mexico State Police, and the San Juan and McKinley County sheriff's deputies."

Leaphorn didn't object to that analysis. "And then they think maybe there might be a drug angle, or a gang angle. All those good things," he added.

"No other theories?"

"Not from what I'm hearing."

"You're telling me something right now," Chee said, unable to suppress a grin, even though it hurt. "I think you're telling me that neither the feds nor anyone else has shown any interest in trying to tie an eleven-year-old run-away-husband case into this felony homicide. Am I right?"

Leaphorn was never very much a man for laughing, but his amusement showed. "That is correct," he said.

"I've been trying to visualize that," Chee said. "You've known Captain Largo longer than I have. But can you visualize him trying to explain to some special agent that I had actually gone out to interview Maryboy to see if he could identify who had climbed Ship Rock eleven years ago, because we were still working on a 1985 missing person case? Can you imagine Largo doing it? Trying to get the guy's attention, especially when Largo doesn't understand it himself."

The amusement had left Leaphorn's face.

"I guessed that's why you were out there," he said. "What'd you find out?"

Chee couldn't pass up this opportunity to needle the Legendary Lieutenant. Besides, Leaphorn was working for McDermott. So Chee said, "Nothing. Maryboy was dead when I got there."

"No. No." Leaphorn let his impatience show. "I meant what had you learned that caused you to go out there? In the night?"

The moment had come:

"I learned that on the morning of September 18, 1985, a dark green, square, ugly recreational vehicle with a ski rack on its roof was driven to the usual climbers' launch site on Maryboy's grazing lease. Three men got out and climbed Ship Rock. Maryboy had given them trespass permission. Now, to bring things up to date, I learned yesterday that John McDermott hands this same Hosteen Maryboy one hundred dollars for trespass rights for another climb. I presume that George Shaw and others intend to climb the mountain, probably just as quickly as they can get a party organized. So, I went out to learn if Hosteen Maryboy remembered who had paid him for climbing trespass rights back in 1985."

Chee recited this slowly, watching Leaphorn's face. It became absolutely still. Breathing stopped. The green vehicle was instantly translated into Breedlove's status truck, the date into a week before Hal had begun his vanishing act, and two days before his all-important thirtieth birthday. All that, and all the complex implications suggested, had been processed by the time Chee finished his speech. Leaphorn's first question, Chee knew, would be how he had learned this. Whether the source of this information was reliable. Well, let him ask it. Chee was ready.

Leaphorn sighed.

"I wonder how many people knew that George Shaw was looking for a team to climb that mountain with him," Leaphorn said.

Chee looked at the ceiling, clicked his tongue against his teeth, and said, "I have no idea." Why did he continue trying to guess how the Legendary Lieutenant's mind worked? It was miles and miles beyond him.

Leaphorn abruptly clapped his hands together.

"Now you've given us the link that can fit the pattern together," Leaphorn said, with rare exuberance. "Finally something to work with. I spent most of my time for months trying to think this case through and I didn't come up with this. Emma was still healthy then, and she thought about it, too. And I've spent a lot of thought on it since then, even though we officially gave up. And in — how many days was it? — less than ten, you come up with the link."

Chee found himself baffled. But Leaphorn was beaming at him, full of pride. That made it both better and worse.

"But we still don't know who killed Hosteen Maryboy," Chee said, thinking at least he didn't know.

"But now we have something to work on," Leaphorn said. "Another part of the pattern takes shape."

Chee said, "Umm," and tried to look thoughtful instead of confused.

"Breedlove's skeleton is found on Ship Rock," Leaphorn said, holding up a blunt trigger finger. "Amos Nez is promptly shot." Leaphorn added a second finger. "Now, shortly thereafter, just as arrangements are being made for another climb of Ship Rock, one of the last people to see Breedlove is shot." He added a third finger.

"Yes," Chee said. "If we have all the pertinent facts it makes for a short list of suspects."

"I can add a little light to that," Leaphorn said. "Actually, it's what I came in to tell you. Eldon Demott told me some interesting things about Hal. The key one was that he'd quarreled with his father, and his family. He had decided to cut the family corporation out of the mining lease as soon as he inherited the ranch."

"Did the family know that?"

"Demott presumed they did. So do I. He probably told them himself. Demott understood Hal had tried to get money out of his father, and got turned down, and came home defiant. But even if he tried to keep it secret, the money people seemed to have known about it. Hal was in debt. Borrowing money. And if the money people knew, I'm sure the word got back to the Breedlove Corporation."

"Ah," Chee said. "So we add George Shaw to the list of people who would be happy if Hal Breedlove died before he celebrated the pertinent birthday."

"Or even happier to prove that Hal Breedlove was murdered by his wife, which would mean she couldn't inherit. I would guess that would put the ranch back into probate. And the Breedlove family would be the heir."

They sat for a while, thinking about it.

"If you want a little bit more confusion, I turned up a possible boyfriend for Elisa," Leaphorn said. "It turns out their climbing team was once a foursome." He explained to Chee what Mrs. Rivera had told him of Tommy Castro and what Demott had added to it.

"Another rock climber," Chee said.

"You think he killed Hal to gain access to the widow? Or the widow and Castro conspired to get Hal out of the way?"

"If so, they didn't do much about it. As far as we know, that is."

"How about Shaw as the man who left Breedlove dying on the ledge? Or maybe gave him a shove?"

Leaphorn shrugged. "I think I like one of the Demotts a little better."

"How about the shootings?"

"About the same," Leaphorn said.

They thought about it some more, and Chee felt himself being engulfed with nostalgia. Remembering the days he'd worked for Leaphorn, sat across the desk in the lieutenant's cramped second-floor office in Window Rock trying to put the pieces of something or other together in order to understand a crime. Stressful as it had been, demanding as Leaphorn tended to be, it had been a joyful time. And damn little paperwork.

"Do you still have your map?" Chee asked.

If Leaphorn heard the question he didn't show it. He said, "The problem here is time."

Lost again, Chee said, "Time?"

"Think how different things would be

if Hal Breedlove's thirtieth birthday had been a week after he disappeared, instead of a week before," Leaphorn said.

"Yeah," Chee said. "Wouldn't that have simplified things?"

"Then the presumption that went with his disappearance would have been foul play. A homicide to prevent the inheritance."

"Right," Chee said.

Leaphorn rose, recovered his Cubs cap from Chee's table.

"Do you think you can get Largo to make Ship Rock off limits to climbers for a few days?"

"Do I tell him why?" Chee asked.

"Tell him that mountain climbers have this tradition of leaving a record behind when they reach a difficult peak. Ship Rock is one of those. On top of it, there's a metal box — one of those canisters the army uses to hold belted machine gun ammunition. It's waterproof, of course, and there's a book in it that climbers sign. They jot down the time and the date and any note they'd like to leave to those who come later."

"Shaw told you that?"

"No. I've been asking around. But Shaw would certainly know it."

"You want to keep Shaw from going up and getting it," Chee said. "Didn't you tell me you were working for him?"

"He retained me to find out everything I could about what happened to Hal Breedlove," Leaphorn said. "How can I learn anything I can depend on from that book if Mr. Shaw gets it first?"

"Oh," Chee said.

"I want to know who was in that party of three who made the climb before Hal disappeared. Was one of them Hal, or Shaw, or Demott, or maybe even Castro? Three men, Hosteen Sam said. But how could he be sure of gender through a spotting scope miles away? Climbers wear helmets and they don't wear skirts. Was one of the three Mrs. Breedlove? If Hal was one of them and he got to the top, his name will be in the book. If it isn't, that might help explain why he went back after he vanished from Canyon de Chelly: to try again. If he got to the top that time, his name and the date will be there. I want to know when he made the climb that killed him."

"It wasn't in the first forty-three days after he disappeared," Chee said.

"What?" Leaphorn said, startled. "How do you know that?"

Chee described Hosteen Sam's ledger, his habit of rolling his wheelchair to the window each day after his dawn prayers and looking at the mountain. He described Sam's meticulous entry system. "But there was no mention of a climbing party from September eighteenth, when he watched the three climb it and then complained to Maryboy about it, through the first week of November. So if Hal climbed it in that period he had to somehow sneak in without old Sam seeing him. I doubt if that's possible, even if he knew Sam would be watching — which he wouldn't — or had some reason to be sneaky. I'm told that that's the starting point for the only way up."

"I think we need to keep that ledger somewhere safe," Leaphorn said. "It seems to be telling us that Breedlove was alive a lot longer than I'd been thinking."

"I'll call Largo and get him to stall off climbing for a while," Chee said. "And I'll call my office. Manuelito knows Lucy Sam. She can go out and take custody of that ledger for a little while."

"You take care of yourself," Leaphorn said, and headed for the door.

"Wait a second. If we get the climbing

stopped, how are you going to get someone up there to look at the register?"

"I'm going to rent a helicopter,"
Leaphorn said. "I know a lawyer in
Gallup. A rock climber who's been up
Ship Rock himself. I think he'd be willing to go up with me and the pilot, and
we put him down on the top, and he
takes a look."

"And brings down the book."

"I didn't want to do that. I'm a civilian
now. I don't want to tamper with evidence. We'll take along a camera."

"And make some photocopies?"

"Exactly."

"That's going to cost a lot of money,
isn't it?"

"The Breedlove Corporation is paying
for it," Leaphorn said. "I've got their
twenty thousand dollars in the bank."

22

The KOAT-TV weather map the previous night had shown a massive curve of bitterly cold air bulging down the Rocky Mountains out of Canada, sliding southward. The morning news reported snow across Idaho and northern Utah, with livestock warnings out. The weather lady called it a "blue norther" and told the Four Corners to brace for it tomorrow. But at the moment it was a beautiful morning for a helicopter ride, if you enjoyed such things, which Leaphorn didn't.

The last time he'd ridden in one of these ugly beasts he was being rushed to a hospital to have a variety of injuries treated. It was better to go when one was healthy, he thought, but not much.

However, Bob Rosebrough seemed to be enjoying it, which was good because Rosebrough had volunteered to climb down the copter's ladder to the tip of Ship Rock, photograph the documents in the box there, and climb back up.

"No problem, Joe," he'd said. "Climbing down a cliff can be harder than climbing up it, but ladders are different.

And I sort of like the idea of being the first guy to climb down onto the top of Ship Rock." Liking the idea meant he wouldn't accept any payment for taking the day off from his Gallup law practice. That appealed to Leaphorn. The copter rental was taking eight hundred dollars out of the Breedlove Corporation's twenty thousand retainer, and Leaphorn was beginning to have some ethical qualms about how he was using that fee.

The view now was spectacular. They were flying south from the Farmington Airport and if Leaphorn had cared to look straight down, which he didn't, he would have been staring into row after row of dragon's teeth that erosion had formed on the east side of the uplift known as the Hogback. The rising sun outlined the teeth with shadows, making them look like a grotesquely over-sized tank trap — even less hospitable than they appeared from the ground. The slanting light was also creating a silver mirror of the surface of Morgan Lake to the north and converting the long plume of steam from the stacks of the Four Corners Power Plant into a great white feather. The scale of it made even Leaphorn, a desert rat raised in the vastness of the Four Corners, conscious of its immensity.

The pilot was pointing down.

"How about having to land in those shark's teeth?" he asked. "Or worse, parachuting down into it. Just think about that. It makes your crotch hurt."

Leaphorn preferred to think of something else, which in its way was equally unpleasant. He thought about the oddity of murder in general, and of this murder in particular. Hal Breedlove disappears. Ten quiet years follow. Then, rapidly, in a matter of days, an unidentified skeleton is found on the mountain, apparently a man who has fallen to his death in a climbing accident. Then Amos Nez is shot. Next the bones are identified as the remains of Hal Breedlove. Then Hosteen Maryboy is murdered. Cause and effect, cause and effect. The pattern was there if he could find the missing part — the part that would bring it into focus. At the center of it, he was certain, was the great dark volcanic monolith that was now looming ahead of them like the ruins of a Gothic cathedral built for giants. On top of it a metal box was cached. In the box would be another piece to fit into the puzzle of Hal Breedlove.

"The spire on the left is it," Rosebrough said, his voice sounding metallic through the earphones they were wearing. "They look about the same height from this vantage, but the one on the left is the one you have to stand on top of if you want to say you've climbed Ship Rock."

"I'm going to circle around it a little first," the pilot said. "I want to get a feeling for wind, updrafts, downdrafts, that sort of thing. Air currents can be tricky around something like this. Even on a calm, cool morning."

They circled. Leaphorn had been warned about what looking down while a copter is spiraling does to one's stomach. He folded his hands across his safety belt and studied his knuckles.

"Okay," Rosebrough said. "That's it just below us."

"It doesn't look very flat," the pilot said, sounding doubtful. "And how big is it?"

"Not very," Rosebrough said. "About the size of a desktop. The box is on that larger flattish area just below. I'll have to climb down to get it."

"You have twenty feet of ladder, but I guess I could get close enough for you to just jump down," the pilot said.

Rosebrough laughed. "I'll take the ladder," he said.

And he did.

Leaphorn looked. Rosebrough was on the mountain, standing on the tiny sloping slab that formed the summit, then climbing down to the flatter area. He removed an olive drab U.S. Army ammunition box from the crack, opened it, removed the ledger, and tried to protect it from the wind produced by the copter blades. He waved them away. Leaphorn, stomach churning, resumed the study of his knuckles.

"You all right?" the pilot asked.

"Fine," Leaphorn said, and swallowed.

"There's a barf bag there if you need it."

"Fine," Leaphorn said.

"He's taking the pictures now," the pilot said. "Photographing one of the pages."

"Okay," Leaphorn said.

"It'll just be a minute."

Leaphorn, busy now with the bag, didn't respond. But by the time the rhetorical minute had dragged itself past and Rosebrough was climbing back into the copter, he was feeling a little better.

"I took a bunch of different exposures so we'll have some good ones," he said, settling himself in his seat and fastening his safety belt. "And I shot the five or six pages before and after. That what you wanted?"

"Fine," Leaphorn said, his mind working again, buzzing with the questions that had brought them up here. "Did you find Breedlove's name? And who else —" He stopped. He was breaking his own rule. Much better to let Rosebrough tell what he had found without intervention.

"He signed it," Rosebrough said, "and wrote 'vita brevis.' "

He didn't explain to Leaphorn that the inscription was Latin and provide the translation — which was one of the reasons Leaphorn liked the man. Why would Breedlove have bothered to leave that epigram? "Life is short." Was it to explain why he'd taken the dangerous way down in case he didn't make it? He'd worry about that later.

"Funny thing," Rosebrough said. "No

one else signed it on that date. I told you I didn't think he could possibly climb it alone. But it looks like maybe I was wrong."

"Maybe the people with him had climbed it before," Leaphorn said.

"That wouldn't matter. You'd still want to have it on the record that you'd done it again. It's a hell of a hard climb."

"Anything else?"

"He said he made it up at eleven twenty-seven A.M. and under that he wrote, 'Four hours, twenty-nine minutes up. Now, I'm going down the fast way.' "

"Looks like he tried," the pilot said. "But it took him about eleven years to make it all the way to the bottom."

"Could he have climbed it that fast alone?" Leaphorn asked. "Is that time reasonable?"

Rosebrough nodded. "These days the route is so well mapped, a good, experienced crew figures about four hours up and three hours down."

"How about the fast way down?" Leaphorn asked. To him it sounded a little like a suicide note. "What do you think he meant by that?"

Rosebrough shook his head. "It took

teams of good climbers years to find the way you can get from the bottom to the top. Even that's no cinch. It involves doing a lot of exposed climbing, with a rope to save you if you slip. Then you have to climb down a declivity to reach the face where you can go up again. That's the way everybody who's ever got to the top of Ship Rock got there. And as far as I know, that's the way everybody always got down."

"So there isn't any 'fast way down'?"

Rosebrough gave that some thought. "There has been some speculation of a shortcut. But it would involve a lot of rappelling, and I never heard of anyone actually trying it. I think it's way too dangerous."

They were moving away from Ship Rock now, making the long slide down toward the Farmington Airport. Leaphorn was feeling better. He was thinking that whatever Breedlove had meant by the fast way down, he had certainly done something dangerous.

"I'm thinking about that rappel route," Rosebrough said. "If he tried that by himself, that would help explain where they found the skeleton." He was looking at Leaphorn quizzically. "You're awfully quiet, Joe. Are you okay? You're looking pale."

"I'm feeling pale," Leaphorn said, "but I'm quiet because I'm thinking about the other two people who made the climb with him that day. Didn't they get all the way up? Or what?"

"Who were they?" Rosebrough asked. "I know most of the serious rock climbers in this part of the world."

"We don't know," Leaphorn said. "All we have are the notes of an old mountain watcher. Sort of shorthand, too. He just jotted down nine slash eighteen slash eighty-five and said three men had parked at the jump-off site and were climbing the —"

"Wait a minute," Rosebrough said. "You said nine eighteen eighty-five? That's not the date Breedlove wrote. He put down nine thirty eighty-five."

Leaphorn digested that. No thought of nausea now. "You're sure?" he asked. "Breedlove dated his climb September thirty. Not September eighteen."

"I'm dead certain," Rosebrough said. "That's what the photo is going to show. Was I confused or something?"

"No," Leaphorn said. "I was the one who was confused."

"You sure you feel all right?"

"I feel fine," Leaphorn said. Actually he was feeling embarrassed. He had been conned, and it had taken him eleven years to get his first solid inkling of how they had fooled him.

23

Chee had decided the grease in the frying pan was hot enough and was pulling the easy-open lid off the can of Vienna sausages when the headlight beam flashed across his window. He flicked off his house trailer's overhead light — something he wouldn't have considered doing a few days ago. But his cracked ribs still ached, and the person who had caused that was still out there somewhere. Possibly in the car that was now rolling to a stop under the cottonwood outside.

Whoever had driven it got out and walked into the headlights where Chee could see him. It was Joe Leaphorn, the Legendary Lieutenant, again. Chee groaned, said, "Oh, shit!" and switched on the light.

Leaphorn entered hat in hand. "It's getting cold," he said. "The TV forecaster said there's a snow warning out for the Four Corners. Livestock warning. All that."

"It's just about time for that first bad one," Chee said. "Can I take your hat?"

Which got Leaphorn's mind off the

weather. "No. No," he said, looking apologetic. He regretted the intrusion, the lateness of the hour, the interruption of Chee's supper. He would only take a moment. He wanted Chee to see what they'd found in the ammunition box on top of Ship Rock. He extracted a sheaf of photographs from the big folder he'd been carrying and handed them to Chee.

Chee spread them on the table.

"Note the date of the signature," Leaphorn said. "It's the week after Breedlove disappeared from Canyon de Chelly."

Chee considered that. "Wow," he said. And considered it again. He studied the photograph. "Is this it? No one else signed the book that day?"

"Only Breedlove," Leaphorn said. "And I'm told that it's traditional for everyone in the climbing party to sign if they get to the top."

"Well, now," Chee said. He tapped the inscription. "It looks like Latin. Do you know what it means?"

Leaphorn told him the translation. "But what did he mean by it? Your guess is as good as mine." He explained to Chee what Rosebrough had told him

about the 'fast way down' remark —
that if Hal had tried this dangerous
rappelling route it might explain how
his body came to be on the ledge where
it was found.

They stood at the table, Chee staring
at the photograph and Leaphorn watching Chee. The aroma of extremely hot
grease forced itself into Leaphorn's consciousness, along with the haze of blue
smoke that accompanied it. He cleared
his throat.

"Jim," he said. "I think I interrupted
your cooking."

"Oh," Chee said. He dropped the
photograph, snatched the smoking pan
off the propane burner, and deposited
it outside on the doorstep. "I was going
to scramble some eggs and mix in these
sausages," he said. "If you haven't eaten
I can dump in a few more."

"Fine," said Leaphorn, who had deposited his breakfast in the barf bag,
had been suffering too much residual
queasiness for lunch, and had been too
busy since to stop for dinner. In his
current condition, even the smell of
burning grease aroused his hunger.

They replaced the photos with plates,
retrieved the frying pan, replenished

the incinerated grease with a chunk of margarine, put on the coffeepot, performed those other duties required to prepare dinner in a very restricted space, and dined. Leaphorn had always tried to avoid Vienna sausages even as emergency rations but now he found the mixture remarkably palatable. While he attacked his second helping, Chee picked the crucial photograph and resumed his study.

"I hesitate to mention it," Chee said, "but what do you think of the date?"

"You mean being a date when the keen eye of Hosteen Sam saw no one climbing Ship Rock?"

"Exactly," Chee said.

"I've reached no precise conclusion," Leaphorn said. "What do you think?"

"About the same," Chee said. "And how about nobody at all signing the book twelve days earlier? What do you think about that? I'm thinking that the three people who old man Sam saw climbing up there must not have made it to the top. Either that, or they were too modest to take credit for it. Or, if his ledger hadn't told me how exactly precise Sam was, I'd think he got his dates wrong."

Leaphorn was studying him. "You think there's no chance of that, then?"

"I'd say none. Zero. You should see the way he kept that ledger. That's not the explanation. Forget it."

Leaphorn nodded. "Okay, I will."

The entry signed by Breedlove was near the center of the page. Above it the register had been signed by four men, none with names familiar to Chee, and dated April 4, 1983. Below it, a three-climber party — two with Japanese names — had registered their conquest of the Rock with Wings on April 28, 1988.

"Skip back to September eighteenth," Leaphorn said. "Let's say that Hal was one of the three Hosteen Sam saw climbing. It sounds like the car they climbed out of was that silly British recreation vehicle he drove. And then let's say they didn't make it to the top because Hal screwed up. So Hal broods about it. He gets the call at Canyon de Chelly from one of his climbing buddies. He decides to go back and try again."

"All right," Chee said. "Then we'll suppose the climbing buddy went with him, they tried the dangerous way down. This time the climbing buddy —

and let's call him George Shaw — well, George screws up and drops Hal down the cliff. He feels guilty and he figures Hal's dead anyway, so slips away and tells no one."

"Yeah," Leaphorn said. "I thought about that. Trouble is, why hadn't the climbing buddy signed the register before they started down?"

Chee shook his head, dealt Leaphorn some more of the Vienna-and-eggs mixture, and put down the pan.

"Modesty, you think?" Leaphorn said. "He didn't want to take the credit?"

"The only reason I can think of involves first-degree murder," Chee said. "The premeditated kind."

"Right," Leaphorn said. "Now, how about a motive?"

"Easy," Chee said. "It would have something to do with the ranch, and with that moly mine deal."

Leaphorn nodded.

"Now Hal has inherited. It's his. So let's say George Shaw figures Hal's going to keep his threat and do his own deal on the mineral lease, cutting out Shaw and the rest of the family. So Shaw drops him."

"Maybe," Leaphorn said. "One problem with that, though."

"Or maybe Demott's the climbing buddy. He knows Hal's going for the open strip mine, so he knocks him off to save his ranch. But what's the problem with the first idea?"

"Elisa inherits from Hal. Shaw would have to deal with her."

"Maybe he thought he could?"

"He says he couldn't. He told me this afternoon that Elisa was just as fanatical about the ranch as her brother. Said she told him there wouldn't be any strip-mining on it as long as she was alive."

"You saw Shaw today?" Chee sounded as much shocked as surprised. "Sure," Leaphorn said. "I showed him the photographs. After all, I spent his money getting them."

"What'd he think?"

"He acted disappointed. Probably was. He'd like to be able to prove that Hal was dead about a week or so before he signed that register."

Chee nodded.

"There's a problem with your second theory, too."

"What?"

"I was talking with Demott on the

telephone September twenty-fourth. Twice, in fact."

"You remember that? After eleven years?"

"No. I keep a case diary. I looked it up."

"Mobile phone, maybe?"

"No. I called him at the ranch. Elisa didn't remember the license number on the Land-Rover. I called him about the middle of the morning and he gave me the number. Then I called him again in the afternoon to make sure Breedlove hadn't checked in. And to find out if he'd had any other calls. Anything worthwhile."

"Well, hell," Chee said. "Then I guess we're left with Breedlove climbing up there alone, or with Shaw, and then taking the suicidal shortcut down."

Leaphorn's expression suggested he didn't agree with that conclusion, but he didn't comment on it directly.

"It also means I'm going to have to run down all these people who climbed up there in the next ten years and find out if any of them got off with a long piece of that climbing rope."

"Not necessarily," Leaphorn said. "You're forgetting our Fallen Man business is still not a crime. It's a missing person case solved by the discovery of an accidental death."

"Yeah," Chee said, doubtful.

"It makes me glad I'm a civilian these days."

The wind gusted, rattling sand against the aluminum side of Chee's home, whistling around its aluminum cracks and corners.

"So does the weather," Leaphorn said. "Everybody in uniform is going to be working overtime and getting frostbite this week."

Chee pointed to Leaphorn's plate. "Want some more?"

"I'm full-filled. Probably ate too much. And I took too much of your time." He got up, retrieved his hat.

"I'm going to leave you these pictures," he said. "Rosebrough has the negatives. He's a lawyer. An agent of the court. They'll stand up as evidence if it comes to that."

"You mean if anyone gets up there and steals the ledger?"

"It's a thought," Leaphorn said. "What are you going to do tomorrow?"

Chee had worked for Leaphorn long enough for this question to produce a familiar uneasy feeling. "Why?"

"If I go up to the ranch tomorrow and show Demott and Elisa these pictures and ask her what she thinks about them, and ask her who was trying to climb that mountain on that September eighteenth date, then I think I could be accused of tampering with a witness."

"Witness to what? Officially there's no crime yet," Chee reminded him.

"Don't you think there will be one? Presuming we're smart enough to get this sorted out."

"You mean not counting Maryboy and me? Yeah. I guess so. But you could probably get away with talking to Elisa until the official connection is made. Now you're just a representative of the family lawyer. Perfectly legit."

"But why would Demott or the widow want to talk to a representative of the family's lawyer?"

Chee nodded, conceding the point.

"And I think there's something else I should be doing."

Chee let his stare ask the question.

"Old Amos Nez trusts me," Leaphorn said, and paused to consider it. "Well, more or less. I want to show him this evidence that Hal climbed Ship Rock just one week after he left the canyon and tell him about Maryboy being murdered, and ask him if Hal said anything about trying to climb Ship Rock just before he came to the canyon. Things like that."

"That could wait," Chee said, thinking of his aching ribs and the long painful drive up into Colorado.

"Maybe it could wait," Leaphorn said. "But you know the other afternoon you decided Hosteen Maryboy couldn't wait and you rushed right out there to see if he could identify those climbers for you. And you were right. Turned out it couldn't wait."

"Ah," Chee said. "But I'm not clear on what makes Amos Nez so important. You think Breedlove might have told him something?"

"Let's try another theory," Leaphorn said. "Let's say that Hal Breedlove didn't live until his thirtieth birthday. Let's say those people Hosteen Sam saw climbing on September eighteenth got to the top, or at least two of them did. One of the two was Hal. The other one — or maybe two — push him off. Or, more likely he just falls. Now he's dead and he's dead two days too soon. He's

311

still twenty-nine years old. So the climbers' register is falsified to show he was alive after his birthday."

Chee held up his hand, grinning. "Huge hole in that one," he said. "Remember Hal was prowling around the canyon with his wife and Amos Nez until the twenty-third of . . ." Chee's voice trailed off into silence. And then he said, "Oh!" and stared at Leaphorn.

Leaphorn was making a wry face, shaking his head. "It sure took me long enough to see that possibility," he said. "I never could have if you hadn't got into old man Sam's register."

"My God," Chee said. "If that's the way it worked, I can see why they have to kill Nez. And if they're smart, the sooner the better."

"I'm going to ask you to call the Lazy B and find out if Demott and the widow are there and then arrange to drive up tomorrow and talk to them about what we found on top of the mountain."

"What if they're not at home?"

"Then I think we ought to be doing a little more to keep Amos Nez safe," Leaphorn said. And he opened the door and stepped out into the icy wind.

24

Elisa Breedlove had answered the telephone. And, yes, Eldon was home and they'd be glad to talk to him. How about sometime tomorrow afternoon?

So Acting Lieutenant Chee showed up at his office in Shiprock early to get his desk cleared and make the needed arrangements. He arrived with tape plastered over the stitches around his left eye and a noticeable shiner visible behind them. He lowered himself carefully into the chair behind the desk to avoid jarring his ribs and gave Officers Teddy Begayaye, Deejay Hondo, Edison Bai, and Bernadette Manuelito a few moments to inspect the damage. In Begayaye and Bai it seemed to provoke a mixture of admiration and amusement, well suppressed. Hondo didn't seem interested and Officer Bernie Manuelito's face reflected a sort of shocked sympathy.

With that out of the way, he satisfied their curiosity with a personal briefing of what actually happened at the Maryboy place, supplementing the official one they would have already received.

Then down to business.

He instructed Bai to try to find out where a .38-caliber pistol confiscated from a Shiprock High School boy had come from. He suggested to Officer Manuelito that she continue her efforts to locate a fellow named Adolph Deer, who had jumped bond after a robbery conviction but was reportedly "frequently being seen around the Two Gray Hills trading post." He told Hondo to finish the paperwork on a burglary case that was about to go to the grand jury. Then it was Teddy Begayaye's turn.

"I hate to tell you, Teddy, but you're going to have to be taxi driver today," Chee said. "I have to go up to the Lazy B ranch on this Maryboy shooting thing. I thought I could handle it myself, but —" He lifted his left arm, flinched, and grimaced. "— the old ribs aren't quite as good as I thought they were."

"You shouldn't be riding around in a car," Officer Manuelito said. "You should be in bed, healing up. They shouldn't have let you out of the hospital."

"Hospitals are dangerous," Chee said. "People die in them."

Edison Bai grinned at that, but Officer Manuelito didn't think it was funny.

"Something goes wrong with broken ribs and you have a punctured lung," she said.

"They're just cracked," Chee said. "Just a bruise." With that subject closed, he kept Bai behind for a fill-in about the pistol-carrying student. Typically, Bai provided far more details than Chee needed. The boy had been involved in a joyride car theft during the summer. He was born to the Streams Come Together people, his mother's clan, and for the Salt clan, for his paternal people, but his father was also part Hopi. He was believed to be involved in the smaller and rougher of Shiprock's juvenile gangs. He was meanness on the hoof. People weren't raising their kids the way they used to. Chee agreed, put on his hat and hurried stiffly out the door into the parking lot. It had been chilly and clouding up when he came to work. Now there was solid overcast and an icy northwest wind swept dust and leaves past his ankles.

The gale was blowing Begayaye back toward him.

"Jim," he said. "I forgot. The wife made

315

a dental appointment for me today. How about me switching assignments with Bernie? That Deer kid isn't going anywhere."

"Well," Chee said. Across the parking lot he saw Bernie Manuelito standing on the sheltered side of his patrol car, watching them. "Is it okay with Manuelito?"

"Yes, sir," Begayaye said. "She don't mind."

"By the way," Chee said, "I forgot to thank you guys for sending me those flowers."

Begayaye looked puzzled. "Flowers? What flowers?"

Thus it was that Acting Lieutenant Jim Chee headed north toward the Colorado border leaning his good shoulder against the passenger-side door with Officer Bernadette Manuelito behind the wheel. Chee, being a detective, had figured out who had sent him the flowers. Begayaye hadn't done it, and Bai would never think of doing such a thing even if he was fond of Chee — which Chee was pretty sure he wasn't. That left Deejay Hondo and Bernie. Which clearly meant Bernie had sent them and made it look like everybody did it so he wouldn't think she was buttering him up. That probably meant she liked him. Thinking back, he could remember a couple of other signs that pointed to that conclusion.

All things considered, he liked her too. She was really smart, she was sweet to everybody around the office, and she was always using her days off to take care of an apparently inexhaustible supply of ailing and indigent kinfolks, which gave her a high score on the Navajo value scale. When the time came he would have to give her a good efficiency rating. He gave her a sidewise glance, saw her staring unblinkingly through the windshield at the worn pavement of infamous U.S. Highway 666. A very slight smile curved the corner of her lip, making her look happy, as she usually was. No doubt about it, she really was an awfully pretty young woman.

That wasn't the way he should be thinking about Officer Bernadette Manuelito. Not only was he her superior officer and supervisor, he was more or less engaged to marry another woman. And he was thinking that way, most likely, because he was having a very

317

confusing problem with that other woman. He was beginning to suspect that she didn't really want to marry him. Or, at least, he wasn't sure she was willing to marry Jim Chee as he currently existed — a just-plain cop and a genuine sheep-camp Navajo as opposed to the more romantic and politically correct Indigenous Person. Making it worse, he didn't know what the hell to do about it. Or whether he should do anything. It was a sad, sad situation.

Chee sighed, decided the ribs would feel better if he shifted his weight. He did it, sucked in his breath, and grimaced.

"You all right?" Bernie asked, giving him a worried look.

"Okay," Chee said.

"I have some aspirin in my stuff."

"No problem," Chee said.

Bernie drove in silence for a while.

"Lieutenant," she said. "Do you remember telling us how Lieutenant Leaphorn was always trying to get you to look for patterns? I mean when you had something going on that was hard to figure out."

"Yeah," Chee said.

"And that's what you wanted me to try to find in this cattle-stealing business?"

Chee grunted, trying to remember if he had made any such suggestion.

"Well, I got Lucy Sam to let me take that ledger to that Quik-Copy place in Farmington and I got copies made of the pages back for several years so I'd have them. And then I went through our complaint records and copied down the dates of all the cattle-theft reports for the same years."

"Good Lord," Chee said, visualizing the time that would take. "Who was doing your regular work for you?"

"Just the multiple-head thefts," Officer Manuelito said, defensively. "The ones which look sort of professional. And I did it in the evenings."

"Oh," Chee said, embarrassed.

"Anyway, I started comparing the dates. You know, when Mr. Sam would write down something about a certain sort of truck, and when there would be a cattle theft reported in our part of the reservation."

Officer Manuelito had been reciting this very carefully, as if she had rehearsed it. Now she stopped.

"What'd you notice?"

She produced a deprecatory laugh. "I think this is probably really silly," she said.

"I doubt it," Chee said, thinking he would like to get his mind off of Janet Pete and quit trying to find a way to turn back the clock and make things the way they used to be. "Why don't you just go ahead and tell me about it."

"There was a correlation between multiple theft reports and Mr. Sam seeing a big banged-up dirty white camper truck in the neighborhood," Manuelito said, looking fixedly at the highway center stripe. "Not all the time," she added. "But often enough so it made you begin to wonder about it."

Chee digested this. "The trailer like Mr. Finch's rig?" he said. "The New Mexico brand inspector's camper?"

"Yes, sir." She laughed again. "I said it was probably silly."

"Well, I guess our theft reports would be passed along to him. Then he'd come out here to see about it."

Officer Manuelito kept her eyes on the road, her lips opened as if she were about to say something. But she didn't. She simply looked disappointed.

"Wait a minute," Chee said, as understanding belatedly dawned. "Was Hosteen Sam seeing Finch's trailer after the thefts were reported? Or —"

"Usually before," Bernie said. "Sometimes both, but usually before. But you know how that is. Sometimes the cattle are gone for a while before the owner notices they're missing."

Bernie drove, looking very tense. Chee digested what she'd told him. Suddenly he slammed his right hand against his leg. "How about that?" he said. "That wily old devil."

Officer Manuelito relaxed, grinned. "You think so? You think that might be right?"

"I'd bet on it," Chee said. "He'd have everything going for him. All the proper legal forms for moving cattle. All the brand information. All the reasons for being where the cattle are. And all cops would know him as one of them. Perfect."

Bernie was grinning even wider, delighted. "Yes," she said. "That's sort of what I was thinking."

"Now we need to find out how he markets them. And how he gets them from the pasture to the feedlots."

"I think it's in the trailer," Bernie said.

"The trailer? You mean he hauls cattle in his house trailer?"

Chee's incredulous tone caused Bernie to flush slightly. "I think so," she said. "I couldn't prove it."

A few moments ago Acting Lieutenant Chee might have scoffed at this remarkable idea. But not now. "Tell me," he said. "How does he get them through the door?"

"It took me a long time to get the idea," she said. "I think it was noticing that now and then I'd see that trailer parked at the Anasazi Inn at Farmington, and I'd think it was funny that you'd drive that big clumsy camper trailer around if you didn't want to sleep in it. I thought, you know, well, maybe he just wants a hot bath, or something like that. But it stuck in my mind."

She laughed. "I'm always trying to understand white people."

"Yeah," Chee said. "Me too."

"So the other day when he parked the trailer in the lot at the station, when I walked past it I noticed how it smelled."

"A little whiff of cow manure," said Chee, who had walked behind it too. "I just thought, you know, he's around feedlots all the time. Stepping in the stuff. Probably gets used to it. Doesn't clean his boots."

"That occurred to me, too," Bernie said. "But it was pretty strong. Maybe women are more sensitive to smells."

Or smarter, Chee thought. "Did you look inside?"

"He's got all the windows all stuck full of those tourist stickers, and they're high windows. I tried to take a peek but I didn't want him to see me snooping."

"I guess we could get a search warrant," Chee said. "What would you put on the petition? Something about the brand inspector's camper smelling like cow manure, to which the judge would say 'Naturally,' and about Finch not liking to sleep in it, which would cause the judge to say 'Not if it smells like cow manure.' "

"I thought about the search warrant," Bernie said. "Of course there's no law against hauling cows in your camper if you want to."

"True," Chee said. "Might be able to get him committed for being crazy."

"Anyway," Bernie said. "I called his office and I —"

"You *what!*"

"I just wanted to know where he was. If he answered I was going to hang up. If he didn't, I'd ask 'em where I could find him. He wasn't there, and the secretary said he'd called in from the Davis and Sons cattle-auction place over by Iyanbito. So I drove over there and his camper truck was parked by the barn and he was out in back with some people loading up steers. So I got a closer look."

"You didn't break in?" Chee asked, thinking she'd probably say she had. Nothing this woman did was going to surprise him anymore.

She glanced at him, looking hurt, and ignored the question.

"Maybe you noticed that camper has just a straight-up flat back. There's no door in it and no window. Well, all around that back panel it's sealed up with silvery duct tape. Like you'd maybe put on to keep the dust out. But when you get down and look under you can see a row of big, heavy-duty hinges."

Chee was into this now. "So you back your trailer up to the fence, pull off the duct tape, lower the back down, and that makes a loading ramp out of it. He probably has it rigged up with stalls to keep 'em from moving around."

"I guessed it would handle about six," Bernie said. "Two rows of cows, three abreast."

"Bernie," Chee said. "If my ribs weren't so sore, and it wasn't going to get me charged with sexual harassment and cause us to run off the road, I would reach over there and give you a huge congratulatory hug."

Bernie looked both pleased and embarrassed.

"You put a lot of work into this," he said. "And a lot of thought, too. Way beyond the call of duty."

"Well, I'm trying to learn to be a detective. And it got sort of personal, too," she said. "I don't like that man."

"I don't much either," Chee said. "He's arrogant."

"He sort of made a move on me," she said. "Maybe not. Not exactly."

"Like what?"

"Well, he gives you that 'doll' and 'cute' stuff, you know. Then he said how would I like to get assigned to work with him. But of course he said 'under' him. He said I could be Tonto to his Lone Ranger."

"Tonto?" Chee said. "Well, now. Here's

what we do. We keep an eye on him. And when he's on the road with a load, we nail him. And when we do, you're the one who gets to put the handcuffs on him."

25

When Officer Bernadette Manuelito parked Chee's patrol car at the Lazy B ranch Elisa Breedlove was standing in the doorway awaiting them — hugging herself against the cold wind. Or was it, Chee thought, against the news he might be bringing?

"Four Corners weather," she said. "Yesterday it was sunny, mild autumn. Today it's winter." She ushered them into the living room, exchanged introductions gracefully with Bernie, expressed the proper dismay at Chee's condition, wished him a quick recovery, and invited them to be seated.

"I saw the story about you being shot on television," she said. "Bad as you look, they made it sound even worse."

"Just some cracked ribs," Chee said.

"And old Mr. Maryboy being killed. I only met him once, but he was very nice to us. He invited us in and offered to make coffee."

"When was that?"

"Way back in the dark ages," she said. "When Hal and George would come out for the summer and Eldon and I would go climbing with them."

"Is your brother here now?" Chee asked. "I was hoping to talk to you both."

"He was here earlier, but one of the mares got herself tangled up in a fence. He went out to see about her. There's supposed to be a snowstorm moving in and he wanted to get her into the barn."

"Do you expect him back soon?"

"She's up in the north pasture," Elisa said. "But he shouldn't be long unless she's cut so badly he had to go into Mancos and get the vet. Would you two care for something to drink? It's a long drive up here from Shiprock."

She served them both coffee but poured none for herself. Chee sipped and watched her over the rim, twisting her hands. If she had been one of the three climbers that day, if she had reached the top, she should know what was coming now. He took out the folder of photographs and handed Elisa the one signed with her husband's name.

"Thanks," she said, and looked at it. Officer Manuelito was watching her, sitting primly on the edge of her chair, cup in saucer, uncharacteristically quiet. It occurred to Chee that she looked like a pretty girl pretending to be a cop.

Elisa was frowning at the photograph. "It's a picture of the page from the climbers' ledger," she said slowly. "But where —"

She dropped the picture on the coffee table, said, "Oh, God," in a strangled voice, and covered her face with her hands.

Officer Manuelito leaned forward, lips apart. Chee shook his head, signaled silence.

Elisa picked up the picture again, stared at it, dropped it to the floor and sat rigid, her face white.

"Mrs. Breedlove," Chee said. "Are you all right?"

She shook her head. Shuddered. Composed herself, looked at Chee.

"This photograph. That's all there was on the page?"

"Just what you saw."

She bent, picked up the print, looked at it again. "And the date. The date. That's what was written?"

"Just as you see it," Chee said.

"But of course it was." She produced a laugh on the razor edge of hysteria. "A silly question. But it's wrong, you know. It should have been — but why

—" She put her hand over her mouth, dropped her head.

The noise the wind was making — rattles, whistles, and howls — filtered through windows and walls and filled the dark room with the sounds of winter.

"I know the date's wrong," Chee said. "The entry is dated September thirty. That's a week after your husband disappeared from Canyon de Chelly. What should —" He stopped. Elisa wasn't listening to him. She was lost in her own memory. And that, combined with what the picture had told her, was drawing her to some ghastly conclusion.

"The handwriting," she said. "Have you —" But she cut that off too, pressed her lips together as if to keep them from completing the question.

But not soon enough, of course. So she hadn't known what had happened on the summit of Ship Rock. Not until moments ago when the forgery of her husband's signature told her. Told her exactly what? That her husband had died before he'd had a chance to sign. That her husband's death, therefore, must have been preplanned as well as postdated. The pattern Leaphorn had taught him to look for took its almost final dismal shape. And filled Jim Chee with pity.

Officer Manuelito was on her feet.

"Mrs. Breedlove, you need to lie down," she said. "You're sick. Let me get you something. Some water."

Elisa sagged forward, leaned her forehead against the table. Officer Manuelito hurried into the kitchen.

"We haven't checked the handwriting yet," Chee said. "Can you tell us what that will show?"

Elisa was sobbing now. Bernie emerged from the kitchen, glass of water in one hand, cloth in the other. She gave Chee a "How could you do this?" look and sat next to Elisa, patting her shoulder.

_____ _____ 'er," Bernie said. "And you should lie down until you feel better. We can finish this later."

Ramona appeared in the doorway, wrapped in a padded coat, her face red with cold. She watched them anxiously. "What are you doing to her?" she said. "Go away now and let her rest."

"Oh, God," Elisa said, her voice muffled by the table. "Why did he think he had to do it?"

"Where can I find Eldon?" Chee asked.

Elisa shook her head.

"Does he have a rifle?" But of course he would have a rifle. Every male over about twelve in the Rocky Mountain West had a rifle. "Where does he keep it?"

Elisa didn't respond. Chee motioned to Bernie. She left in search of it.

Elisa raised her head, wiped her eyes, looked at Chee. "It was an accident, you know. Hal was always reckless. He wanted to rappel down the cliff. I thought I had talked him out of it. But I guess I hadn't."

"Did you see it happen?"

"I didn't get all the way to the top. I was below. Waiting for them to come down."

Chee hesitated. The next question would be crucial, but should he ask it now, with this woman overcome by shock and grief? Any lawyer would tell her not to talk about any of this. But she wouldn't be the one on trial.

Bernie reappeared at the doorway, Ramona behind her. "There's a triple gun rack in the office," she said. "A twelve-gauge pump shotgun in the bottom rack and the top two empty."

"Okay," Chee said.

"And in the wastebasket beside the desk, there's a thirty-ought-six ammunition box. The top's torn off and it's empty."

Chee nodded and came to his decision.

"Mrs. Breedlove. No one climbed the mountain on the date by your husband's name. But on September eighteenth three people were seen climbing it. Hal was one of them. You were one. Who was the third?"

"I don't want to talk to you anymore," Elisa said. "I want you to go."

"You don't have to tell us anything," Chee said. "You have the right to remain silent, and to call your lawyer if you think you need one. I don't think you've done anything you could be charged with, but you never really know what a prosecuting attorney will decide."

Officer Manuelito cleared her throat. "And anything you say can be used against you. Remember that."

"I don't want to say any more."

"That's okay," Chee said. "But I should tell you this. Eldon isn't here and neither is his rifle and it looks like he just reloaded it. If we have this figured out right, Eldon is going to know there is just one man left alive who could ruin this for him."

Chee paused, waiting for a response. It didn't come. Elisa sat as if frozen, staring at him.

"It's a man named Amos Nez. Remember him? He was your guide in Canyon de Chelly. Right after Hal's skeleton was found on Ship Rock last Halloween, Mr. Nez was riding his horse up the canyon. Someone up on the rim shot him. He wasn't killed, just badly hurt."

Elisa sagged a little with that, looked down at her hands, and said, "I didn't know that."

"With a thirty-ought-six rifle," Chee added.

"What day was it?"

Chee told her.

She thought a moment. Remembering. Slumped a little more.

"If anyone kills Mr. Nez the charge will be the premeditated murder of a witness. That carries the death penalty."

"He's my brother," Elisa said. "Hal's death was an accident. Sometimes he acted almost like he wanted to die. No thrills, he said, if you didn't take a chance. He fell. When Eldon climbed down to where I was waiting, he looked like he was almost dead himself. He was devastated. He was so shaken he could hardly tell me about it." She stopped, looking at Chee, at Bernie, back at Chee.

Waiting for our reaction, Chee thought. Waiting for us to give her absolution? No, waiting for us to say we believe what she is telling us, so that she can believe it again herself.

"I think you were driving that Land-Rover," Chee said. "When police found it abandoned up an arroyo north of Many Farms they said there was a telephone in it."

"But what good would it have done to call for help?" Elisa asked, her voice rising. "Hal was dead. He was all broken to pieces on that little ledge. Nobody could bring him back to life again. He was dead!"

"Was he?"

"Yes," she shouted. "Yes. Yes. Yes."

And now Chee understood why Elisa had been so shocked when she learned the skeleton was intact — with not a bone broken. She didn't want to believe it. Refused to believe it still. That made the next question harder to ask. What had Eldon told her of the scene at the top? Had he explained why Hal had started his descent before he signed the book? Why he falsified the register? Had he —

Ramona rushed into the room, sat beside Elisa, hugged the woman to her. She glared at Chee. "I said go away now," she said. "Get out. No more. No more. She has suffered too much."

"It's all right," Elisa said. "Ramona, when you came in did you see the Land-Rover in the garage?"

"No," Ramona said. "Just Eldon's pickup truck."

Elisa looked at Chee, sighed, and said, "Then I guess he didn't go up to see about the mare. He would have taken his truck."

Chee picked up his hat and the photographs. He thanked Mrs. Breedlove for the cooperation, apologized for bringing her bad news, and hurried out, with Bernie trotting along behind him. The wind was bitter now, and carrying those dry-as-dust first snowflakes that were the forerunners of a storm.

"I want to get Leaphorn on the radio,"

he said, as Bernie started the engine, "and maybe we'll have to make a fast trip to Canyon de Chelly."

Bernie was looking back at the house. "Do you think she will be all right?"

"I think so," Chee said. "Ramona will take good care of her."

"Ramona's pretty shaken up, too," Bernie said. "She was crying when she helped me look for the rifle. She said it was always the wrong men with Elisa — always having to take care of them. That Hal was a spoiled baby and Eldon was a bully. She said if it wasn't for Eldon she'd be married to a good man who wanted to take care of her."

"She say who?"

"I think it was Tommy Castro. Or maybe Kaster. Something like that. She was crying." Bernie was staring back at the house, looking worried.

"Bernie," Chee said. "It's starting to snow. It's probably going to be a bad one. Start the car. Go. Go. Go."

"You're worried about Amos Nez," Bernie said, starting the engine. "We can just call the station at Chinle and have them stop any Land-Rover driving in. Bet Mr. Leaphorn already did that."

"He said he would," Chee said. "But I

want to get a message to him about Demott taking off with his thirty-ought-six loaded. Maybe Eldon won't be driving in. If you can climb seventeen hundred feet up Ship Rock, maybe you can climb down a six-hundred-foot cliff."

26

They drove into the full brunt of the storm halfway between Mancos and Cortez, the wind buffeting the car and driving a blinding sheet of tiny dry snowflakes horizontally past their windshield.

"At least it's sweeping the pavement clear," Bernie said, sounding cheerful.

Chee glanced at her. She seemed to be enjoying the adventure. He wasn't. His ribs hurt, so did the abrasions around his eye, and he was not in the mood for cheer.

"That won't last long," he said.

It didn't. In Cortez, snow was driving over the curbs and the pavement was beginning to pack, and the broadcasts on the emergency channel didn't sound promising. A last gasp of the Pacific hurricane system was pushing across Baja California into Arizona. There it met the first blast of Arctic air, pressing down the east slope of the Rockies from Canada. Interstate 40 at Flagstaff, where the two fronts had collided, was already closed by snow. So were high-ways through the Wasatch Range in

Utah. Autumn was emphatically over on the Colorado Plateau.

They turned onto U.S. 666 to make the forty-mile run almost due south to Shiprock. With the icy wind pursuing them, the highway emptied of traffic by storm warnings, and speed limits ignored, Bernie outran the Canadian contribution to the storm. The sky lightened now. Far ahead, they could see where the Pacific half of the blizzard had reached the Chuska range. Its cold, wet air met the dry, warmer air on the New Mexico side at the ridgeline. The collision produced a towering wall of white fog, which poured down the slopes like a silent slow-motion Niagara.

"Wow," Bernie said. "I never saw anything quite like that before."

"The heavy cold air forces itself under the warmer stuff," said Chee, unable to avoid a little showing off. "I'll bet it's twenty degrees colder at Lukachukai than it is at Red Rock — and they're less than twenty miles apart."

They crossed the western corner of the Ute reservation, then roared into New Mexico and across the mesa high above Malpais Arroyo.

"Wow," Bernie said again. "Look at that."

Instead Chee glanced at the speed-ometer and flinched.

"You drive," he said. "I'll check the scenery for both of us." It was worth checking. They looked down into the vast San Juan River basin — dark with storm to the right, dappled with sun-light to the left. Ship Rock stood just at the edge of the shadow line, a grotesque sunlit thumb thrust into the sky, but through some quirk of wind and air pressure, the long bulge of the Hogback formation was already mostly dark with cloud shadow.

"I think we're going to get home before the snow," Bernie said.

They almost did. It caught them when Bernie pulled into the parking lot at the station — but the flakes blowing against Chee as he hurried into the building were still small and dry. The Canadian cold front was still dominat-ing the Pacific storm.

"You look terrible," Jenifer said. "How do you feel?"

"I'd say well below average," Chee said. "Did Leaphorn call?"

"Indirectly," Jenifer said, and handed Chee three message slips and an enve-lope.

It was on top — a call from Sergeant Deke at the Chinle station confirming that Leaphorn had received Chee's message about Demott leaving his ranch with his rifle. Leaphorn had gone up the canyon to the Nez place and would either bring Nez out with him or stay, depending on the weather, which was terrible.

Chee glanced at the other messages. Routine business. The envelope bore the word "Jim" in Janet's hand. He tapped it against the back of his hand. Put it down. Called Deke.

"I've seen worse," Deke said. "But it's a bad one for this time of year. Still above zero but it won't be for long. Blowing snow. We have Navajo 12 closed at Upper Wheatfields, and 191 between here and Ganado, and 59 north of Red Rock, and — well, hell of a night to be driving. How about there?"

"I think we're just getting the edge of it," Chee said. "Did Leaphorn get my message?"

"Yep. He said not to worry."

"What do you think? Demott's a rock climber. Is Nez going to be safe enough?"

"Except for maybe frostbite," Deke

said. "Nobody's going to be climbing those cliffs tonight."

And so Chee opened the envelope and extracted the note.

"Jim. Sorry I missed you. Going to get a bite to eat and will come by your place — Janet."

Her car wasn't there when he drove up, which was just as well, he thought. It would give him a little time to get the place a little warmer. He fired up the propane heater, put on the coffee, and gave the place a critical inspection. He rarely did. His trailer was simply where he lived. Sometimes it was hot, sometimes it was cold. But otherwise it was not something he gave any thought to. It looked cramped, crowded, slightly dirty, and altogether dismal. Ah, well, nothing to do about it now. He checked the refrigerator for something to offer her. Nothing much there in the snack line, but he extracted a slab of cheese and pulled a box of crackers and a bowl with a few Oreos in it off the shelf over the stove. Then he sat on the edge of the bunk, slumped, listening to the icy wind buffeting the trailer, too tired to think about what might be about to happen.

Chee must have dozed. He didn't hear the car coming down the slope, or see the lights. A tapping at the door awakened him, and he found her standing on the step looking up at him.

"It's freezing," she said as he ushered her in.

"Hot coffee," he said. Poured a cup, handed it to her, and offered her the folding chair beside the fold-out table. But she stood a moment, hugging herself and shivering, looking undecided.

"Janet," he said. "Sit down. Relax."

"I just need to tell you something," she said. "I can't stay. I need to get back to Gallup before the weather gets worse." But she sat.

"Drink your coffee," he said. "Warm up."

She was looking at him over the cup. "You look awful," she said. "They told me you'd gone up to Mancos. To see the Breedlove widow. You shouldn't be back at work yet. You should be in bed."

"I'm all right," he said. And waited. Would she ask him why he'd gone to Mancos? What he'd learned?

"Why couldn't somebody else do it?" she said. "Somebody without broken ribs."

344

"Just cracked," Chee said.

She put down her cup. He reached for it. She intercepted his hand, held it.

"Jim," she said. "I'm going away for a while. I'm taking my accrued leave time, and my vacation, and I'm going home."

"Home?" Chee said. "For a while. How long is that?"

"I don't know," she said. "I want to get my head together. Look forward and backwards." She tried to smile but it didn't come off well. She shrugged. "And just think."

It occurred to Chee that he hadn't poured himself any coffee. Oddly, he didn't want any. It occurred to him that she wasn't burning her bridges.

"Think?" he said. "About us?"

"Of course." This time the smile worked a little better.

But her hand was cold. He squeezed it. "I thought we were through that phase."

"No, you didn't," she said. "You never really stopped thinking about whether we'd be compatible. Whether we really fit."

"Don't we?"

"We did in this fantasy I had," she

said, and waved her hands, mocking herself. "Big, good-looking guy. Sweet and smart and as far as I could tell you really cared about me. Fun on the Big Rez for a while, then a big job for you in someplace interesting. Washington. San Francisco. New York. Boston. And the big job for me in Justice, or maybe a law firm. You and I together. Everything perfect."

Chee said nothing to that.

"Everything perfect," she repeated. "The best of both worlds." She looked at him, trying to hold the grin and not quite making it.

"With twin Porsches in the triple garage," Chee said. "But when you got to know me, I didn't fit the fantasy."

"Almost," she said. "Maybe you do, really." Suddenly Janet's eyes went damp. She looked away. "Or maybe I change the fantasy."

He extracted his handkerchief, frowned at it, reached into the storage drawer behind him, extracted paper napkins, and handed them to Janet. She said, "Sorry," and wiped her eyes.

He wanted to hold her, very close. But he said, "A cold wind does that."

"So I thought maybe as time goes by

everything changes a little. I change and so do you."

He could think of nothing honest to say to that.

"But after the other evening in Gallup, when you were so angry with me, I began to understand," she said.

"Remember once a long time ago you asked me about a schoolteacher I used to date? Somebody told you about her. From Wisconsin. Just out of college. Blonde, blue eyes, taught second grade at Crownpoint when I was a brand-new cop and stationed there. Well, it wasn't that there was anything much wrong with me, but for her kids she wanted the good old American dream. She saw no hope for that in Navajo country. So she went away."

"Why are you telling me this?" Janet said. "She wasn't a Navajo."

"But I am," he said. "So I thought, what's the difference? I'm darker. Rarely sunburn. Small hips. Wide shoulders. That's racial, right? Does that matter? I think not much. So what makes me a Navajo?"

"You're going to say culture," Janet said. "I studied social anthropology too."

"I grew up knowing it's wrong to have more than you need. It means you're not taking care of your people. Win three races in a row, you better slow down a little. Let somebody else win. Or somebody gets drunk and runs into your car and tears you all up, you don't sue him, you want to have a sing for him to cure him of alcoholism."

"That doesn't get you admitted into law school," Janet said. "Or pull you out of poverty."

"Depends on how you define poverty."

"It's defined in the law books," Janet said. "A family of *x* members with an annual income of under *y*."

"I met a middle-aged man at a Yeibichai sing a few years ago. He ran an accounting firm in Flagstaff and came out to Burnt Water because his mother had a stroke and they were doing the cure for her. I said something about it looking like he was doing very well. And he said, 'No, I will be a poor man all my life.' And I asked him what he meant, and he said, 'Nobody ever taught me any songs.' "

"Ah, Jim," she said. She rose, took the two steps required to reach the bunk where he was sitting, put her arms carefully around him and kissed him. Then she pressed the undamaged side of his face against her breast.

"I know having a Navajo dad didn't make me a Navajo," she said. "My culture is Stanford sorority girl, Maryland cocktail circuit, Mozart, and tickets to the Met. So maybe I have to learn not to think that being ragged, and not having indoor plumbing, and walking miles to see the dentist means poverty. I'm working on it."

Chee, engulfed in Janet's sweater, her perfume, her softness, said something like "Ummmm."

"But I'm not there yet," she added, and released him.

"I guess I should work on it from the other end, too," he said. "I could get used to being a lieutenant, trying to work my way up. Trying to put some value on things like —" He let that trail off.

"One thing I want you to know," she said. "I didn't use you."

"You mean —"

"I mean deliberately getting information out of you so I could tell John."

"I guess I always knew that," he said. "I was just being jealous. I had the wrong idea about that."

"I did tell him you'd found Breedlove's body. He invited Claire and me to the concert. Claire and I go all the way back to high school. And we were remembering old times and, you know, it just came out. It was just something interesting to tell him."

"Sure," Chee said. "I understand."

"I have to go now," she said. "Before you guys close the highway. But I wanted you to know that. Breedlove had been his project when the widow filed to get the death certified. It looked so peculiar. And finally, now, I guess it's all over."

Her tone made that a question.

She was zipping up her jacket, glancing at him.

"Lieutenant Leaphorn gave Mr. Shaw that photograph of the climber's ledger," she said.

"Yeah," Chee said. The wind buffeted the trailer, made its stormy sounds, moved a cold draft against his neck.

"She must have thought that terribly odd — for him to just leave her at the canyon, and then abandon their car, and go back to Ship Rock to climb it like that."

Chee nodded.

"Surely she must have had some sort of theory. I know I would have had if you'd done something crazy like that to me."

"She cried a lot," Chee said. "She could hardly believe it."

And in a minute Janet was gone. The good-bye kiss, the promises to write, the invitation to come and join her. Then holding the car door open for her, commenting on how it always got colder when the snowing stopped, and watching the headlights vanish at the top of the slope.

He sat on the bunk again then, felt the bandages around his eye, and decided the soreness there was abating. He probed the padding over his ribs, flinched, and decided the healing there was slower. He noticed the coffeepot was still on, got up, and unplugged it. He switched on the radio, thinking he would get some weather news. Then switched it off again and sat on the bed.

The telephone rang. Chee stared at it. It rang again. And again. He picked it up.

"Guess what?" It was Officer Bernadette Manuelito.

"What?"

said. "You're looking at a photograph the Breedloves had taken at a studio in Farmington on their wedding anniversary — the summer before they came out here and got you to guide them."

Nez stared at the photograph. "Well, now," he said. "It sure is funny what white people will do. Who is that man she was here with?"

"You tell me," Leaphorn said. He handed Nez two more photographs. One was a photocopy he'd obtained, by imposing on an old friend in the Indian Service's Washington office, of George Shaw's portrait from the Georgetown University School of Law alumni magazine. The others had been obtained from the photo files of the *Mancos Weekly Citizen* — mug shots of young Eldon Demott and Tommy Castro wearing Marine Corps hats.

"I don't know this fella here," Nez said, and handed Leaphorn the Shaw photo.

"I didn't think you would," Leaphorn said. "I was just making sure."

Nez studied the other photo. "Well, now," he said. "Here's my friend Hal Breedlove."

He handed Leaphorn the picture of Eldon Demott.

"Not your friend now," Leaphorn said, and tapped Nez's leg cast. "He's the guy that tried to kill you."

Nez retrieved the photo, looked at it, and shook his head. "Why did he do —" he began, and stopped, thinking about it.

Leaphorn explained about ownership of the ranch depending on the date of Breedlove's death, and now depending upon continuing the deception. "There were just two people who knew something that could screw this up. One of them knew the date Hal Breedlove and Demott climbed Ship Rock — a man named Maryboy who gave them permission to climb. Demott shot him the other day. That leaves you."

"Well, now," Nez said, and made a wry face.

"A policeman who is looking into all this sent me a message that Demott loaded up his rifle this morning and headed out. I guess he'd be coming out here to see if he could get another shot at you."

"Why don't they arrest him?"

"They have to catch him first," Leaphorn said, not wanting to get into the complicated explanation of legalities — and the total lack of any concrete evidence that there was any reason to arrest Demott. "My idea was to take you and Mrs. Benally into Chinle and check you into the motel there. The police can keep an eye on you until they get Demott locked up."

Nez gave himself some time to think this over. "No," he said. "I'll just stay here." He pointed to the shotgun in the rack on the opposite wall. "You just take old lady Benally there. Look after her."

Mrs. Benally may not have been able to translate "bikini" into Navajo, but she had no trouble with "motel."

"I'm not going into any motel," she said.

For practical purposes, that ended the argument. Nobody was moving.

Leaphorn wasn't unprepared for that. Before he'd parked at the Nez hogan, he had scouted up Canyon del Muerto, examining the south-side cliff walls below the place where the ranger had reported seeing the man with the rifle. Sergeant Deke had said it was just five or six hundred yards up-canyon from the Nez place. Leaphorn had seen no location within rifle range where the top of the south cliff offered a fair shot at the Nez hogan. But about a quarter mile up-canyon a huge slab of sandstone had given way to the erosion undercutting it.

The cliff had split here. The slab had separated from the wall. He'd studied it. Someone who knew rock climbing, had the equipment, and didn't mind risking falling off a forty-story building could get down here. This must have been what Demott had been doing here — if it was Demott. He was looking for a way in and out that avoided the bottleneck entrance.

It was certainly conveniently close for a climber. Or a bird. Being neither meant Leaphorn would have to drive about fifteen miles down Canyon del Muerto to its junction with Canyon de Chelly, then another five or six to the canyon mouth to reach the pavement of Navajo Route 64. Then he'd have to reverse directions and drive twenty-four miles northeastward along the north rim of del Muerto, turn southwestward maybe four miles toward Tsaile, then complete the circle down the brushy dirt-and-boulder track that took those foolhardy enough to use it down that finger of mesa separating the canyons.

The last six or seven miles on that circuit would take about as long as the first fifty.

Leaphorn hurried. He wanted enough daylight left to check the place carefully — to either confirm or refute his suspicions. More important, if Demott was coming Leaphorn wanted to be there waiting for him.

He seemed to have managed that. He stopped across the cattle guard where the unmarked track connected with the highway, climbed out, and made a careful inspection. The last vehicle to leave its tracks here had been coming out, and that had been shortly after the snowfall began. Eight or nine jolting miles later, he pulled his car off the track and left it concealed behind a cluster of junipers. The wind was bitter now, but the snow had diminished to occasional dry flakes.

The west rim of Canyon del Muerto was less than fifty yards away over mostly bare sandstone. If he had calculated properly, he was just about above the Nez home site. In fact, he was perhaps a hundred yards below it. He stood a foot or two back from the edge looking down, confirming that the Nez hogan was too protected by the over-hang to offer a shot from here. He could see the track where Nez drove in his truck, but the hogan itself and all of its outbuildings except a goat pen were hidden below the wall. But he could see from here the great split-off sandstone slab, and he walked along the rim to-ward it. He was almost there when he heard an engine whining in low gear.

Along the cliff here finding conceal-ment was no problem. Leaphorn moved behind a great block of sandstone sur-rounded by piñons. He checked his pistol and waited.

The vehicle approaching was a dirty, battered, dark green Land-Rover. It came almost directly toward him. Stopped not fifty feet away. The engine died. The door opened. Eldon Demott stepped out. He reached behind him into the vehicle and took out a rifle, which he laid across the hood. Then he extracted a roll of thin, pale yellow rope and a cardboard box. These two also went onto the hood. From the box he took a web belt and harness, a helmet, and a pair of small black shoes. He leaned against the fender, removed a boot, replaced it with a shoe, and repeated the process. Then he put on the belt and the climbing harness. He looked at his watch, glanced at the sky, stretched, and looked around him.

He looked directly at Joe Leaphorn, sighed, and reached for the rifle.

"Leave it where it is," Leaphorn said, and showed Demott his .38 revolver.

Demott took his hand away from the rifle, dropped it to his side.

"I might want to shoot something," he said.

"Hunting season is over," Leaphorn said.

Demott sighed and leaned against the fender. "It looks like it is."

"No doubt about it. Even if I get careless and you shoot me, you can't get out of here anyway. Two police cars are on their way in after you. And if you climb down, well, that's hopeless."

"You going to arrest me? How do you do that? You're retired. Or is it a citizen's arrest?"

"Regular arrest," Leaphorn said. "I'm still deputized by the sheriff in this county. I didn't get around to turning in the commission."

"What do you charge me with — trespass?"

"Well, I think more likely it will start out being attempted homicide of Amos Nez, and then after the FBI gets its work done, the murder of Hosteen Maryboy."

Demott was staring at him, frowning. "That's it?"

"I think that would do it," Leaphorn said.

"Nothing about Hal."

"Nothing so far. Except that Amos Nez thinks you're him."

Demott considered that. "I'm getting cold," he said, and reopened the car door. "Going to get out of the wind."

"No," Leaphorn said, and shifted the pistol barrel before him.

Demott stopped, shut the door. He smiled at Leaphorn, shook his head. "Another weapon in there, you think?"

Leaphorn returned the smile. "Why take chances?" he said.

"Nothing about Hal," he said. "Well, I'm glad of that."

"Why?"

Demott shrugged. "Because of Elisa," he said. "The other cop, Jim Chee I think it was, he was coming up to see us. He said you had looked at the climber register. What did Elisa say about that?"

"I wasn't there. Chee showed her the page with Hal's name on it, and the date. He said she sort of went to pieces. Cried." Leaphorn shrugged. "About what you'd expect, I guess."

Demott slumped against the fender. "Ah, hell," he said, and slammed his fist against the hood. "Damn! Damn! Damn! Damn!"

"It made it look premeditated, of course," Leaphorn said.

"Of course," Demott said. "And it wasn't."

"An accident. If it wasn't, it may be hard to keep her out of it."

"She was still in love with the bastard. Didn't have a damn thing to do with it."

"I'm not surprised," Leaphorn said. "But considering what's involved, the Breedloves will probably hire a special prosecutor and they'll be aimed at getting the ranch back. Voiding the inheritance."

"Voiding the inheritance? What do you mean? Wouldn't that sort of be automatic? I mean, with what you said about Nez knowing . . . You know, Hal didn't inherit until he was thirty. The way the proviso read, if he didn't reach that birthday, everything was voided."

"Nez thinking you were Hal isn't the only evidence that he lived past that birthday," Leaphorn said. "There's his signature in the climbers' register. That's dated September thirty. You know of any evidence that he died before that?"

Demott was staring at Leaphorn, mouth partly open. "Wait a minute," he said. "Wait. What are you saying?"

"I guess I'm saying that I think there's sometimes a difference between the law and justice. If there's justice here, you're going to spend life in prison for the premeditated murder of Mr. Maryboy, with maybe an add-on twenty years or so for the attempted murder of Amos Nez. I think that would be about right. But it probably won't work quite like that. Your sister's probably going to be charged with accessory to murder — maybe as a conspirator and certainly as an accessory after the fact. And the Breedloves will get her ranch."

Demott inhaled a deep breath. He looked down at his hands, rubbed at his thumb.

"And Cache Creek will be running water gray with cyanide and mining effluent."

"Yeah," Demott said. "I really screwed it up. Year after year you're nervous about it. Sunny day you think you're clear. Nothing to worry about. Then you wake up with a nightmare."

"What happened up there?" Leaphorn said.

Demott gave him a questioning look. "You asking for a confession?"

"You're not under arrest. If you were, I'd have to tell you about your rights not to say anything until you get your lawyer. Elisa told Chee she didn't get all the way to the top. Is that right?"

"She didn't," Demott said. "She was getting scared." He snorted. "I should say sensible."

Leaphorn nodded.

"This birthday was a big deal for Hal," Demott said. "He'd say, Lord God Almighty, I'll be free at last, and get all excited thinking about it. And he'd invited this guy he'd known at Dartmouth to bring his girlfriend to see Canyon de Chelly and Navajo National Monument, the Grand Canyon, all that. Meet him and Elisa at the canyon for a birthday party for starters. But first he wanted to climb Ship Rock before he was thirty. That proved something to him. So we climbed it. Or almost."

Demott looked away. Deciding how much of this he wants to tell me, Leaphorn thought. Or maybe just remembering.

"We stopped in Rappel Gulch," Demott said. "Elisa had dropped out about an hour before that. Said she would just wait for us. So Hal and I were resting for that last hard climb. He had been talking about how the route up involves so much climbing up and then climbing back down to get to another up-route. He said there surely had to be a better way with all the good rappelling equipment we had now. Anyway, he edged out on the cliff. He said he wanted to see if there was a faster way down."

Demott stopped. He sat on the fender, studying Leaphorn.

"I take it there was," Leaphorn said.

Demott nodded. "Partway."

"Gust of wind caught him. Something like that?"

"Why are you doing this?"

"I like your sister," Leaphorn said. "A kind, caring woman. And besides, I don't like strip miners ruining the mountains."

The wind was blowing a little harder now, and colder. It came out of the northwest, blowing the hair away from Demott's face and dust around the tires of the Land-Rover.

"How does this come out?" Demott said. "I don't know much about the law."

"It will depend mostly on how you handle it," Leaphorn said.

"I don't understand."

"Here's where we are now. We have three felonies. The Maryboy homicide and the related shooting of a Navajo policeman. The FBI is handling that one. Then there is the assault upon Amos Nez, in which the FBI has no interest."

"Hal?"

"Officially, formally, an accident. FBI's not interested. Nobody else is, except the Breedlove Corporation."

"Now what happens?"

"Depends on you," Leaphorn said. "If I were still a Navajo Tribal Policeman and working this case, I'd take you in on suspicion of shooting Amos Nez. The police do a ballistics check on that rifle of yours and if the bullets match the one they got from Nez's horse, then they charge you with attempted murder. That gets Nez on the witness stand, which makes Elisa an accessory after the fact but probably indicted as coconspirator. That leads the Breedloves to file legal papers to void the inheritance. And what Nez says wakes up the FBI and they make the Maryboy connection. The ballistics test on whatever you shot him with, which I suspect we'll find either in your glove compartment or under the front seat, nails you on that one. I'd say you do life. Elisa? I don't know. Much shorter."

Demott had been following this intently, nodding sometimes. Sometimes frowning.

"But why Elisa?"

"If they can't make the jury believe she helped plan it, you can see how easy it is to prove she helped cover it up. Just get Nez and some of the people at the Thunderbird Lodge under oath. They saw you there with her."

"You mentioned an option. Said it depends on me. How could it?"

"We go into Gallup. You turn yourself in. Say you want to confess to the shooting of Hosteen Maryboy and Jim Chee. No mention of Nez. No mention of Hal. No mention of climbing Ship Rock."

"And what do you say? I mean about where you found me. And why and all that."

"I'm not there," Leaphorn said. "I park where I can see you walk into the police station and wait awhile and when you don't come out, I go somewhere and get something to eat."

"Just Maryboy, then, and Chee?" Demott said. "And Elisa wouldn't get dragged into it?"

"Without Nez involved, how would she?"

"Well, that other cop. The one I shot. Doesn't he have a lot of this figured out?"

"Chee?" Leaphorn chuckled. "Chee's a genuine Navajo. He isn't interested in revenge. He wants harmony."

Demott's expression was skeptical.

"What would he do?" Leaphorn asked. "It's obvious why you shot Chee. You were trying to escape. But you have to give them some plausible reason for shooting Maryboy. Chee isn't going to rush in and say the real motive was some complicated something or other to cover up not reporting that Hal

Breedlove fell off the mountain eleven years ago. What's to be gained by it? Except a lot of work and frustration. Either way, you are going to do life in prison."

"Yes," Demott said, and the way he said it caused Leaphorn to lose his cool.

"And you damn sure deserve it. And worse. Killing Maryboy was cold-blooded murder. I've seen it before but it was always done by psychopaths. Emotional cripples. I want you to tell me how a normal human can decide to go shoot an old man to death."

"I didn't," Demott said. "They found the skeleton. Then they identified Hal. The nightmare was coming true. I got panicky. Nobody knew I'd climbed up there with Hal and Elisa that day but the old man. We went to ask him about trespassing, but that was eleven years ago. I didn't think he'd remember. But I had to find out. So I drove down there that evening, and knocked on the door. If he didn't recognize me I'd go away and forget it. He opened the door and I told him I was Eldon Demott and heard he had some heifers to sell. And right away I could see he knew me. He said I was the man who'd climbed up there with Mr. Breedlove. He got all excited. He asked how I could have gone off and left a friend up there on the mountain. And now that he knew who I was, he was going to tell the police about it. I went out and got into the car and there he was coming out after me, carrying a thirty-thirty, and wanted me to go back into the house. So I got my pistol out of the glove box and put it in my coat pocket. He went into his house and put on his coat and hat, and he was going to take me right into the police station at Shiprock. And, you know . . ."

"That's how it was, then?"

"Yeah," Demott said. "But if I can just keep Nez out of it, maybe we save Elisa?"

Leaphorn nodded.

Demott reached his hand slowly toward the rifle.

"What I'd like to do is slip the bolt out of this thing so it's harmless."

"Then what?"

"Then I walk five steps over there to the cliff, and I toss it down into that deepest crack where nobody could ever find it."

"Do it," Leaphorn said. "I won't look."

Demott did it. "Now," he said. "I want

just a few minutes to write Elisa a little letter. I want her to know I didn't kill Hal. I want her to know that when I climbed on up there and signed that register for him, it was just so she wouldn't lose her ranch."

"Go ahead."

"Got to get my notebook out of the glove box then."

"I'll watch," Leaphorn said. He moved around to where he could do that.

Demott dug out a little spiral notebook and a ballpoint pen, closed the box, backed out of the vehicle, and used the hood as a writing desk. He wrote rapidly, using two pages. He tore them out, folded them, and dropped them on the car seat.

"Now," he said, "let's get this over with."

"Demott," Leaphorn shouted. "Wait!"

But Eldon Demott had already taken the half dozen running steps to the rim of Canyon del Muerto and jumped, arms and legs flailing, out into empty space.

Leaphorn stood there a while listening. And heard nothing but the wind. He walked to the rim and looked. Demott had apparently hit the stone where the cliff bulged outward, down some two hundred feet. The body bounced out and landed on the stony talus slope just beside the canyon road. The first traveler to come along would see it.

Demott had left the door open on the Land-Rover. Leaphorn reached in and picked up the letter, holding it by its edges.

Dear Sister:

The first thing you do when you read this is call Harold Simmons at his law office don't tell anyone anything until you talk it over with him. I've made an awful mess of things, but I'm out of it now and you can still have a good life taking care of the ranch. But I want you to know that I didn't kill Hal. I'm ashamed to tell you a lot of this but I want you to know what happened.

About a week after Hal disappeared from the canyon I got a call from him. He was in a motel in Farmington. He wouldn't tell me where he had been, or why he was doing this, but he said he wanted to climb Ship Rock right away, before it got too cold. I said hell no. He said if I didn't I was fired. I wouldn't anyway. Then he said if I would and I didn't say anything to you, he would decide against signing that strip mining contract and put it off for another full year. He said he wanted to explain everything to you after we got down. So I said okay and I picked him up at the motel about five the next morning. He wouldn't tell me a word about where he'd been and he was acting strange. But we climbed it, up to Rappel Gulch, and there he insisted on edging out on the cliff face to see if there was a way good hands with rope could get down. A gust of wind caught him and he fell.

That's it, Elisa. I've been too ashamed to tell you all these years and I'm ashamed now. I think it's made me crazy. Because when I went to see Mr. Maryboy about his stock getting onto our grazing over on the Checkerboard Reservation, we got to yelling at one another and he got his rifle down and I shot him and then I shot the policeman to get away. I checked on the penalty I can expect and it's life in prison, so I'm going to take the quick way out of it and set an all-time record getting down that 800-foot cliff into Canyon del Muerto.

Remember I love you. I just got crazy.
Your big brother, Eldon

Leaphorn read it again, refolded it carefully, replaced it on the seat. He took out his handkerchief, pushed down the lock lever, wiped off the leather seat where he might have touched it, and slammed the door.

He drove a little faster than was smart down the track, anxious to get out before somebody spotted Demott's body. He didn't want to meet a police car coming in, and if he didn't, the dry snow now being carried by the wind would quickly eliminate any clue that Demott had had company. He was almost back to Window Rock before a call on his police monitor let him know that the body of a man had been found up Canyon del Muerto.

He turned up the thermostat beside his front door, heard the floor furnace roar into action, put on the coffeepot, and washed his face and hands. That done, he checked his telephone answering machine, punched the button and listened to the first words of an insurance agent's sales pitch, and hit the erase button. Then he took his coffee mug off the hook, got out the sugar and cream, poured himself a cup, and sat beside the telephone.

He sipped now, and dialed Jim Chee's number in Ship Rock.

"Jim Chee."

"This is Joe Leaphorn," he said. "Thanks for the message you sent me. I hope I'm not calling at a bad time."

"No. No," Chee said. "I've been wondering. And I've been wanting to tell you about an arrest we made today in our cattle-rustling case. But by the way, have you heard they found a man's body in Canyon del Muerto? Deke said it was near the Nez place. He said it's Demott."

"Heard a little on my scanner," Leaphorn said.

Brief silence. Chee cleared his throat. "Where are you calling from? Was it Demott? Were you there?"

"I'm at home," Leaphorn said. "Are you off duty?"

"What do you mean? Oh. Well, yes. I guess so."

"Better be sure," Leaphorn said.

"Okay," Chee said. "I'm sure. I'm just having a friendly talk with an unidentified civilian."

"Tomorrow, you're going to get the word that Demott killed himself. He jumped off the cliff above the Nez place. About like diving off a sixty-story building. And he left a suicide note to his sister. In it he said he got into a quarrel with Mr. Maryboy over some cattle and shot him. Shot you while escaping. He told Elisa that he didn't kill Hal. He said Hal had called him from Farmington a week after vanishing from his birthday party, offered to delay signing the mining lease he had cooking for a year if Demott would climb Ship Rock with him the next day. Demott agreed. They climbed. Hal fell off. Demott said he kept it a secret because he was ashamed to tell her."

Silence. Then Chee said, "Wow!"

Leaphorn waited for the implications to sink in.

"I'm not supposed to ask you how you know all this?"

"That is correct."

"What did he say about Nez?"

"Who?"

"Amos Nez," Chee repeated. "Oh, I guess I see."

"Saves you a lot of work, doesn't it?"

"Sure does," Chee said. "Except for when they find the rifle. Body near the Nez place, rifle nearby I guess. Nez recently shot. Two and two make four and the ballistics test raises a problem. Even the FBI won't be able to shrug that off."

"I think the rifle doesn't exist," Leaphorn said.

"Oh?"

"It's my impression that Demott didn't want to involve his sister. So he didn't want the Nez thing connected to the Maryboy thing because with Nez, you have his sister indicted as an accessory."

"I see," Chee said, a little hesitantly. "But how about Nez? Won't he be talking about it?"

"Nez isn't much for talking. And he's going to think I pushed Demott off the cliff to keep Demott from shooting him."

"Yeah. I see that."

"I think Demott did this partly to keep

the Breedlove Corporation from strip-mining the ranch. Ruining his creek. So he left the world a suicide letter certifying that he was on Ship Rock with Hal a week after the famous birthday. Add that to Hal signing the register a week after the same birthday."

"One's as phony as the other," Chee said.

"Is that right?" Leaphorn said. "I would like to sit there and listen while you try to persuade the agent in charge that he should reopen his Maryboy homicide, throw away a written point-of-death confession on grounds that Demott was lying about his motive. I can just see that. 'And what was his real motive, Mr. Chee?' His real motive was trying to prove that accidental death that happened eleven years ago actually happened on a different weekend, and then —"

Chee was laughing. Leaphorn stopped.

"All right," Chee said. "I get your point. All it would do is waste a lot of work, maybe get Mrs. Breedlove indicted for something or other, and give the ranch back to the Breedlove Corporation."

"And get a big commission to the attorney," Leaphorn added.

"Yeah," Chee said.

"Tomorrow, when the news is out, I'll send Shaw details about the suicide note. And give him back what's left of his money. Now, what were you going to tell me about cattle rustling?"

"It sounds trivial after this," Chee said, "but Officer Manuelito arrested Dick Finch today. He was loading Maryboy heifers into his camper."

Tony Hillerman is past president of the Mystery Writers of America and has received their Edgar and Grand Master awards. Among his other honors are the Center for the American Indian's Ambassador Award, the Silver Spur Award for best novel set in the West, and the Navajo Tribe's Special Friend Award. His many bestselling novels include *Finding Moon*, *Sacred Clowns*, and *Coyote Waits*. He lives with his wife, Marie, in Albuquerque, New Mexico.

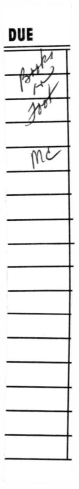

DUE

Books
Fri
Zoo

MC

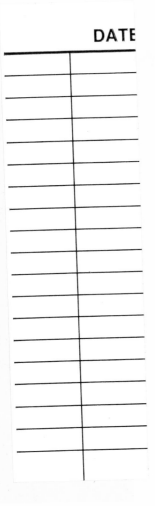

DATE